MW00780127

Not Okay

Not Okay

Brett Axel

Brett Axel

Published by Vinal Publishing Inc.
193 Delaware Ave Buffalo NY 14202
ISBN: 978-1-7345036-1-6

Not Okay

"Did you do it?"
Do what?
"Did you kill this guy?"
Well, yeah.
"Why?"

1.

Now my lawyer, she's looking at me and I'm looking at her and she's looking at me and I'm not saying anything and she's not saying anything and this has gone on long enough that I think maybe the first one of us who speaks is just going to pop like a balloon. I'm thinking this is a challenge to her, like who's going to be dominating who, make me speak and she's in charge, I make her speak and I'm in charge, that kind of thing. But I don't care who's in charge, I don't really get that sort of thing anyway, I'm just worried I'll be popping like a balloon. Or she will be, that wouldn't be any good either. I'm already in trouble. I bet they'd blame me for that too.

She deserves an answer. Even if it is an answer she can't use in court. It is my turn. She spoke last, it is my damned turn. I am going to pop. I just know it.

Sabrina! Yeah. Her name is Sabrina. I don't know why it isn't Mrs. something or miss something or Ms. something even. Lawyers aren't this informal on TV. We don't know each other. She's just a court appointed lawyer. And she's still waiting. She still hasn't said anything again, at least I don't think so. I haven't either. Maybe she knows about the popping. She could know she could pop if she speaks. Most likely not. People never know. They never know when they could pop if they speak. They never know that. I don't know why they don't ever know that. It is important enough to want to know. But I can't tell them. I've learned that much. If I tell someone they might have popped but they didn't, they think, just because they didn't pop that time that they couldn't have. I guess it makes life easier for people not to know how dangerous life really is.

Not Okay

I don't know Sabrina's story. I hate not knowing anything, so I start thinking about it. I bet she's hot stuff. Wants to win herself a case and look good for her bosses. She's so young and pretty. She must not have been out of school long. I bet she passed the BAR exam last week and this is her first case ever. Shit damn! Her first case and she gets stuck with a loser like me. That's pretty bad luck. I was born guilty. Before I ever killed anyone I was guilty. She's not going to build her resume on this case. I'm going down.

She looks short to me, so I start to wonder if she's short. You can't always tell when people are sitting down. That's Sabrina, my lawyer, appointed by the court from the Orange County, New York public defender's office. She's ambitious, fresh out of law school. I am going to be such a disappointment.

I'm thinking five foot three. Five four. She's short all right. Look at her shoes. An extra inch of sole. Short girls wear shoes like that. She's short. She's got on the thickest socks she can find too. Anything to add a little height. She's so insecure about her height.

"You look good to me; I don't think you are too short."

Fuck, shit, damn, that was me! It was. I said something. I didn't pop though. That was a stupid thing to say. I don't know what made me call her a tiny midget. I know how insecure she is about her height. Stupid stupid stupid. But I didn't pop. That is the good thing. There is a good thing.

"Let's keep this about you."

Oh, she's smooth. If I didn't tell you already, her hair is brown. Not too many girls have brown hair. I mean, really brown hair. Not dark brown or dirty blonde but actually regular sort of brown. Girls think regular brown hair is too plain maybe. If they have it they dye their hair darker or bleach it lighter. Not Sabrina though. She's good with being plain. That kind of makes her beautiful, you know. It is kind of straight, her hair. A little wave to it but I bet she puts that in. Not a big deal but a few minutes every morning I bet.

I can't believe I didn't say anything about her eyelashes yet. I should have. Just because they are long the way we are told eyelashes are supposed to be. Pretty too. She doesn't work at being pretty. She is anyway. Plain and pretty too. That makes her prettier I think. And the eyelashes are the best. They are suspended over liquid brown eyes. I didn't notice the eyes at first. I'm not so good at looking people in the eye, especially not when the people are my lawyer and I am being held on a murder charge. Not that this has happened before. This is my first time. Not my first murder, just my first arrest. Maybe I'll be more confident the next time. Shit damn this Sabrina's got pretty eyes.

Shit, I'm objectifying her. I shouldn't be thinking about what she looks like. That's what Sharon says. Men are judged by what they do, women by what they look like. I'm not supposed to do that. I'm supposed to be better than that.

We are still looking at each other. If I don't start talking, I mean really talking, we run the risk of maybe popping again. Just because we didn't before doesn't mean we couldn't have, I told you that much already. You have to pay attention.

Spending a night in jail shakes you up. Even people who don't get shook up easily. I get shook up really easy, so it was worse for me. 16 hours. I'm looking at the clock and counting back and I think yeah, they brought me in here 16 hours ago. It's not an accident either. They design the whole thing to shake you up. The toilet is stainless steel, which is cold on your butt. Not only that, but it is right in the room with you. You don't go to the bathroom when you are in jail, you are already there.

They don't need to do that. It isn't cost efficient to have a toilet for every person; I'll tell you that. Not to mention, if everybody took a shit at once, I mean, if everybody flushed at once, I bet the whole building would run out of water.

The toilet is like bolted to the back wall which is cement. The bed is bolted to the wall on the right. I mean, it is the wall on the right if you are facing the toilet. If you are facing the bars it is the wall on the left. I'm pretty sure anyway. I never was really good with right and left but I've gotten better, so I think I've got it now. I was facing the bars more than I was facing the toilet so I guess I should say the bed was bolted to the wall on the left. Nothing was bolted to the other wall. It was just cement.

They make you walk through corridors like Pac-man. I really felt like I was Pac-man going through the old jail's corridors, turning right then turning left then turning left again then turning right and more of the same again. The guards were like Blinky and Stinky and whatever the ghosts' names were. I would have called one Stinky, but I was afraid of them. They are pretty scary. I bet they try to be scary because it is their job. Maybe they aren't as scary when they are off duty, like at home or something. Maybe some of them are, but they are pretty scary here in the jail. There aren't any power pills either. I can't eat a power pill and make them turn blue and become vulnerable I don't think. Maybe I could. I'll have to keep my eyes out for a power pill when they bring me back to my cell. I bet I won't find one though. There weren't any dots in any of the halls. If there aren't any dots there aren't going to be any power pills either. It is a jail. I can understand them not wanting prisoners to get super powered. They must clean up all the power pills and dots long before they let any prisoners go through. I would if I were running a jail.

The whole jail smells like Play-Doh. I'd smelled that before. It was the smell of poverty. Old city buildings smelled like this. Kindergartens smell like this too. Kindergartens are always older than high schools if you noticed that. They build a new high school and let the less important little kids use the old building as a kindergarten. The older you are, the more important you are. Everyone in the jail is older but that's different. If they put you in the jail you get demoted. You get an old building again, like you are in Kindergarten.

The room I'm in now is bigger than my cell. There are three chairs, but we are only using two. Big old chairs, like schools have too. They are heavy as hell, so I think they are oak. I remember something about oak chairs being big like this and heavier than other wooded chairs. As heavy as these are, if they aren't oak they must be iron. Some kind of iron wood. Oh, and there's a really worn table too. The table is twice as solid even as the chairs. All cement walls still, but a real door rather than a door made out of bars.

I'm objectifying the room now by talking about what it looks like, but Sharon would be fine with that. Rooms can't be marginalized.

Sabrina is sitting on one side of that table in one of the iron oak chairs and I'm on the other side of the table in the other chair. Don't ask me which one is the right, and which one is the left though. I wouldn't be able to figure that out.

Not Okay

She might have just said something. I don't know what it was. I was thinking about the chairs or maybe it was when I was thinking about being Pac-Man. I could ask her, but I bet she doesn't know I was thinking about Pac-Man at all, she isn't going to know when I was. People just don't know things I know. They don't know what they ought to know.

I wanted to tell her about the way the one corrections officer yelled at me even though I didn't do anything. That's Stinky. He is pretty single-minded. All he cares about is that I stay on the white line and keep my eyes forward. He told me a couple of times that if I looked at him I'd end up with an indentation the shape of his club in my skull. The same about going off the white line. He told me he wasn't playing with me either. I didn't go off the white line or look at him or anything, but he kept on saying it like as if I wasn't doing what he said which kind of got me flustered. When I'm flustered I can't concentrate on what I am doing. When I can't concentrate on what I am doing I mess things up so if he didn't want me to mess up what he was telling me he really should have been nicer about the whole thing.

Maybe it was his way of striking up conversation. Maybe if I had told him how nice a white line it was or like, that whoever painted it did a really nice job on it, maybe things would have gone from there. I didn't though because I was scared. Damn being scared. I bet I miss a lot of social opportunities because I'm scared. Maybe he painted the white line and that was why he was so proud of it, or maybe a friend of his painted it. I should have complimented the white line. I hope I'll have a chance when he takes me back to my cell.

Sabrina told me her name, but I didn't have to tell her mine. It was written right on the file folder in front of her. Peter Wilson big as fireworks. It looked like it was written with a Sharpie too. I love Sharpies. If I had one, I'd write on my cell wall. I could ask her for hers, but I don't think they would let me keep it. I wouldn't write anything very bad, just Peter Wilson was here or something like that. Plus, maybe flowers and a peace sign and maybe a rifle with curly hair coming out of the barrel. I'm not a great artist or anything but I like drawing and I can draw a rifle with curly hair coming out of the barrel. I can do that. When I've got a Sharpie marker in my hand I really feel like an artist though.

I was glad Sabrina already knew my name because jail kind of takes the name right out of you. I hadn't even been there a full day and I already had trouble remembering who I had been before I was in jail.

Sabrina is patient. I just noticed that. People usually don't give me enough time to think and she does. People usually snap at me to answer when I'm off thinking about Sharpies or Pac-Men or whatever it is I'm thinking about. Not Sabrina though. She went at my pace. That's about as good a thing as you can do with me. It made me kind of trust her even though I didn't know her.

Right then I started to be suspicious of her. I mean, because she made me trust her so quickly and we didn't know each other. Maybe that's what she does with her long eyelashes and liquid brown eyes and patience. Maybe she tricks people like me into trusting her and then, wham! But if that was what she did then she'd be good enough at it that I wouldn't even suspect, so because I suspected her I figured out that I didn't need to. I reached over to her little tape recorder. I pressed the button that turns it off.

"I hope no one is expecting you home for dinner," I said real dramatic like.

"We have hours," she said back, looking at her watch, "an hour and a half left."

"Won't be enough time," I answered.

"I can come back tomorrow," she replied.

"Alright," I answered.

Then one of those long silences started. You can just tell when those things start even before they have gone on a long time. I just couldn't deal with another one of those, so I cut it off.

"What do you know about monsters?"

Next was more of a dramatic pause then an uncomfortable silence. She reached into her black leather portfolio and pulled out a green and white pack of cigarettes.

"Do you mind?"

"Not if you share," I answered eagerly.

Soon 2 cigarettes were in her mouth. She lit them both at once, using a disposable lighter, leaned over the table and put one in my mouth. In a different setting, it might have been erotic. So maybe it was a little erotic, but I bet that wasn't her intention.

I fucking hate menthol.

I hadn't had a cigarette for a day, but shit fuck if it wouldn't have been nice for her to be a Winston smoker. Someone told me that after I'm in general population there is a store of sorts, then I'd be able to buy cigarettes. I had cigarettes when I got here though, and the fuck stains took them from me and put them in an envelope. I wouldn't need to buy them if they'd just give me the pack they took. They say I'll get them back when I get out, but I kill motherfuckers. Want to guess how stale they'll be when I get out? Fucking stale, no doubt. And what little money I had on me they took too so don't even ask me what I'm going to be able to pay with at that store of theirs.

I took a deep drag off the cigarette Sabrina gave me.

My lungs had gotten a little used to not having smoke in them after almost a day. They seemed to like it, even if I didn't. They balked at first. I took two more drags. After a while, they realized they had no choice, that I was going to do what I was going to do, and they gave in.

"Where were we?" I asked.

"Nowhere yet, Peter," Sabrina replied.

I bet she was hoping there was a chance that the entire story wouldn't be necessary. She was right. Everything wasn't important. But I'd never been arrested for murder before, so I didn't know what would be or wouldn't be important. The only way I could be sure I didn't leave out some critically important detail would be to tell her everything.

"I guess I'll start with my birth," I said, knocking the first ash off my cigarette.

"Go ahead then," Sabrina nodded, resigned to a long afternoon. She leaned back in her chair, making an effort to be comfortable despite the inhospitable surroundings.

I talked for an hour at least, telling a story that is all lost now. two, maybe three chapters worth, all of it really good, but I couldn't even try to recreate it now.

Sabrina put some things that were on the table back into her briefcase just as I was starting to talk about Woodbridge New Jersey in 1980. I didn't know this at the time, but when she did this she flipped her tape recorder back on. From then on everything I said to her was recorded so that's how you can know about it now.

Not Okay

2.

It wasn't summer yet, but it was the first summer kind of day in Woodbridge, New Jersey, and I was out in it. Teenagers kind of stayed in their various worlds if it wasn't warm out, but let the sun come shining and we filled the parks, sidewalks, pizza shops, and pinball arcades like roaches on puppy shit.

I wasn't free like they all were, but I went out into town with them and acted free. I belonged to Uncle Will. Uncle Will picked me up hitchhiking when I was 12, which was, like, four years before this.

Not that much had changed since before Uncle Will picked me up. Some of the pinball machines turned into video games. That wasn't so bad. Oh, and the jukeboxes didn't have The Doors on them all. There used to be like 10 different songs by The Doors on every jukebox. Now you'd be more likely to find 10 different songs by Blondie. That part was kind of sad. But I bet if you go look at those jukeboxes right now The Doors will be on there again. See, that's the thing about good music. You can't think Blondie will ever come back like The Doors will. Blondie was the music of the moment.

I was 16 in Woodbridge.

Uncle Will didn't let me make friends. I mean, not real friends. The kind of people who you called or called you, people you'd visit at their house or would come over to your house. It wasn't so bad. We moved around a lot; this way I didn't have to leave good friends behind.

I did have 'hi, how's it hanging' friends. Most of us knew each other's names and knew like, if we smoked pot or not or if we drank beer or not, like that. My friends were the people I'd run into and say hi to or ask 'how's it hanging' to and then maybe I'd ask if they had some pot or they'd ask if I had some, you know, like that. Thing is that most of the time no one ever had pot. If we did, we'd be home smoking it instead of out bumming around. We just asked each other if we did, that's all. It was kind of the way 16-year-olds said hi to each other in Jersey in 1980, other than saying 'hi' I mean. That was the first way. 'Got any pot' would be like an extra way.

I was thinking about girls almost all of the time then. Of course, I didn't tell Uncle Will. I mean, I was supposed to be gay. I was supposed to like sucking his cock. Truth is, I liked when he sucked mine, but I couldn't tell him I'd have my eyes closed pretending it was a girl doing it. No one particular girl. I mean, not the same one with any regularity or anything like that. Girls from TV shows mostly. Valerie Bertinelli sometimes. Pam Dawber sometimes. I was just getting interested in girls but the only ones I knew were on TV and this was way before I knew I shouldn't objectify them. Those girls on TV, I objectified the shit out of them.

Really, I'd been thinking about girls a lot for a long time. Girls and my shit ass life. I had been thinking about girls and my shit ass life for a long time. The difference was that this year I was thinking I wanted to do something that was more interesting than just thinking, with one of them or, preferably, both.

There was butt stuff too. With Uncle Will I mean. I don't like talking about that. It makes me feel uncomfortable thinking about that. You know what really fucks you up? When your mind doesn't like what someone is doing to you but your body does. I just won't talk about it and you can assume whatever you assume.

Not Okay

I couldn't do anything with girls or my life. Not in the situation I was in. In order to ever do something, first I needed to get away from Uncle Will.

I tried that when he first picked me up and it didn't work out well for me. For two months I think, he locked me in a basement and kept me in the dark. By the time he'd open the door to throw me a bag from McDonalds or something the light would hurt my eyes, I'd be so hungry I'd eat it too fast and end up throwing it right up, which didn't help my hunger at all.

I suppose I don't have to tell you that Uncle Will wasn't my uncle. He had me call him Uncle Will, that was all. I did what he told me.

Uncle Will was a fucker when I disobeyed him. At sixteen, half the time I couldn't believe I was even thinking about leaving, the other half I couldn't believe I just did what he said all the time and stayed with him for so long. I was pretty fucked up then. Not like now. Then I thought that I wasn't OK and then I thought, if I'm OK then other people are not OK. That was before I read a book that set me straight about that.

I didn't know much of anything. Still, I knew I needed money to get away. That meant I needed a job.

I got one cleaning the floors at the DeVry Institute, a kind of college for people who were too stupid for college but too smart for Vo-Tech. At DeVry, you could learn how to put transistors and light emitting diodes and shit like that on circuit boards in order to make electronic shit work. I learned the names of the stuff because when I went and applied for the job I stole a couple handfuls of the shit. I thought maybe they'd be worth something, but it turned out that Radio Shack didn't even want it.

I worked a week without telling Uncle Will. I was going to tell him at first and then it just got harder. I knew he wasn't going to be happy. I thought, if I told him just right he'd let me keep the job though. I mean, if I made it clear to him that I didn't want the money to get away, which I actually did.

I was pretty ungrateful really. Uncle Will was the only family I had. I was nothing without him and we both knew it. Just in case I didn't know, he told me pretty often, especially when I wasn't giving him the proper gratitude. Of course, I was nothing without him. But I was nothing with him too. Still, I kind of thought, if I got away from him, I might be able to become something.

I don't want to give you the impression that it was awful with Uncle Will. It wasn't most of the time. I mean, it was awful sometimes but that was only when I didn't do what I was supposed to. He only locked me in the basement when I was really bad and even that he hadn't done for a long time.

As long as I was good though, he treated me well. I had an Atari video game machine and a Beta Max for movies, there was always ice cream and cookies in the house, really, I had a much better life than the one I'd run away from when I was 12. I want you to understand. My real mother was a cunt. She hit me more and harder than Uncle Will did and for no reason I could figure out. The food always sucked, the house was always cold, and I never got anything I wanted. Overall, Uncle Will was a real step up for me. And sucking his dick wasn't so bad.

I had to tell him before the second work week started. I knew if I waited any longer he would suspect something and then I wouldn't be able to tell him without his totally blowing up. So, I served him his dinner and let him get settled into his chair and start eating. As he did this, I worked on gathering my nerve.

"Why aren't you eating?" he asked me.

"I will..," I started, "I just wanted to talk to you about something."

"Spit it out" he said, continuing to eat. A few kernels of corn fell out of his mouth as he spoke and chewed at the same time.

"I applied for a job today," I said.

"What the fuck did you do that for?" I demanded.

"I wanted something to do during the day," I said.

He looked angry but I expected that. I was only worried about how angry he would be.

I think waiting for him to say something then, I mean, right then, is what made me learn to hate long silences. When he did speak, it was like his cheeks had been pressurized. He opened his mouth and the air rushed out before he said a word. He looked and sounded like he had just popped.

"You can work.."

He said it calmly, but he didn't look calm. After a few seconds he slammed his fork down hard-on the glass top table.

"Bring your paycheck to me. I'll take care of your money. You don't know how to handle money."

I hadn't thought of that.

"But" I started.

"Are you thinking about leaving? Looking to make some money to run away with you ungrateful piece of shit? Is that it?" He demanded.

"No," I lied.

"You better not be, you know that? You know what will happen if I even think I can't trust you, right?"

He couldn't lock me in the basement again because this apartment didn't have one. I thought about it long enough to know that I didn't know, but I said I knew anyway. This was not a good time for getting technical.

"You fucking better. Now go to your fucking room, you aren't eating with me tonight you piece of shit, you turn my fucking stomach."

I stood for a moment. This had actually gone better than I had expected. I mean, he didn't tell me I couldn't have the job and there was a good chance that after a while he'd let me keep some of the money I made.

"Go!" he yelled, starting to rise from the table.

I went.

Things changed some after that. Uncle Will became more interested in other boys. For a long time, I was the only one, or at least, he kept me from knowing about the others. Now he was bringing other boys home once or twice a week.

It might have been coincidence. I was 16 and starting to look more like a man than a boy. He picked me up when I was 12, like I said. The other boys were all around 12 or maybe even younger, none of them were as old as I had become.

You might not believe it but I kind of felt jealous. I mean, it was great. I didn't like sucking his stupid cock and now I didn't have to, but it was because I wasn't good enough for him anymore and I didn't like that, if that makes any kind of sense to you.

The only time he did anything with me sexually, after I got the job I mean, was when he needed me to be in pictures with the new boys he brought home. I didn't dare refuse, but there was no way to pretend I was enjoying it. Not getting a hard-on was kind of a giveaway.

He never hurt these kids, but he didn't keep them either. They went home between sessions, and they kept quiet about it too. He still threatened me with hurting them if I didn't go along. I did what he said so I don't really know what he would have done, but I was pretty sure he could kill if he wanted to.

Oh, also, he traded the pictures he took with other people like him all over the place. He had lots of pictures too. Boxes full. Some of them were scenes way worse than what he'd done with me. I mean, like boys tied up and long needles in their nipples and shit I don't even want to say but you get the idea. He didn't do that with me, but I thought he could. I was always scared of him I guess, but I was especially scared of him when he showed me those stupid pictures.

I still did all the cooking and cleaning, but I had time to work at my job, so I did. I don't know exactly how or when I got smarter being that I didn't go to school from 12 years old on, but somehow I got smart enough to think my way around problems. My first real success at this was making a deal with my boss, to get half my pay in cash and the rest in my paycheck. What I told Larry (that was my boss, Larry) was that my dad made me turn over my paycheck, which was almost the truth. I never had a dad and Uncle Will did take care of me. Larry was cool about it.

Larry was a pot smoker and for him, the world was divided into two groups: people who smoked pot and people who didn't. No matter what the situation and no matter if it had anything to do with pot, he would always side with a pot smoker against someone who didn't smoke pot.

To Larry, pot smoking was a religion, a philosophy, a political party and an ethnicity. That meant I was getting

21

smoked up with some regularity. I can't tell you what a difference it made as far as coping with a life that wasn't really good. Pot was great. I couldn't believe people weren't packaging it and sell it in the supermarket.

Larry said pot was illegal because William Randolph Hearst was afraid the hemp industry would cut into his profits from paper mills. I didn't know who William Randolph Hearst was but I went ahead and repeated it as if it were true to my hi how's it hanging friends and they were all pretty impressed with how fucking smart I was.

Larry was the most pot obsessed person I had ever met so had no reason not to believe he knew what he was talking about when it came to pot.

Uncle Will let me keep most of my paychecks. He didn't care about the money; he just didn't want me to have too much on me at one time. Whatever he gave me back I was sure to spend right away on things he could see. I wanted him to think I couldn't save money to save my life, which was what I was trying to do. That was me being smart again. See. I was getting smarter all the time. In five months, I had about a thousand dollars. When the right moment came, when I did get away, damned if I wouldn't have the money to set myself up pretty good.

Things were going well for some time. Uncle Will had three regular boys and one he only saw once in a while and they kept him pretty busy.

Then the bastard got sick. I mean, he was really sick.

His skin turned yellow, he was throwing and he had a fever. The doctor said it was hepatitis. I don't remember who it was who told me you get it was from ass-fucking but someone said it and I believe it.

Not Okay

I got a shot to keep me from getting it and I guess I was lucky because I didn't, but I didn't fuck anyone's ass either, so I guess I wasn't in the high-risk category.

The thing was, because Uncle Will was sick, I couldn't go to work. I had to stay home and take care of him. Really, he should have had me working more because he wasn't going to his job. He had a good enough job as a service representative for high technology medical equipment. Fucking eye surgery lasers and shit like that, you know. And he didn't save money. He said his insurance covered him, but he started worrying about money, which he never had to do before, so I knew the insurance wasn't paying as much as he was used to spending.

I should have taken off then. I had enough money. I don't know why I stayed. Maybe I liked it. I didn't think I did, but if I didn't like it I would have left, I guess.

My boss liked me, so he called every few days to see when I'd come back. Uncle Will intercepted more than one of these calls and one of the times he was talking to my boss he found out I was getting paid more than I brought home this whole time. That was the beginning of the end for me and Uncle Will.

I almost saw it coming. When he was on the phone I had thought he was talking to Larry. But Uncle Will didn't call me to the phone. Instead, he called me over and told me to go to the pharmacy in Pathmark.

"Who was on the phone?" I asked.

"The doctor, he said he was calling a new prescription into the pharmacy. Go now. You may have to wait. You might get there before the doctor calls it in, but go, sit there and wait, I want it as quick as possible," He said.

You understand I was on a fool's errand. One that would keep me out of the house an hour or longer. There

23

wasn't any call coming into the pharmacy from Uncle Will's doctor. I was sent there to get me out of the house. I was to wait at the pharmacy until I gave up, which wasn't going to be too quickly since I was afraid of how Uncle Will would react to my coming back empty handed.

Uncle Will knew that and took his time searching my room. He found some pot, which was bad enough, and he found my money. A little over $1100.00, under the top drawer of my dresser, so you had to pull out the entire drawer to find it.

I called home from the pay phone in front of Pathmark before I gave up on the prescription.

"Just come back then," he said, "It can wait till tomorrow,"

Fuck if I'm not smart, I'm thinking. If I had just come home I'd have been in for it. I walked back so proud of myself for having thought to call, successfully avoided getting Uncle Will pissed off.

I walked up to the door to find him standing near the doorway looking mad.

"You should be in bed," I said, trying to hide my fear behind concern for the bastard's health.

"What the fuck is this?" he yelled, throwing the wad of bills on the ground in front of me. A couple of the 20s scattered blew around the courtyard.

"What are doing searching my room?" I yelled back in an uncharacteristic display of assertiveness. I think, because I was so pleased with myself about avoiding making Uncle Will mad and here he was, not just mad but furious, I was caught off guard. I forgot for a second how afraid of him I was.

That was a bad thing to forget.

"Your room? You don't have a room you little shit,

you don't have anything but what I give you!" He screamed at me.

It had been so long since I started tucking that money away I wasn't even thinking about what might happen if he found out. When I had thought about it, I didn't think about ways to try to get out of it. I just thought that it would be the end of the world. So, I surprised myself even more with an elaborate lie that I'd come up with right there. I was getting so smart it was becoming automatic.

I started with the truth, which is a terrific place for a lie to start.

"I had my boss give me half of my pay in cash," I told him.

It was lucky for me I went that way since he already knew that from talking to Larry on the phone.

I guess I was inspired by the fact that I got angry at Uncle Will and yelled. Now I was going with a story that would explain my having a right to be mad at him rather than him having a right to be mad at me and it was flowing out of me. I thought I could have been a politician, I was lying so well, or a lawyer. No offense Sabrina, but you are a lawyer.

"It was a secret. I wanted to give you something special for your birthday," I lied.

He didn't look impressed, but I stayed with my story hoping my confidence in it would give me credibility.

"My birthday isn't for three months!" Uncle Will yelled.

"Uncle Will, I've been saving for six months, since May. Fuck, I'm trying to earn $1600.00, that takes a while," I'm still yelling, but not as loudly. While yelling at him will piss him off, the fact that I am will make him think I'm too upset to lie. This whole lying thing is a science and right here is where I'm earning my merit badge in it. For example, there is such a thing as overkill. So, I stop yelling and I go for upset and disappointed. The idea was that my beautiful surprise has been spoiled.

"I was going to buy you a video camera from the mall. Because you love pictures so much, I thought you'd really love making home movies. You can call the store. Ask them, they'll tell you. I'm in the store every few weeks looking at it, it's the one that's $1600.00, well, $1599.00, same thing, right. I wanted it to be a big surprise."

I took a big chance. I really didn't know how much video cameras cost, much less if there was one for just that price. Shit, I didn't even know which store in the mall sold video cameras, but I went all the way. Even if he found out I was lying tomorrow, he'd have calmed down first.

I could see on his face he was thinking about it.

"Why the fuck should I believe you? You lying sack of shit!" He demanded, "You already lied to me about hiding this money. Don't you think that counts? Give me one reason I shouldn't think you were going to run away with this money?"

And the reason was right there. It was the most obvious reason. So obvious it convinced me.

"Are you kidding me? How much money does it take to run away? I saved enough to bring a family with me. If I wanted to run away I would have long before I passed $1100.00."

I think he believed me. But he was worked up and ready to hit so he had to hit me anyway. I took a good hard smack in the followed by hard punches. Uncle Will was depleted from being sick. He was puffing and panting in no time. Realizing his blows weren't effective, he picked up the brass floor lamp next to him and hit me with that.

Not Okay

It really hurt but I'd already learned how to kind of go inside myself, to a place that doesn't feel. A place deep inside me. In a few minutes I was just numb physically and emotionally too. I wasn't thinking about how I lost my chance to leave because I knew I didn't want to leave. Instead, I was thinking about what a waste of a loser I was to want to stay.

When he got too tired to swing the lamp anymore, Uncle Will pulled me by my hair into the house and across the floor, then pushed me into my room. He told me that I'd better not leave that room for anything until he came and got me out.

I stayed limp on the floor as I heard my door slam closed and Uncle Will angrily stomp away. I don't know how I slept but I did. I slept right on that floor all bruised and bloody until way into the morning.

When I went to open my door a crack, just to listen for Uncle Will, I found that I was locked in. During the night Uncle Will had put a bolt on the outside of the door and locked me in. After all these years I was being retrained.

The first time I was locked in was when Uncle Will first picked me up.

It was worse the first time because I didn't know what was going on or what he was going to do. That time I didn't have a television or a clock or a window or even light. Most importantly, I didn't have a bathroom. In my room this time I had all those things, although I wished I had a fresh roll of toilet paper under the sink for when the one on the spindle was used up. It was already more than half gone.

I didn't even know how much time had passed the first time. After a few days it was just one big expanse of unmeasured time. A little at a time I was granted small rewards for cooperating with Uncle Will.

27

Food, a light, then a radio. Uncle Will was God. He alone controlled my pleasure or my pain, my comfort or my discomfort. And what he wanted wasn't much. Just my devotion. Like any God, he wanted to be worshiped, honored, and obeyed.

However long it was, in less than six months I had earned the right to go out with him. After a year I was allowed to go out by myself and I was trusted to return, which I did. In May of 1980 I was able to come and go fairly freely. As long as I knew I wasn't really free, I was given freedom.

This time around was much better. I had an Atari with 20 or so game cartridges, a stereo and tons of records, books, and lots of other stuff both that I'd bought with my own money from my job and that I'd earned from doing what Uncle Will wanted me to do.

I passed the time listening to music with my headphones on or watching TV with the sound really low so that Uncle Will wouldn't hear it, realize his mistake and come take it from me. I didn't play any Bruce Springsteen, for fear that I'd start singing along without realizing it and give myself away.

I loved Bruce Springsteen then. I didn't know anything about the stuff Sharon taught me yet. I know better now. I mean when you think about it, he is saying this:

'Ridin in my car, I turn on the radio, I pull you close, and you say no. You say you don't like it,' …and that should be enough. No means no. But instead he calls her a liar because when they kiss he enjoys it. What a pig. Hardcore disrespect that is.

I set new all-time records on Asteroids and Space Invaders which, I was absolutely sure no one anywhere could ever beat.

Not Okay

Every day or so Uncle Will would open the door and throw in a bag of cold fast food. He didn't think to get me toilet paper but if I used the napkins on the fast food bags sparingly it was good enough.

I enjoyed myself more of the time than I was stressed out. I mean, I wasn't really captive. My window looked out on the courtyard of the apartment complex. I could have opened it, wiggled out and just walked away.

For the first month or so I figured he would let me out sooner or later. I started to worry when my food started getting delivered by a boy instead of him. This was a new boy. One I hadn't seen before. He might have been my replacement. I think he brought me my food as a warning. So, he would know what might happen to him if he betrayed Uncle Will.

I had a pile of books I thought I might want to read one day but hadn't up to that point and went through them. That was when I first read the book that explained everything.

I'm OK - You're OK by Thomas Anthony Harris. I didn't just read it, I read the shit out of it. In it I learned that other people were just like me, going around thinking they were not OK, and I needed to learn that I was OK. But then when people come to realize that they are OK the next thing they do is think that other people are not OK, so the next step is to realize that other people are OK too. That was the secret to being OK. To accept that I am OK and other people are OK too.

It wasn't easy. I didn't feel like I was OK and, just like the book said, when I did believe that I was OK it made Uncle Will seem to be not OK at all. But I wanted to be OK, so I started working at it. As soon as I believed that I was OK and Uncle Will was OK too I would actually be

OK. Becoming OK was important to me, so I tried. I read it so many times because it didn't work easily.

On a few occasions there wasn't any napkins in the food bag, so I had to use my hand to wipe my ass and wash it off in the sink. These were the times when it was especially hard to feel like I was OK. Feeling like you are OK isn't easy under any circumstances, but it is especially hard when you are washing poop off your hand.

Then the door to my room opened and stayed open.

I didn't come out at first. I waited until Uncle Will told me to come out. When he called me, I came timidly, and followed him into the kitchen.

On the table was a video camcorder. It looked nice, really expensive, you know, with all kinds of special features.

"Thank you so very much for your thoughtful gift," He said blankly.

I realized that Uncle Will had waited to release me on his birthday.

"Now you will help me use it," He told me. I didn't dare say no.

Uncle Will picked up the camcorder with one hand and directed me to the library with his other. But it wasn't a library anymore. During the three months of my exile he had converted the room into a kind of torture chamber. One wall looked like an old timey dungeon wall, but it was printed on paper and stapled up. There was a whip hanging on the wall as well as little chains with adjustable clips on either ends. There were other things I didn't understand but had to assume were used to hurt people. All of these were hanging on hooks that were screwed into the ceiling. The hooks were the ones you would find at Home Depot for hanging plants. They were for show. There was no way they were strong enough to hold if someone pulled on them.

In the center of the room was a platform that stood about knee high from the floor. It was padded, but not enough to make it comfortable. Strapped to the platform was the boy who had been bringing me food for the last few weeks of my imprisonment. I couldn't really tell before, but now, getting a good look at him, I could see he was younger. About 10. He had what looked like a big rubber ball in his mouth and running right through the ball was a leather strap which held it in as a gag. He could make whimpering noises, which he did, but he couldn't scream.

This part wasn't for show. He was really strapped down. I could see fresh tears over dried ones.

Uncle Will secured the camcorder into a black tripod at the corner of the room farthest from me and pointed it at the boy. He turned the lens to adjust the focus as the boy squirmed with fear and fought against the restraints.

"This naughty young man," Uncle Will told me, "went and told his poor dear mother that I, of all people, tried to touch him in a private area. You can't imagine how very deeply that hurts me, can you?"

I took a step back, into the doorway.

"I had to take time away from my personal activities," Uncle Will continued, to go over to the sweet woman's house and set her mind at ease. I explained how this misbegotten child wanted me to buy him some ice cream and I said I wouldn't."

He spoke dispassionately, which was even scarier than when he was yelling. It was as if he was talking about something as emotionless as the weather forecast for a city far away.

"That wasn't nice of him, was it, Peter? Was it nice, Peter?" He asked.

31

"No," I whispered.

I bit my upper lip to try to keep myself from crying. It didn't really work, but it helped a little.

I whispered to myself, "I'm OK. I'm OK. I'm OK."

"Do you know how to work a cane?" Uncle Will asked, handing me a long, kind of skinny plastic baton. It left an ominous empty hook where it used to hang.

My heart was beating so fast I thought it would work its way up and out of my mouth. I knew what he was expecting me to do. I was pretty sure I couldn't do it, at the same time, I was pretty sure Uncle Will would kill me if I didn't. As soon as I felt OK I was flooded with feeling that Uncle Will was not OK, just like the book said I would. I whispered to myself, "you're OK, You're OK, You're OK."

I wanted it to work but it wasn't.

I needed there to be a God.

Right then I worked it out in my head, and I knew there wasn't any God up there or out there or anywhere else. If there was a God this would never have happened. From that moment, the moment I knew there wasn't a God, I started praying. I prayed asking the God that didn't exist to kill me rather than make me choose between doing what Uncle Will expected me to do or being on that slab myself.

I felt a little dizzy, like the room had become a carnival ride. Something between the Tilt-A-Whirl and the Graviton. Spinning, and getting darker the more I tried to focus on the I'm OK - You're OK words but they melted away. I think, just before I passed out, I puked all over the place.

3.

The Red and Tan Bus Line takes care of all of the public transportation needs for Rockland County, New York, a suburban county about 40 minutes North of New York City. From within a mile of just about anywhere in Rockland County to within a mile of just about anywhere else in Rockland County, there was a bus.

Transportation meant freedom. None of the towns that Uncle Will and I lived in before were like Spring Valley in this respect. I discovered the bus soon after we moved here and was taking full advantage of it almost immediately. I spent most of my days traveling to Suffern to hang out with friends I had made there, Nanuet to hang out at the area's mall, which is where I met those friends, and Nyack to buy comic books from M and M's Cards and Comics, the one only real comic book store in the county. There must be a half a dozen places now, but back then, M and M was all we had.

The two people that were behind the counter at M and M's were a younger guy and an older woman. The older woman called the younger guy Mike, and, in turn, Mike called the older woman Mom, so as far as I was concerned, the store was named M and M for Mike and Mom. No one ever told me that, I just assumed it. For all I know it stood for something completely different. Hell, it could have stood for Mom and Mike's and I wouldn't have known otherwise. But I thought of it as Mike and Mom's. They weren't friends with me exactly, but I would call Mike Mike when I was in there. I didn't call the woman Mom because she wasn't my Mom even if she was Mike's.

I liked comic books, so I said hi to Mike at as often as I said hi to my actual friends. I don't think he ever called me by my name, but he knew which comic books I read.

I walked shorter distances, like to the indoor flea market on Route 59. It was a big flea market but not a very good one. Most of the dealers sold new merchandise. We're talking cheap crap made in Japan and Hong Kong. There was a guy that sold some comic books in there but his was much smaller and I didn't know his name, so I never bought comic books from him. Other than the occasional good deal on a video game cartridge, there wasn't much there I was interested in, but I went just for the sake of something to do. Even something stupid was better than staying around home. Anywhere was better than home and all of a sudden anywhere could be a lot of different places.

Uncle Will had eased up on me since we moved to Spring Valley. I was 18 years old now. That meant I wasn't a threat to him at all. I came and went as I pleased with few restrictions, but I was still his property.

When I thought about it I knew I had to break free, but it was easier to distract myself with running around and smoking pot when I could get it than it was to think about solving problems. It was a shitty life, Sure, but I never had a better life to compare it to. I sure didn't think I could survive in the world if I were to suddenly find myself alone in it, and that's the truth.

Money wasn't as good as it had been before he had gotten sick. Before, when we would move, Uncle Will would plan it out and have his work transfer him. When we left Woodbridge New Jersey, it was in the night. He left the job behind and started fresh with a new last name.

Don't ask me what happened to the boy. I didn't see anything, honest. When I came to I was back in my bed with the door bolted closed. The next time Uncle Will opened the door, it was for me to get in the truck. The apartment was empty. And no, I didn't ask about the kid. The whole thing could have been a show, like, to test my loyalty, but I didn't think so, especially not after the way we left in the night and Will changed his name. More likely, Uncle Will killed him. That was another thing I tried not to think about and another thing that running around and smoking pot helped to put out of my mind.

Right away when we got to Spring Valley Uncle Will helped me to get on Public Assistance. This gave him some money for my upkeep and gave me a little something to spend on getting around without my needing to go to work. I didn't argue of course. I just did what I was told.

Uncle Will didn't stop messing around with little boys. If anything, he was doing it more, and, as he got older, the boys got younger. He was a Big Brother now. Big Brothers is an organization that matches fatherless, vulnerable little boys with pedophiles. I'm not sure why, but people seem to think it is a good thing. They get grant money from the government and single mothers are delighted to hand their little boys over to be molested.

10-year-olds mostly. The thought of Uncle Will having sex with 10-year-olds made me feel nauseous all over again. I was 12 when he took me. That didn't seem as bad. 12-year-olds get hard-ons, 12-year-olds think about sex. Well, I did when I was 12 anyway. But I hadn't yet at 10. I don't know why I felt like that makes a difference, but I did. Now, instead of just wanting to leave Uncle Will, I wanted to stop him.

I met Little Willie once. That was what Uncle Will called him, because his name was Will too. Well, really, his name was actually Will. Uncle Will's name wasn't really Will, it was Bradley or Bentley or some other really stupid name like that.

Little Willie was introverted. Whatever he had gone through in his first 10 years must have been a bitch. Poor kid. Now that he was hooked up with Uncle Will, you have to know that worse is coming.

This Little Willie kid had me all twisted up. Sometimes I didn't give a turtle's ass about him. It's a bad world my friend, the sooner you learn that the better off you'll be, you know, like that.

Other times I'd just start crying and hating myself like it was my fault, or at least, my responsibility. Like right now I was in a position to do something about it. Like Uncle Will trusted me. I was the one person who was close enough to Uncle Will to kill him in his sleep. It wasn't exactly like I wanted to, but I felt like I was supposed to.

It was kind of a coincidence that the Department of Social Services was on this Community Campus in the town of Pomona. It looked like it should have been a college, but it was everything else instead, including the county mental health center. I was trying to sort things out in my head all the time then, and not making a shit load of progress either. After two years of trying I still didn't feel OK and when I did I couldn't convince myself for very long that Uncle Will was OK. So, one time I was on the Community Campus, on a lark, I walked into the mental health clinic and asked to talk to somebody.

It wasn't that big a deal when I walked in the big glass front doors, but, by the time I got to the right window on the third floor and had a receptionist in front of me I had gotten pretty stressed up.

"Is this an emergency?" The girl on the other side of the window asks me. I'm gone then. I hope you know what I mean by gone. If not, you'll know in a minute.

"What constitutes an emergency?" I asked.

She looks startled, like she's a client rather than an employee. She opened her mouth to answer me, but I didn't give her time. Like I said, I was gone.

"Isn't life just one long emergency? Like Bruce Springsteen says, come on, Greetings From Asbury Park, it's a fucking classic. No, forget that, life is really a series of small emergencies strung together like cranberries on a Christmas tree, we step from one to another to another until we find one we can live with or one that fails to support our weight. No, this isn't an emergency. This is an average day for me. Oh, I know what you mean, like an emergency, like a time when someone could intervene and save the mother fucking day, is that what you mean?"

I paused to take a breath. She tried to interject but still wasn't fast enough.

"Lady, my emergency came and went. I'm what is left when there was an emergency, and no one came to the rescue. The damage is done here. But why do people have to wait until there's an emergency to take any action? Wouldn't it be easier to come to the rescue before it's an emergency?"

I kept going. The receptionist must have forgotten most of my questions around the same time she figured out that I wasn't looking for answers to them. Now I'd call them rhetorical questions, but I wouldn't have then because I didn't know what rhetorical meant yet. Imagine that. One of my favorite things now and at 18 I didn't even know what they were. I kept on going a while longer. At some point I stopped paying attention to what I was saying so I can't tell you what it was now, but I'm pretty sure I didn't say anything important.

"Excuse me!"

The girl behind the window found her voice and I'll be shit damned if it wasn't a loud one.

"I'm sorry I bothered you, really, I don't need anything," I said, calmer.

She relaxed her tone a little.

"You don't have to leave, just hold on a minute and one of our counselors will be able to speak with you."

"Just a counselor? I don't warrant a damn doctor? I whole fucking team of them? Nets, strait jackets? Nothing like that?" I started, but she cut me off.

"I can see you are getting agitated, just take a seat and try to relax."

"Agitated, fucking agitated, you have no idea..," she tried not to say anything else, instead, she used a hand to make a motion like a flag man would on the side of the road when there's construction going on. It was a motion that kind of said slow down. It should have worked but it didn't. Maybe I was fucking with her a little.

"Oh yeah, I get agitated, sure, I do that all the time, I kind of like it, I think it gives my personality charm, that's not the problem," I said.

"Oh?" She responded, looking more than a little agitated herself.

"Then what is the problem?" She asked.

"I'm having trouble expressing myself," I said as deadpan as I could. I didn't want to give her any indication that I was kidding her. It worked. She must have thought I was totally bonkers.

This worked pretty well for me. I got pushed ahead of everyone else waiting and got to see the next available psychiatrist. I hate waiting so I'm thinking I handled things perfectly.

I wasn't even finished filling out the forms when I got called in, and didn't bother to finish them after, but I did steal the pen.

On the way in I pointed to the woman I had talked to and said, "You're OK."

But about the psychiatrist. The guy was like Indian or Pakistani or something like that. I don't know but I do know that when a doctor is Indian or Pakistani or whatever he was, they never understand what I say to them. Believe me, I've met a few of them. I don't think I'm prejudice, well, I mean, not like prejudice against the people that most people are prejudice against like black people or Jewish people, or people like that. I mean, I'm in there and I'm a homosexual. Maybe. Maybe not. I guessed I was. I was 18 years old and I'd never kissed a girl but I sure sucked dick a lot of times. I didn't know what I was. Maybe that was one of those things I was all twisted up about.

The thing is though, that I didn't think I had a right to be a bigot what with me maybe being something bigots are bigoted against, but I still didn't like those doctors from that country, whatever it is, that seems to exist just to send us doctors that don't understand me.

I guess you could say I was a reluctant bigot.

"Why are you here?" He asks me.

I'm thinking now that this is his standard first question for everyone, but at the time it sounded like he was just asking me, like he didn't think I should be there, like I had to prove I deserved to be talking to a psychiatrist. I don't know. That sort of thing just pisses me off. I might have gone in there to get untwisted but at that moment I was there to fuck with him.

"Everybody has to be some place."

Then he asked, "What is your problem?" but let me tell you, he didn't ask it quite as clearly as that. I'd do the accent for you, but if I did that I think that would make me sound even more racist. Even if I am racist, I'm not racist on purpose and I don't want to sound racist.

I could have told him that I came there to find out what my problem was and if he needed to ask me we were both fucked. That was the truth. It really was, and now I was kind of interested in getting some help again. But sometimes it's hard to keep track of what I am doing.

"I don't feel OK no matter how hard I try and when I do feel OK I don't feel like other people are OK," I told him.

"Do you feel depressed?" The guy asks.

"Oh, sure. Who the isn't depressed?" I told him.

That was another one of those rhetorical questions.

I went on, "You'd have to be pretty stupid to look around you and not be at least a little depressed."

"Have you been thinking about killing yourself?" He asked me dead serious.

Now I'm sure his questions are on a cheat sheet.

"Kill myself?" I repeated, "Why would I do that?"

"You tell me," He says. Oh damn, he's a smug fuck stain too.

"Well, it isn't like there is some pleasure in living, but what would being dead accomplish, right? Do you honestly think an after-life is going to be any better than this shit? Come on! I can't see that being likely. My experience has been that everything pretty much sucks ass. Even new things. Isn't it safe to assume that everything I haven't experienced yet, like death, will suck too? You have to be pretty optimistic to be suicidal if you ask me.

Not Okay

I should tell you at this point, that I asked a lot of rhetorical questions in there. I mean, I still do, but I don't say them as if they were questions anymore. I'll tell you why that is. One day I learned what a rhetorical question was, and I kind of misunderstood and thought that meant that you shouldn't say it like a question, so I stopped. I found out later that it was fine to do that, but I'd already got into the habit and it just stuck. I bet you think that makes me weird, but I don't. I kind of think it makes me unique. Anyway, I was going on at the psychiatrist who I bet understood every third word I said and I'm telling him, "I think killing yourself would have to make your situation worse for the one reason that you would be trying to make things better for yourself and every fucking time you try to make things better for yourself you know what happens? You make things worse, that's what."

When I stopped talking and the psychiatrist started, I didn't hear him. He had me thinking about suicide, which, up until that point, I hadn't even considered. It was an option, after all. It didn't solve the problem of stopping Uncle Will fucking ten-year-old Little Willie. If it had, I might have liked the idea better. But it took me a minute or so to come to that decision and whatever doctor foreigner said was lost. When I realized he was talking he was just about finished.

"I can't help you if you don't listen," is all I caught.

"We're not discussing your problems right? You'll need to find your own shrink for that," I answered.

"What do you want from me?" He finally asked. Now that was the question he should have started with. That was a question I could understand.

I started thinking about myself.

"The thing is, I'm 18 years old and I don't have a clue how to take care of myself. I need to become my own person, become like, self-sufficient and shit. I'm totally dependent on an asshole who isn't nice to me and I think I could leave if I got some kind of training, you know? Training on how to be a grown up. Do you have anything like that in your bag of tricks?"

Surprisingly, the guy said yes. Well what he actually said was, "I think I can help you."

"No offense, but I'm really, I mean, I need an American, I'm sure you are a great doctor and shit, but you hear with an accent."

"You misunderstand me," The doctor says.

"Yes, exactly," I say back.

But he tells me that what he means is that there is a program they call 'Day Treatment' which is three days a week for 15 weeks and it is just for what I'm talking about. Just going will help me learn to structure my day, be places I'm supposed to be when I'm supposed to be there like jobs and shit. I had nothing to do during the days, so I signed up.

As it turned out, a new 15 week session just started. At first the doctor thought it was too late to get me in and I'd have to wait 15 weeks to start, but he made a short phone call while I was in his office and it turned out that I could start the very next day. I had only missed the first session, and nothing had really happened yet, just orientation. I already knew what direction to face: toward the person talking, right? I didn't need orientation.

Day Treatment was like kindergarten right down to the plastic chairs being too small and the halls smelling like Play-Doh. Kindergarten level was at mental capacity for most of the people there too. Damn if I didn't feel superior to them. I called them all wackos. Really, only three were total out-there wackos. three were depressed and the rest (the majority) suffered from being overly melodramatic.

I guess you could say that I fit most snugly into that category myself.

Day treatment really helped me. Right off it improved my self-image. I mean, I saw how totally bonkers some poor saps had allowed themselves to become. One girl was always going on about monsters, and I mean, she really believed in them, she'd talk about them so creepy I'd start to believe in them too.

"What do you think monsters are?" She'd ask, kind of like that, "They prey on the weak, the innocent, children, virgin children. You don't even know you are a victim until they're long gone and then, either you're destroyed, or you've been turned into one of them. That's what monsters are."

Once she said that killing monsters isn't really murder because they aren't human, and that's when I started thinking of people like Uncle Will as monsters and taking the idea of killing them seriously. I already wanted to kill him, but after listening to her it didn't feel like a very wrong thing to do, you know, because they weren't really people, they were monsters.

There was another girl who said that the leprechaun on her cereal box was telling her she was worthless and should kill herself.

All of these people were trying to learn to live on their own. If they could even think about it, I knew for sure that I could do it.

I an asshole to the staff. I was smart and could compete with them for the admiration of the fruit loops. I had my own agenda. Some of those girls were fucking hot. Not like, girls on TV hot, but hot for being real life people.

I wouldn't really know, I told myself, if I was gay or not if I didn't get to bang a girl. I'm not saying I would think like that now, but I did then right, and I'm trying to be honest. I don't try to take advantage of mentally disturbed girls now, I'm just a killer. See, I'm way more moral now than I was before.

It doesn't matter if I was potentially immoral or not though, because I wasn't able to make time with any one of them while I was in program. Even if I would have taken advantage of one or two of those nutty girls, I didn't and what counts it what you do, not what you would have done.

I was able to swipe a lot of neat stuff from the center. I mean, art supplies and books and shit. That was cool. Stuff stolen is way better than stuff you bought yourself, I mean, because it was stolen.

Another thing that was good about day treatment was that I could practice being assertive on those losers and if I fucked things up it wouldn't matter. After 15 weeks I never had to see any of them again. So, I became like another person with them. A strong minded, self-assured, demanding person. It was neat as hell. At first I did it with everyone, but the wackos were too, well, wacko. They weren't a fair sampling of how normal people would react. I mean, that was what I thought at the time. It wouldn't be until I really got out on my own that I learned that there are damned few actual normal people. People are fucking crazy, if you hadn't noticed. I mean, you might be crazy too and I'm not trying to offend you. Crazy people can do a lot, but still, it is something to think about how few people are really sane if you get to know them well enough to know.

I know I'm really going on about this program I went to, but it was important to me. It helped to turn me into a killer and believe me, that is a good thing. I really started liking myself after that. It was like, what I was supposed to do. Fulfilling, if you can understand that. So, I think it is important that I talk about it.

It is how I feel like I'm OK and as far as anyone who isn't OK, once I've killed every one of them there will only be OK people.

I spoke in the group therapy part of the day all the time. I mean, I really participated. Not just talking about myself, which I loved to do, but responding to other people and their stupid, pathetic, meaningless problems. Sometimes I felt like I had helped them a lot. Which was a real kick since the staff were supposed to be there for that.

Being encouraged to talk about myself was like a God damned holiday. The other clients had to be prodded to open up and when they did they bawled like stupid babies. It was as if there was so little substance to them that only their most deeply painful revelations were available to them as topics of conversation.

I had no such problem. I had so much unimportant drivel I could talk about that I'd never have to bring up a difficult or painful subject. I may have cried just a little, when talking about some stupid meaningless thing, but I only did that to fit in. The thing was though, that I really couldn't have talked about my real problems.

These people were in there crying over liking a boy that didn't like them back or having a parent that didn't understand them and dip shit stuff like that. Could you imagine how they'd react if I told them the shit I was dealing with? It'd be like Julius Erving playing basketball with a junior high school basketball team.

I wasn't really going to tell Uncle Will at all, but around the end of the 10th week I did. He didn't object as I expected he would. First he wanted to know how I was paying for it. I told him Social Services picked up the whole bill. Other than that, he only had one concern.

"Who did you tell them I am to you?" he asked.

"It doesn't really come up," I said, "I think once I mentioned that I live with my lover. I'm an adult, I can have a lover if I want to. It isn't what I'm there about though, so I didn't need to go into any details."

That seemed to satisfy Uncle Will well enough.

I was starting to get tired of the program around that same time. The most use it had been was done after two weeks. I felt better about myself, I was more assertive, and I could get where I was supposed to be on time. Day treatment wasn't much use for bigger problems. Not for me, and not for the other clients either.

One of the last times I went to day treatment, group therapy, I was half listening to this one girl going on about her parents not accepting that she didn't eat meat. Once again, her mother served a meal for dinner with meat in it, and no alternative selection. It wasn't the first time her mother had done this, and it wasn't the first time we all had to hear about it.

Out of boredom more than anything else, I gave in to a temptation I had managed to keep under control the last time and the time before that this issue had come up. I'm talking about the temptation to give her some honest, kick-in-the-ass feedback.

It was a good thing I had waited. I'd had weeks to roll around what I would say in my head. If I'd let her have it the previous week or three weeks before it wouldn't have been nearly as biting.

What I said was, "You are what? 30 years old? And still living at home which is, I think, no small imposition on your parents who surely thought their child raising years would end when you were 18 or 20, surely at 22, what do you think? And on top of this, you expect your mommy to feed you, and feed you what you want to eat. Do I have this right?" I yelled. Well, not yelled exactly, but louder than a normal voice.

I'm sure it was yelling to her. She started crying 10 words in.

"That's rather harsh, Peter, perhaps you could tell Sharon how you feel without hurting her feelings," One of the meddlesome staff members told me.

I swear, that was the first time right then, after like 30 sessions of group, that one of the other clients had a name. Until then they were just the wackos. And it wasn't because she was crying, I mean, this girl was crying all the time. Maybe because I was making her cry, maybe because of that, her tears got real to me. I didn't want to let on that I was starting to care about the stupid little wacko, but it must have shown because I did ease up on her.

"You may think your eating habits are the most important thing in the whole world, but I doubt if your mother's life revolves around what you put in your mouth. She isn't being insensitive or cruel, she's just putting food on her family's table. If you don't want to eat it, use the refrigerator and the stove like every other 30 year-old on the planet and feed your own damn self."

I said it then. I had done a good job of ripping her apart too, so I settled back in my chair.

Sharon's reaction wasn't at all what I was expecting. The little butterfly grew a set of teeth.

"You're one to talk!" She yelled at me.

Apparently she wasn't the only one who could use Day Treatment Program to practice assertiveness.

"Me? When have you ever heard me complaining and whining about some stupid problem? Never, That's when!" I yelled back at her.

The staff had completely lost control of the group now, which was just as well, really.

"That's right, Peter doesn't have any problems at all. Then what the hell are you doing here?" Sharon demanded.

"I have my problems," I shouted back at her, "and they aren't stupid, unimportant problems like who doesn't want to date me or what I don't like to eat. My problems would make you and your petty little bullshit problems wilt away from unmitigated embarrassment!" I told her. Maybe I didn't say that exactly. Maybe I didn't know what unmitigated meant then, but I do now and that is what I would have said if I had known the word then. OK, so maybe I am not really sure now either what unmitigated actually means, but it is a word I have heard used in a sentence like this and it sounds to me like it would fit here. I didn't say it then, but I would have if I'd heard the word before.

I don't know why you are making such a big deal out of it. It doesn't matter. What matters is that then I was in for it. I realized as soon as the words fell out of my mouth that I had inadvertently brought massive amounts of grief on myself. I would have to spill my guts or be prodded relentlessly like the others were for the remaining three weeks of the program.

None of them were going to let me get away with talking about anything less than *the* problem now. That's the thing. Once these damn people catch the smell of a juicy story they are on it like a pack of wild dingoes on an injured kangaroo in the Australian outback: they are going to hunt it down and devour it.

Not Okay

Did I mention I've watched a lot of National Geographic specials? I know more about kangaroos and dingoes than I do about people.

Anyway, while I'm shaking like a fucking epileptic, one of the staff people steps in.

"Yes, Peter, I would like to know more about your problems too," She says.

I'm sorry, the truth is, I don't know what an epileptic shakes like. I never saw a special about them. I bet most of the time they don't shake at all. I shouldn't have said that, it was insensitive to epileptics. I guess I should have said I was shaking like something else. But what? Shaking like a Chevy Suburban with a broken tie rod? That sounds good. Fuck it, though the point is I was shaking.

I had lost it. I had been maneuvered into this and now there was nothing I could do. I tried to breathe but I really couldn't. No matter how much I inhaled nothing would really come out, so I'd inhale a little more.

"The man I live with isn't really my lover," I said between inhales. I couldn't believe I was saying it. But it wasn't to the whole group, I was talking just to Sharon.

Believe this, nobody was interrupting me. Fuck, no. I mean, this was the good part, right. I was already starting to cry.

God damn, I thought. I'd avoided this for two months. I was almost home free and now look at me.

"I guess he is, in a way. I don't know what else to call him," I said.

Now I was really crying. I was crying all over the place, thick, itchy tears. I was just like the wackos when they cried, really, I was no better than any of the wackos, crying and sniffing and none of them could have possibly known the reason why.

I can't begin to tell you how much I wanted to stop right there, how much I needed to stop. I'd had so much more than enough. But if I had shut up at that point, I'm telling you, the whole group would have been sitting around wondering what the hell I had been crying about.

I don't want to get soppy, but this was the thing and it is a soppy kind of thing. The thing was that I started to understand the others a little bit for the first time. Right then, with me in the same place, I got what I didn't get before. That they started crying when they got close to the really hard problem. That just getting close to it hurts so bad that you're crying and torn up long before you can get out exactly what is making you cry, you know.

I mean, these people don't know anything about what I'm dealing with and I'm being a total fucking mess.

"You were doing so well, go on," Someone told me. I don't know who.

"That was when I was yelling at her," I said, pointing at Sharon.

It was so true. In a rage, I could yell it, but now, quietly, I couldn't get enough air in my lungs to say anything important.

"What did he do to you?" Someone asked. It was a guy and he asked in a tone that suggested he already knew.

"He used me," I said, really low. I guess I shouldn't have been ashamed of myself, but I was.

"He used me, and he made me feel like it was normal, like I was supposed to be used. He kept on using me and I stayed. I'm still there. I mean, he stole me from me," I managed to get out.

I recognized what I had been feeling as panic only after it started to subside. Well, not really subside, more like turn to euphoria. Maybe from hyperventilating, panic was giving way to a dreamy kind of high only without smoking any pot.

"I guess I'm here because I want to get my 'me' back" and let me tell you, that was it for the day.

I didn't bother to go out with the group to play volleyball. I stayed inside and worked on putting myself back together.

I thought about what I had revealed, and I cried a shit load and a half more before I was done.

When I left that day, I really did have a better understanding of the other members of the group, each with their own problems. They weren't nearly as wacko as I thought they were. Except the one who has cereal mascots talk to her. She's batshit crazy. The others though, they were the same as I was: damaged goods. People who were not OK and no amount of thinking they were OK was going to change that.

I may not have said enough for any of them to really have a clue what I was so upset about, but it still did me a lot of good. I figured out what had eluded me for so long. I entered a phase of my life where I thought that the I'm OK You're OK book was total shit.

4.

I didn't go to program the next day or the day after that. The first 10 weeks of it had been boring. It was a lot more real now. And not real in a good way.

Told myself I had better things to do with my time then get all cry baby in front of a bunch of wackos. Could you blame me? This was some difficult shit and they hadn't warned me it would happen. What if I get to be crying so much I end up like them? I mean, come on.

I scored a dime bag of pot from a kid named Zipper on the Hill. Really, there are lots of hills in and around Spring Valley, but only one was known as 'The' Hill. It was kind of a housing development that was built in the '50s and wasn't taken good care of. Mostly black families and white people on welfare lived there. Zipper was like 13 and black enough.

His mom was white and lived there with some other black guy that wasn't Zipper's dad. I think, maybe, because she was the only white person with black kids in the development, she worked extra hard to talk what white people think of as the black talk. She talked that kind of black as if it were a second language though. I mean, you could tell she had to learn it. You could tell she'd practiced. She threw the slang around just enough thicker, and drawled her a's and u's just enough longer, I thought, to know she was putting it on.

On TV they really put it on. No black person I ever saw talked like the black people on TV. She was something in between real black person and TV black person. Not that I'm an expert or anything.

Not Okay

I kind of figured Zipper was selling for his mom, since she'd always be checking on him out the window, and one time she sent him to the store for a whole bunch of shit and didn't give him any money. I'd just copped some pot from him so I figured she must have known he had money on him from that.

Once, when Zipper didn't have anything, he offered to swing by my place later that night. I nearly knocked a Neighborhood Watch sign off its pole when I said no, swinging my arms. Zipper is a good-looking boy, I thought, if Uncle Will got a look at him...shit.

I wasn't ever a big pot head or anything, but right then I needed it. I got good and high a few times over the three days after my difficult group. Once or twice, as I was coming down, I smoked up some more and brought myself right back up. It was therapeutic, I think. If I were running group therapy, I'd get everybody really baked. I think it would be easier for people to open up, and I bet there'd be quite a bit less crying too.

The third day after, which wasn't a group day, I'm naked on the sofa, smoking a badly rolled joint. I'm buzzed but I'm not totally stoned yet, and there's a knock at the door. It was fucked up, because I wouldn't have expected a knock. I mean, we've got a fucking doorbell.

Who knocks on a door even though there is a doorbell? In case you are wondering, who would be Sharon, from the program. She knew where to find me because I had let her drive me home from group a couple of times.

"I just wanted to know if you were going to come back to group?" she said, as if it were a question rather than a statement. I don't know what you would call that. An unrhetorical statement maybe, but that's what she said.

Her dark brown eyes seemed to sparkle like there was a reflection of a campfire in them. You can believe magazines and movies and shit if you want to. That guys like girl's asses and legs and tits and all, but fuck that. I'm telling you, sexy is all in the eyes. You get a girl like Sharon in front of you, and she's not what any magazine would call pretty, and she's way old, I mean, 30, and her tits aren't for nothing and her legs are kind of short and dumpy, but then she looks at you with those eyes and right when you get in her line of sight, then her eyes get a little bigger like she's trying to drink more of you in, now that is sexy.

I'm telling you; I never notice what people are wearing. I mean, maybe I do, but if I do, I don't remember it later. I mean, unless it's like clown shoes or something. But Sharon, I guess because I noticed her eyes I started noticing everything else too. Medium blue Corduroy skirt, lighter, powder blue blouse. Oh, and a silver brooch that looked really old, like an antique, with silvery kind of stones in it, shaped like a garlic bulb.

Now that I think about it, Sharon never looked this good in group. Her hair was always pretty flat, now it waved around her shoulders like a shampoo model's. I mean, she dressed up for me and did her hair and put on makeup too. She wasn't good at it or anything, but she did it and that was really sweet, you know.

I told her I was coming back, but that I'd needed a break from it.

"Tomorrow?" she asked.

"Yeah, sure. I'll be there tomorrow," I answered.

I might never have gone back had Sharon not come over. And even then, well, let me tell you., she stood around long enough for it to get awkward, like I was supposed to invite her in or something, but I didn't. I mean, not just that

Not Okay

I had my pot right out on the coffee table, but if I'd opened the door any wider she would have seen that I had no clothes on.

We stood looking at each other long enough for it to be clear that I wanted her to go away, then she said she had to get going, as if it were her idea, then she left.

The next morning though, she was right at my door making sure I would keep my word to her. She brought me to program in the new car her father bought her.

That kind of pissed me off.

I mean, not that she picked me up and not that she had a new car or even that her father bought it for her, but that she was always bitching about how awful her parents treated her and how much they hate her.

Nice way to show your hate, I thought, buying her a new fucking car. I could use some enemies like that.

People at group welcomed me back and, just as I expected, they pressured me to talk about my problems. I declined as politely as I could, and they relented for then, but we all knew it wasn't over.

This time I played a little basketball. I played a little harder than usual, thinking about how I couldn't put them off for three weeks. They were going to make me spill and I didn't want to do it. I thought about what it was about my story that was so hard to say.

After a lot of thinking I decided it was that I stayed with Uncle Will. I let things go on and on and I could have left, but I didn't.

It was that and it was what that must have said about me. That was what was bothering me the most. When I did start talking, about a week later, that was what I talked about.

It must have sounded ridiculous to the group. I mean, I hadn't told them what it was I had been staying with.

They still didn't know who Uncle Will was to me, but I went on as if they knew the whole story. Disjointed and fragmented was the only way I was able to tell it, so that was the way they would have to hear it.

"When I was 12 I didn't have a choice. He just took me," That's what I said. And I was crying again.

"I never should have stayed this long. It just became what I knew," I said.

People asked questions which was good in one way, because it kept me talking when I got stuck, but it was bad too because it sent me off on tangents that made it even harder to follow what I was saying.

I answered one question with "Yeah, Uncle Will tried to stop me from leaving, but if I really wanted to go, wouldn't I have found a way? Wouldn't I have? I didn't try very hard."

"Where did you go to school this whole time?" Someone in the group asked.

"Oh, Uncle Will didn't let me go to school," I answered, "I haven't been to school since 9th grade."

And then the simplest wacko in the group asked the simplest question.

"If you didn't go to school, how did your mind know you had gotten older?"

That set me thinking. The stupid wacko was right. He really was.

Things were going great, I mean great, and when things are going great in group, when the group is really doing some good for someone, that's when a stupid staff member is going to butt in and ruin it. I mean it, it's true, we do fine without their psychology educated shit.

"Peter, are you saying this Will fellow was a stranger who kidnaped you?"

"Yes," I said low.

"And you were 13 years old?"

"12," I cried.

"You were not allowed to grow intellectually or grow emotionally since then. Inside, you remained a frightened and confused little boy. You may have aged on the outside, but you were stalled on the inside. You can't continue to blame that helpless little boy for his inability to defend himself. It wasn't his fault then, and it isn't your fault now," I was told.

I sat and listened. I was learning a lot. I could believe what the staff guy was telling me, I could believe it in my mind, but it was going to take some time before I would really believe it, I mean, believe it in my heart.

"Who thinks it was Peter's fault?" Another of the staff members chimed in as if right and wrong could be determined by popular opinion. This one was an assistant and a college student. She usually didn't say anything. My problems were getting the attention of everyone, I can tell you that. It was real entertaining shit.

Not one person in the group thought it was my fault. Not one except, to some lessening degree, myself.

"But where does that leave me?" I asked, and nobody knew what I meant.

I clarified, "I'm 12 years old for the sixth year, it still isn't my fault, big whoopidi-shit, but I'm still there. Like Mike Mulligan and his steam shovel, Mary Anne, 'how am I going to get out?'"

"The same way you should have gotten out six years ago. You will get out with help," Sharon responded.

I was being offered all kinds of assistance now, from most of the members of the group. Some were available to help me move my things, one offered to put me up at his apartment until I found my own place, several offered to beat Uncle Will into a bloody sack of meat.

I hadn't even thought of asking anyone to rescue me before, but that really was what I needed.

I turned them all down, but the invitations were left open. I could take anyone up on their offer after I thought about it.

"I have a question," Reluctantly interjected a young man from the far end of the semicircle we sat around.

"Go ahead," A therapist encouraged.

"Who is Mike Mulligan?" He seriously asked.

Well then people started arguing over if Mike Mulligan said that he and his steam shovel could dig as much in one day as a 100 men could dig in a week, or if it was 20 men, and one wacko tried to say it was in one 100 weeks, which really opened it up. When someone else asked if it was a diesel shovel a couple of the other members of the group sent cookies and empty plastic juice cups flying in his direction.

All of this helped as much as anything else that had happened in group. It got my mind off the pain that the first half of group had brought up. I actually felt pretty good after program and continued to feel good until I got home. It wasn't so good then because Uncle Will wasn't alone. He had that neighbor kid, Little Willie with him. They were in Uncle Will's bedroom. That was it. Uncle Will was doing it with the 10 year-old. A fucking 10 year-old. I was feeling sick again.

The big way I could tell that program was helping me was that as I got a little better, I could see how awful what Uncle Will did to me and Little Will really was. I had a little bit of pot left in a ziplock bag. Not really enough to get stoned but I smoked it and the last nibs of three roaches, which gave me a comfortable little buzz: just enough to fall asleep with.

In group the next day I wanted to talk about Little Willie, but I didn't get the chance. Instead, we focused on one of the other members of the group. He had a moment of weakness the night before and went out and got drunk. It was hard-on him because he had managed to stay sober for six months and just a week ago was showing off his six month chip from AA as if it were made of gold.

Nothing had set him off, there wasn't any event in his life that made him sad or angry or depressed or anything, he just did it. I think it was getting the chip that did it. The one thing that pushed him through the month or two before getting it was that goal. Once he achieved it, he didn't have the goal anymore.

I didn't say that though, because I was pissed at him for having the problem when I wanted to talk about my problems. His problem had monopolized the entire session. My problem had monopolized the whole session the day before, but that was different. My problems were more important than his were.

The next day wasn't a program day, then it was the weekend and then it was the first session of the next week. This was when, finally, I got to bring up my concerns about Little Willie. I didn't get much time. My chance was last in the session and there were only a few minutes until we were done. Sometimes, when it was important, we ran over on our sessions and cut into the next period, which was playing volleyball or basketball or capture the flag.

I thought this was important enough to run over time, but the staff didn't. Really, they seemed to gloss over the whole thing.

When program was over I was privileged to have a private consultation with Dr. Denton himself, the actual psychologist in charge of the program.

Those members of the group who made fun of the names of people like bosses, teachers, and doctors, called this guy doctor Denthead. I called him Doctor Underwear which I thought was much funnier, but they didn't get it at all. His name, Dr. Denton that is, is the brand name of an underwear that nobody actually wears.

So, there's Doctor Underwear in his office, looking at me like he's the headmaster and I'm a badly behaved student, and he starts like this, "Child molestation is a very serious charge."

I don't know where he is going yet but things are getting worse with each word, and he goes on, "Your Uncle Will could be arrested, he could even go to jail. This would be a very bad thing to happen if he were innocent,"

"What are talking about?" I ask, and he tells me.

"You are getting a lot of attention with this story of yours. It is perfectly natural for you to want to continue to get that attention. But you should give some thought to who you might be hurting in the process."

"Wait a fuck!" I said loudly, "I'm not lying."

Doctor Underwear continued. He'd already made up his mind, and being so well educated and shit, he didn't consider it too possible that he'd made a mistake.

"I had some concerns about your accusations, Peter. I spoke to your Uncle Will," And right there, my stomach was in my mouth.

While he's talking I'm repeating under my breath, "You idiot. You fucking idiot. You shit stained fucking idiot. I am in so much trouble now. You fucking idiot. You stupid shit fucking idiot," and on like that.

"Your Uncle Will is worried about you. He would like to come in. That way the three of us can have a little talk," Doctor Underwear is saying and I'm glaring at him. Fuck, I'm trying to burn a hole through him with my eyes.

"Doctor, you are a fucking idiot. You don't have any idea what kind of danger you've put me in do you. You stupid fucking idiot. Did you even think it was possible I was telling the truth? What the fuck were you thinking?" I asked, but I already knew what he was thinking.

My story was too unpleasant to accept, so he didn't. This is really the thing that makes it possible for monsters like Uncle Will to do what they do. The fact that people don't want to believe it so much that they'll pretend it isn't real even when it is right in front of them.

"What about patient confidentiality? What the fuck about that? You stupid piece of shit," I shouted. I'm standing now. Doctor Underwear is still in his chair.

"How much did you tell him?" I asked.

"Well, I" he hedged.

"Tell me!" I yelled.

"I was only thinking about what would be in your best interest," He responded.

I'd heard that before and let me tell you, it is never a good thing.

"The road to hell man, the fucking road to hell," I said, and then I left.

That was a reference to a quote, 'The road to hell is paved with good intentions.' I thought it was Samuel Johnson who said it, but once, when I said so someone else told me that Johnson was quoting someone else. Whatever was the case Doctor Underwear's good intentions had paved my road to hell.

There was nothing I could do but go home and deal with the disaster. I was sure he would already be packing. Whenever there was a chance of exposure we would start packing and pretty soon we would just be gone.

Of course, Uncle Will was waiting for me when I got home.

"I had an interesting talk with your psychiatrist today," He said, much calmer than I expected him to be.

"He's not my shrink, just an ass wipe," I replied, trying not to care.

"He said you were troubled. He wanted me to shed some light on your emotional state," Uncle Will told me.

"Did you?" I asked.

"I told him you were always making up outlandish stories, even when you were little. That it was too much for your dear mother to deal with, so she sent you off to live with me, your Uncle Will. I told him I'm afraid you haven't improved any over the years though. We hoped you might, but you were still the same. I told him I hoped this treatment program was finally going to help you," He said.

"That's not exactly the truth though, is it?" I asked.

"No, but I didn't know what you might have told him, or what you were about to. This way he won't believe anything you say. You might as well not go back to your little therapy group at all Peter,"

Uncle Will said this as if it were a suggestion, but I promise you, it was not open for negotiation.

"No problem," I answered, "Shit wasn't helping me anyway."

"Did you tell them anything you shouldn't have?" He asked.

Shit fuck, I thought. The motherfucker doesn't know anything.

"I mostly listened," I said, acting like I didn't care.

"Good!" Uncle Will said, and it really looked like he was believing me.

My big crisis had passed uneventfully. And this time I wasn't going to wait until there was another one. In the morning, after Uncle Will left for work, I called Sharon and asked her to help me move.

She agreed right away and said she would be at my house at ten the next morning. It was a group day and she had never missed one in the entire twelve weeks, but she was giving one up for me.

It was perfect.

I needed the help, I guess, but I needed a friend more than anything. I didn't really have one. I mean, there were a few people I was friendly with, like Zipper, but I didn't have a real friend. Sharon might not have been my first choice, if I were picking, but she was really eager to be my friend and that had to count for something.

Uncle Will didn't come home that night until well after midnight. I figured he must have taken a boy on one of those special outings of his. This worked great for me. I didn't really want to see him before my vanishing act unless I had to.

I left his dinner wrapped on a plate in the refrigerator and turned in early. I didn't sleep, but I laid in my bed telling myself that I was going to fall asleep any minute. When Uncle Will did come home, I heard him rummage around in the kitchen. He heated up his dinner and ate it.

I clenched my eyes tight when he opened my door to check on me. I stayed as still as I could. I tried to breathe evenly. It worked. Uncle Will believed I was asleep and moved on.

I heard the television in his bedroom for another hour or so before he turned it off and went to sleep.

That was it. When I got up in the morning he would already be at work, when he returned home I would be gone.

I would never have to see him again.

That thought helped me to relax enough that I might have fallen asleep. But I was also thinking about what I would do next and I couldn't think of a single thing. After tonight I didn't know where I would sleep, what I would eat, how I would live, nothing. And that sure as fuck kept me awake.

I had no plans, no hope, no life.

When Sharon knocked on the door I was still in my bed, even though I hadn't gotten any sleep at all.

I answered the door half dressed.

"Why don't you ring the doorbell?" I asked.

"Doorbells can be rigged up to check your fingerprint," she told me, "they use doorbells to trace your comings and goings."

"Oh, of course," I said, not asking who 'they' were or why 'they' cared where anyone came or went.

She may have been a wacko but she was bright-eyed and getting more beautiful every day. She was flowing with positive energy, something she never did in group. It was as if, in her whole life, no one had ever let her help them with anything ever before, and now that she had her chance she was going all out.

She was wearing a perfectly white sweatshirt and jeans that were so crisp they still had the bends where they were folded on the store shelf. Sharon must have gone shopping for clothing to move someone in and this is what she came up with.

"Ready to get started?" She asked me, glowing with a strange enthusiasm.

"I just have to grab a thing or two," I answered.

"More than a thing or two, I hope," She said.

"I don't own very much," I told her.

"Oh," She pouted.

"What?" I asked.

She opened my door wider and pointed out into the parking area. There was a large yellow rental truck sitting there. She apparently thought she was helping someone move rather than helping someone escape.

I didn't want her to feel disappointed, so we used the truck. The truck, and everything else she bought for the occasion. I'm talking boxes, packing tape, bubble wrap. Sharon really went for it. I mean, even after we removed everything boxable from the apartment, we still had a good-sized stack of empty boxes and rolls of tape left over.

Even with all the personal property loaded up, mine and Uncle Will's, the truck looked empty, so we started loading furniture too.

While dragging Uncle Will's sofa out, Little Willie stopped us.

"You moving?" He asked surprised.

"Yeah, moving," I said, realizing that school had let out. Little Willie's bus goes right past our complex. He must have seen the moving truck and ran here when he got off his bus.

It was 3:00 in the afternoon, give or take. The clocks had gotten packed and we were working so hard we didn't notice five hours pass. Thing was, Uncle Will would be home from work in less than three hours and I wanted to have a shitload of miles between us and Spring Valley by then.

There was a lot of nothing left in the apartment so it looked like we would have no difficulty making that happen. After Sharon and I struggled with the cherry wood entertainment center, which was really too heavy for us to manage by ourselves, scratching and banging it and the door jam along the way, then heaving it onto the truck, it didn't look like there was room for much more.

We left the beds behind, but not much else. Before leaving I made a sweep of the apartment, checking every room for anything of value that we might have missed. There was nothing to remember.

I unscrewed the light bulb in the refrigerator and took it with me, along with the partial rolls of toilet paper in our bathrooms and the plastic spindles so that new rolls could not be put on. Sharon had already closed the back of the truck, so I took these things up into the cab with me.

At 3:30, maybe 3:45, we pulled out leaving an apartment stripped to its walls. Sharon asked me where we were going and I shrugged.

"I thought you knew," I said.

"All right," she replied as though she expected this, "I have a little money. We will find you an apartment."

"Not near here," I said.

"No," She replied.

"I need to be somewhere with good public transportation. Buses and stuff," I told her, knowing I would need to get myself a job and would need a way to get to it and back.

Sharon decided that it would be hardest for Uncle Will to find me in Manhattan, so that is where we headed. Once we were on the New York State Thruway, I tossed the toilet paper spindles out of the cab window and watched one of them get crushed by the tires of an oncoming RV.

"What did you do that for?" Sharon asked.

"I didn't need it," I replied.

"Then why did you take it?"

"I didn't want Uncle Will to have it," I answered, then turned away to look out the window.

I didn't realize I was singing to myself, but I was.

"... Strung from pages on highway 9, chrome wheeled, fuel injected, and steppin out over the line...," I sung until Sharon reached over and turned the radio on.

"Don't tell me you don't like Bruce," I said surprised.

"I don't," She said, and told me why, then added, "but your singing is even worse."

"Oh, that's so much better," I grumped.

"Oh honey, don't get dejected. There are plenty of things I'm sure you are very good at. You didn't want to be a singer did you?"

I didn't know what dejected meant but I went on as if I did. Once, months after that, I looked it up, but I still didn't understand. It's just one of those words that smart people use to feel smarter than stupid people.

"I wanted to be Bruce Springsteen," I said in mock disappointment.

"I think he's already being him," she said.

"Fuck Bruce Springsteen anyway. Whose boss is he? He isn't my boss. Fuck him, who needs him," I said.

The thing is, I would have been pouting anyway. I couldn't help it, even being embarrassed by it. So, I did it a little more, you know, to make it look like I was pretending.

Sharon though, she took it seriously.

I looked at her and imagined her saying I could be a mime. I mean, I could see her lips moving too, it was like

67

she wanted to say it, but now that I was pouting she didn't want to hurt me. I got so mad at her right there, you know. I mean, imagining mad because I'd only imagined her saying I should be a mime. But when she got teary I realized I'd said, "fuck you bitch" aloud.

"I didn't say that to you," I clarified, which helped a little, but not completely.

"Voices?" She asked.

It wasn't but I just shrugged.

"It's OK," she told me, "I have them too. They get to you sometimes. Sometimes you have to tell them off."

I might have tried to explain but I saw the lights of the city and that became more important. I thought we were going right into the city, but we didn't. Instead, we pulled off into a Budget Lodge in Jersey City, just across the river from Manhattan, and Sharon rented us a hotel room.

We went into the room for a minute or two and went right back out. Sharon had an overnight bag packed and she put that on the one double bed. She turned on the air conditioner even though it was plenty cool in there and checked inside the mini fridge. It was cold, so she put a bottle of grape juice from her bag in it.

"Hungry?" She asked.

"Yeah!" I said and we were out the door again.

We left the truck in the hotel parking lot and walked next door to the Denny's restaurant. I'd actually never eaten in a Denny's before. I'd seen them all over the place, but the thing was, either Uncle Will and I were eating cheap, that was Burger King or McDonald's, or we were eating nice, like Red Lobster. We just didn't do much in between. We weren't like that. Well, Uncle Will wasn't like that. I didn't know what I was like. I could learn to be like whatever I wanted now.

After I bit into my hamburger I thought, shit, this isn't any better than Burger King and it's twice the price. Fuck that.

Sharon was eating some kind of salad with gross looking crumbly cheese on it. I didn't want to leave so much of my food on my plate, especially after saying I was hungry. That's the only reason I offered her a bite. I really wasn't thinking about her stupid vegetarianism crap.

You can bet she took it personal though. The way I was going, I wouldn't have blamed her if she took me right back to Uncle Will. She didn't though, and she dealt with my being an asshole better than she would have from most anyone else, I think.

She started giving me the vegetarian pitch, starting with something about human digestive systems not being like those of carnivorous animals and ending with a load of cruelty to animals shit.

I told her I thought animals, having legs, have at least a chance to get away, where a carrot is just fucked.

"Someone should be looking out for the poor carrots!" I said, "Those carrots are helpless."

"Be serious, Peter, do you really think animals should be brutally slaughtered?" she asked, and I thought about Uncle Will.

"Some."

Sharon looked at me. I mean, she looked right at my eyes as if she was looking through them. I looked back and I couldn't tell if I was seeing sadness or what. Maybe I never looked at someone's eyes for a long time before that moment. But it was like she understood what I was feeling when she did that.

"I wouldn't have thought bad of you if you had killed him," She said.

I kept looking at her eyes. I didn't say that I should have, but my feelings were leaking right through my eyes and she was grabbing them right up.

"He's not human, you know. That's why I had to help you. He's one of them. He's a monster, Peter,"

"Oh, shit," I said, "That was you? In group? I totally didn't realize you were the monster wa...,"

Lucky for me I caught myself before I said 'wacko.' Unlucky, that I couldn't think of another word that starts with 'w' to say to finish my sentence. And I'd said 'wacko' in group enough times that she must have known what I was saying, so I guess it wasn't very lucky after all.

Sharon was being very nice to me. I liked her. And yet I kept being mean.

"Peter, really, he preys on the weak and the helpless, he infects you with his evil and goes on to the next victim. That's what a monster does. It may have been human once, but when you do what people like Will did to you, you give up your humanity."

I knew Sharon was right a month before, when she said it in group. I mean, she might have believed Uncle Will was a monster literally. You can't forget, nice as she is, that she's a wacko. Metaphorically, he was a monster. I mean, there are no such thing as the other kind of monster, so metaphorical monsters are the only real monsters if you think about it. I was thinking about it.

I was thinking about what an asshole I was being to Sharon too. I didn't want to be, but I was anyway. Sharon got me thinking that it was because of the evil Uncle Will infected me with. What he did to me turned me into a monster, I started thinking. And that made what he did worse than I thought even. It made me think more than ever that I shouldn't have just left him like that. He shouldn't have been left to keep on turning more innocent boys into monsters I thought. I should have killed him while I had the chance. I really should have.

Did I tell you Sharon got really into looking at my eyes? After dinner, back in the hotel room, it was starting to creep me out.

I turned on the television and started watching the rerun of M*A*S*H* when Frank Burns is left in charge and it goes to his head. I didn't like the show but I'd still seen that episode before. I didn't like M*A*S*H because it was bloody. It was supposed to be a comedy, but I don't think it is very funny to have people bleeding and dying and shit. Maybe it's just me. Anyway, Sharon went into the bathroom and didn't come back out for a long time.

The shower water came on and I turned the TV off. She wouldn't be able to hear it with the shower on and I only had it on to make her stop looking at me.

She stayed in there a long time. Long enough that I needed to piss and wished she would hurry up. She left the door open, which was kind of creepy too, but fuck if I was going to go in there and piss while she was showering.

I was sweaty and stinky too from all that moving and shit, but I wasn't going to shower. I don't really tell people this, but I'll tell you, I kind of like the smell of my own stink. I mean, not a day later, but right then, when I'd been sweaty an hour or so after working hard, I just kind of like it.

Enough time passed that I went ahead and pissed in the outer sink. I ran the water to wash it down. I'm not disgusting. After that I put myself under the covers of one of the beds with one of the pillows from the other bed as well as both of the pillows from the bed I was in.

When she came out she got into the same bed I was in. Not only that but she got much closer to me than she needed to. I mean, it was a big fucking bed.

My heart went off like a coffee percolator even before she started stroking me. I didn't just pull away, I jumped out of the bed and away.

"You don't like me?" she asked.

I was circling the room, looking at her and down and down and at her.

"Fuck. Fuck shit. Shit. Shit fuck," I said holding my hair to keep it from falling out.

"If I was going to find someone attractive, sure, you'd be attractive, but shit shit shit I don't want to be attracted. If you did all of this to get at my cock I'm sorry, you should've said something. I'm not a sex toy anymore. I'm not for sale. I don't want to be anyone's thing again."

And Sharon tried to tell me she didn't think of me like that, but it didn't matter what she said. I was circling the floor and sputtering, "no no no no" and shit like that.

The truth was, right up until dinner I might have wanted to bang this girl. A little bit at least. I kind of wanted to see if I was gay or not, you know. I'd thought about banging a real actual girl for years. But it was the way it went down that fucked it up. I couldn't tell her that, it would really have fucked her up, but the truth was, if she had let me make the move, if she had acted like she wasn't really interested, you know, like her letting me bang her was doing me a favor, I bet I'd have made that move. I bet she'd have gotten everything she wanted. But she didn't do it like that, and I didn't want to be the one on the bottom, you know, the one being taken. Not ever again.

In the morning I knew that sex was what she had wanted from me. Or love, or some kind of combination of them both. I also knew that she gave up on getting either one. Sleeping in one big bed alone with one pillow while I slept in the other bed with three.

That was the end of the game for her, and she accepted defeat. Too bad. By respecting my wishes and backing off, I felt a little more like I could trust her. Like, if given a little time, I would have wanted to kiss her and after that maybe more.

She got me an apartment in the Bronx just one stop north of Manhattan on the A train. It was a lot cheaper than Manhattan and worked just fine. She paid security and three months' rent but that was it. She didn't leave me with any money and when we said goodbye it was hardly even a goodbye. No hug and no eye contact. And I mean, I looked at her. If she had glanced up once our eyes would have met and maybe things would have ended up different, but that didn't happen.

It wasn't her fault. I could have said, 'hey' or something. Instead I said, "Sorry," and she said, "Me too," and she walked out the door.

I grabbed my hair with both of my hands and looked up, seeing a crack in my ceiling for the first time. It had a wet stain around it, as if it was a place where the rain leaked in, but this was the third floor of a six floor building.

In a little time, I would learn that the bathtub drain upstairs leaks. That every time the upstairs neighbors take a bath their dirty bath water drips down on my stuff. It is pretty gross really, but the upstairs people were pigs that didn't take a lot of baths, so I kept a galvanized washtub that I found at a thrift shop for $2.00 under the leak and learned to deal with it.

Really, the thing that pissed me off about it the most was that it reminded me that they had a bathtub in their apartment and I only had a shower. I liked baths more than showers, but I wasn't going to ask them to use their bathtub because I didn't want to make the crack in my ceiling any worse than it had to be.

Oh, but the first thing to deal with was that I had three months to find a job and start paying my own rent. three months. As I thought about it I thought about the bottle of grape juice Sharon had put in the hotel refrigerator. We forgot it and right then I'd have liked a swig of it.

The neighbor across the hall from me introduced himself and his family in Spanish, which I didn't understand, but I managed to trade him some of Uncle Will's classical music records for some food.

I didn't go back to Orange County to complete the last couple weeks of program, but I didn't really need to. I had gotten more out of it than I had expected. I was 18 years old and free. Not only that, but a girl was willing to bang me. Who cares if we did it or not, she wanted to. That meant there had to be other girls out there who would want to bang me too.

I fell asleep on a couple of blankets on the floor wishing I had taken one of the beds after all. and thinking about all the girls there were in New York City. How, out of all of them, there had to be hundreds that would want to bang me. You can bet I had a hard-on but I didn't do anything about it. I just let myself fall asleep with it all stiff and solid. Fuck, I thought. I better save it for all those New York City girls.

Not Okay

5.

Some subway train cars are covered with graffiti, others have nearly none. Either way they send their roars through miles of tunnels like dragons in caves. I'd be standing on the platform waiting for the train, I mean, wanting it to come because that was what I was there for, yet when I heard it scream I'd always jump with fear.

People who worked for a living were idiots. They really were. I don't mean it in a bad way, I was trying to become one of them even, but still they were. They'd be on the platform with me and when the scream happened they hardly moved. Every time they assumed it was the train, never thought for a minute that it could be a dragon. So far it always did turn out to be a subway train, but that doesn't mean it couldn't have been a dragon. They should have jumped I think, a little anyway, because every time it really could be a dragon, but they just don't know. Like I said, they are idiots.

I was job hunting. Had been for weeks. I didn't start until after my rent credit was used up and I was behind on my rent, otherwise I wouldn't have had many worries.

I was smoking too, right on the platform next to one of the red and white "No Smoking" signs. Uncle Will put little "no smoking" signs in the house and on the dashboard of his car. Fuck Uncle Will, I was thinking, and fuck anyone who puts up "no smoking" signs. Right then, anyway. I hated those signs. At the same time, I would have stolen one for my apartment if the fucking things weren't bolted to the posts. It was the stupidest thing they could do, bolting the "No Smoking" signs to the posts. I mean, who would want to steal a "No Smoking" sign? Other than me, I mean.

75

I don't know if I told you, but I started smoking when I got to the city. I would have tried it years before but Uncle Will didn't like smokers, so you can bet I didn't. But Uncle Will wasn't with me now. I tried it and I tried it again until I got it down. Maybe I thought, if Uncle Will found me and I was a smoker he wouldn't want to take me back. Maybe I just like to smoke. You know, the bad thing about going to therapy is you start analyzing everything with shrink think. I shouldn't have even been concerned with why I was smoking, not when there were fucking dragons traipsing through the fucking subway tunnels.

When the train pulled up it turned out to be one of the ones that did have graffiti all over it and not a clean one or a dragon. I got in starting to breathe a little easier. I looked around at the other riders taking their seats, not one of them knowing how lucky they were that they were getting into a subway car rather than getting gobbled up by a dragon. Once in the train, I buttoned up my shirt and put on my clip-on tie. I bought a regular tie to job hunt in at first but brought it back to the store to have them help me figure out how to work it. After half an hour of trying they took it back and sold me the clip-on tie instead.

Being so far up town on the A train, I always got a seat. But come 125th street I always gave it up for some pregnant woman or old lady or some shit like that. It wasn't that I was all that nice, but fuck, if I didn't give up my seat they'd stare at me and pretty soon they'd have other folks staring at me too. That's the way it worked; they stare at you until you give up your fucking seat. Not everyone. They would leave some people alone. Old people. Women. Little kids. They all got to keep their seats. Me. I was always the one getting stared at.

This time was no exception, and when I got up I looked over at the next well built, young adult male with a seat thinking, he knew he was lucky, if I hadn't been there it would have been him. If I hadn't looked healthier than him he'd be the asshole standing instead of sitting.

I opened a bottle of Dr. Pepper and took a big swig, hanging onto a rail and looking at the spill stains on the floor and walls. There weren't any surfaces in the Subway system that didn't have stains on top of stains. There was so much filth that you couldn't really identify it. It wasn't like, oh, look there, it is a coffee spill, or oh, look there, someone threw up. Nothing that easy. It was so many stains on top of stains on top of stains that it all blended together into a monumental work of deranged contemporary art.

I kind of liked it, I thought, as I spit a little of my Dr. Pepper.

"Look at that!" I said to the old bitch who had stared me out of my seat, "I'm a mother fucking artist."

I should say that the reason I sold off Uncle Will's stuff and took so long to go job hunting was that the apartment was small. It was so small that I couldn't unpack all that stuff, not even a fraction of it. To get space as much as to make money I started selling things on the street.

I tried a few places but ended up around Astor Place and Saint Marks. That was on the East side. There were a few other people doing the same thing and the cops mostly left us alone. The thing was, it made me enough money to eat and do anything else I wanted until my rent credit ran out. It didn't make enough to pay my expenses and pay for rent too. That was why I was job hunting, but so far, trying to make things better was only making things worse. I must have spent fifty dollars on clothes and newspapers looking for a job, I'd be out on interviews instead of making money selling stuff on the street, and I was spending 10 times as much on subway fare.

A few more weeks of this and I'd be broke.

If I had bothered to keep in contact with Sharon I could have hit her up for more money. Maybe rent for a couple more months. If I'd slept with her once in a while I could have kept that up indefinitely. The longer I went without getting a job the less awful I thought fucking for my keep was. There were even a few times when I wondered, if I called Uncle Will, would he take me back. Once, I thought, if I still had his stuff, I'd have done it, but I'd sold half of it already. It was too late to realize that not working sucked as bad as working, so I'd better get a job and get working.

My resume was a work of fiction. It checked out well enough though, thanks to a friend in Suffern whose mother owned a store. She agreed to give me a good reference even though I had never worked for her, and I wrote down that I had worked there full time for years. It would have checked out if they had called to check, but for all those interviews, not one checked.

The interview I was going for this time was pushing a vending cart around New York, selling soda. I was overdressed and appeared to be very overqualified. My competition for the job was a scruffy looking guy who didn't even bother to put on clean clothes.

We both got hired and told to start the next day.

The other guy's name was Jason or Jeremy. Some kind of "J" name, but I called him Dirtbag. The first time I called him that he looked like he was mad. He said that was what his stepfather called him, and I said that was cool, and asked him if he thought I was psychic, or if maybe it really was a name that fit him. He laughed after that and from then on didn't seem to mind when I called him Dirtbag.

Not Okay

Dirtbag was a hard worker. Harder than me. He would heave the heavy carts up the ramp onto the truck and roll them down pretty easily. He also jumped up to move cases of soda whenever the boss wanted. None of that extra work translated into extra pay. We sold our soda for a buck each and got to keep twenty cents of it. When it came to money, we made about the same.

We saw each other on the subway platform 15 minutes or so after we got hired. I recognized him right away, so I yelled over to him, "Hey Dirtbag, you wanna come downtown with me and celebrate?"

He just said, "Fuck you," to me though.

"Your loss," I said, and then he said something else, but the dragon was screaming in the tunnel ahead of us, so I didn't hear what it was. Then the train arrived, and we got into separate train cars.

Dirtbag was sexy despite being dirty and mean. Maybe even a little because of it. I looked at his crotch and saw something of a bulge and it turned me on a little. I thought, if Uncle Will hadn't picked me up, I mean, if I had just been left to my own devises, I probably would have turned out gay, but Uncle Will fucked me out of that. He made sex with guys feel creepy and unsafe. Thanks to that piece of shit, I thought, I was just stuck with women and there was nothing I could do about it.

My apartment might have been way up town, but I lived in the East Village. That's where the clubs I liked were, that's where the clothing stores I liked were, and that's where the people I liked were. So that's where I headed.

I bought a pair of cool looking sunglasses from a street vendor on Saint Marks, then sat down in a coffee shop on Avenue A and wrote a song. It wasn't my first song, but it was the first one I still liked an hour or so after I wrote it

79

so I didn't throw it away. I never let anyone see my songs up until that point, but I never really had a friend I thought would be interested in them either. I think I remember Dirtbag being a musician or something, but I got the feeling we weren't hitting it off really well, so I thought he might not be interested in my song. Too bad for him, he might have been able to record it and have a huge hit or something.

We could have ended up partners and lovers and big stars and shit. Me writing the songs and him recording them. His loss, I thought. He should have been nicer to me.

For a musician, Dirtbag got way too into selling soda. Whenever I tried to talk to him about girls or songs or movies or anything he always brought it back to selling soda. He'd say, "Just sell your soda," or "Why don't you keep your mind on selling your soda and don't worry about me," or something else like that. It was an easy job though. You really didn't have to pay attention to very much. People who wanted a soda would walk up to your cart and buy one. People who didn't want a soda didn't come up. It wasn't like you had to sell them on soda.

I could work extra when I wanted to and take several days off in a row when I wanted to. It was like that most of the time with this job. But big events everybody had to work. I mean, like a concert in Central Park or a parade; for those, you had to work. The thing was though, that you sold a shitload of soda for those events anyway, so everybody wanted to work.

You could always count on thirsty, brainless masses to be attracted to loud noises and bright lights.

I wore my everyday clothes at work, but I was still better dressed than most of my co-workers. Part if that was because I bought my clothes in the East Village where clothes were cool. They weren't that expensive either. My black and grey jeans were $20.00 and regular jeans that weren't even cool were $16.00. I liked two-tone jeans, but the black and grey ones were my favorite.

I had a lot of sparkly black button up shirts too. One with genuine mother of pearl buttons that looked great with my black and grey, two-tone jeans.

On an average day, I'd take home $35.00 - $50.00 if I got an early start and stayed out late. But when I wore my sparkly black shirt with the genuine mother of pearl buttons and my back and grey, two-tone jeans, I'd make fifty bucks without working extra hours. People just liked how I looked in that outfit. I did too.

Guys flirted with me too. Girls didn't, but guys did. I guess they could tell, even if I was back and forth on the subject. I never got a number or a date or anything, but I liked that I got flirted with and sometimes at home I jerked off thinking about what might have happened if I did see one of those guys after work.

I made enough, not only to pay my rent and expenses, but to save money too, which, of course, I didn't. There were far too many things I wanted that I didn't have, like more two-tone jeans and more sparkly shirts.

I did save for a few weeks to get a computer. It was an Apple, but not really. It ran the same programs the Apple computer ran, and it worked the same way, but it was called a Franklin and it cost half what a real Apple did.

I was going to use it to create music to go with my songs, but I ended up just buying video games and playing them. Music making was really difficult, you know. And there weren't any exploding aliens or anything like that.

I bought myself a 10-speed bicycle too. I tried, but I couldn't quite get the hang of riding it, so I just hung it on my wall as a decoration. I bought myself a lot of other cool stuff too, but no matter how much stuff I bought I just wanted more.

I wanted copies of my favorite movies on video tape, a good stereo, a microwave oven, a reclining chair with vibrating massage, and, and, and.

I told myself I was fulfilling my wish list, but it was a list that grew faster than I could buy and half of the things I bought weren't even on it.

Most people wouldn't have called this a good job, but I got to buy all kinds of stuff. What wasn't good about that? So, I had no medical benefits, I hardly ever got sick anyway, and I didn't make much money if it rained, but it didn't rain that much. I was living in the working world and I was making it. That was better than I ever expected.

Oh shit, let me tell you about one time, when I was working the corner of 67th Street and 7th Avenue. I had my head down in my cart, repositioning the bottles of soda and the ice like I sometimes had to do so I had three or four of every flavor cold and ready when I needed them. I'm digging to find another root beer when I hear a familiar voice.

"Let me have a black cherry," The voice says and I smile because I know that voice from the movies.

I look up from my cart and there's Dustin Hoffman standing right in front of me, I swear to God.

"Ratso!" I shouted out. And he smiled back at me.

"Not Tootsie?" He asked surprised.

"Oh, I didn't see that, sorry, was it good?" I asked, handing him the soda.

"No, it sucked, everybody and their dogs loved the thing. I'd rather be remembered for Midnight Cowboy or Little Big Man, or Death of a Salesman," He says and I say back, "I didn't see them either, other than Midnight Cowboy, but I loved you in that. How about an autograph?"

Not Okay

He nods, I hand him a felt tip pen and, like that, Dustin Hoffman was signing my soda cart. I was still looking for some paper or something in my pockets with balls of dollar bills and shit, but he went right for the cart.

"There you go," He said, handing the pen back to me with the cap on its back end.

I shoved the pen back in my back pocket without noticing that the felt tip was now exposed. I didn't find out until I took off my pants that night that a crystal-like black ink stain was expanding from the felt point of that pen messing up the grey denim ass of my favorite two-tone pants. It would be longer before I found out the ink wouldn't come out in the wash and longer still to find out that they weren't in stores anymore so I couldn't replace them. That Dustin Hoffman, he may be a great actor, but when it comes to handing pens back to people, he's a stupid shit.

I was so excited about my encounter with fame that I told everybody at work and not one person was impressed. Half of them tried to tell me about all the famous people they had sold soda to, and how famous people in New York City was no big deal.

The boss was the worst though. I didn't tell you her name because I never really remembered it. I mean, she was always telling me, but it was just not a name that could stay in my head, you know. She was just, The Boss, or Boss, and that was her name. Anyway, the boss bitched about my letting someone put graffiti on her expensive pushcart.

"That isn't graffiti! I insisted, it's Dustin Hoffman," The Boss, Dirtbag, and three other people all said, "So what" or "Big Deal" or "Who Cares" all at the same time.

83

I felt so disappointed after that, that I went to Saint Marks Place and looked at all the stuff the street vendors had, looking for something neat to buy.

I found it too. An acoustic guitar for thirty bucks. The guy tuned it for me too. I think he just did it to say goodbye, like that guitar and him were pals and he hated to sell it. Now that shit happens a lot in New York City. I bet that's more common than a movie star signing someone's soda cart.

I went home and started strumming on the guitar right away. It turned out that guitars were just as hard to figure out how to work as neckties and bicycles. After three hours it still sounded like shit. But I wanted to learn so the next day I bought a book.

The thing is, you can't spend as much time in the East Village as I did without owning a guitar. In the week or so that followed I brought my guitar to work with me so that after work I could go to Saint Marks Place and ask people on the stoops to show me how to play. You may not think something like that would work, but it really did. The book didn't help much. But people on stoops, they taught me quite a lot. In no time at all I was playing four or five different chords and sounding slightly better than awful.

Not only did I make up alternative music for the songs I liked but I started writing new songs and keeping them. The new ones sounded better because they used the chords and rhythms that I had figured out how to play.

I named my guitar, Baby, and it turned out to be a much better friend than Dirtbag.

I stopped working Mondays in order to get to this one club on MacDougal Street called Speak Easy in time to sign up for the open mike. At first I didn't think I would ever get on the stage, but it turned out that everyone who went there were musicians. As such, they never listened to anyone on the stage other than themselves, so they never knew how bad a musician I was.

Sometimes I'd even get a compliment from someone who was hoping I'd then give them a compliment because that's also how things worked in the music scene, but I didn't care. I loved it all.

Everyone smoked in there and not too many of them bought their own. At first, I would go through most of a pack every time I went, then I learned to go without any and sponge off of other people too. I wasn't as into smoking then as much as I am now. I liked it but I didn't need it like I do now. I wish I had known. Maybe I would have left them alone. I didn't know a lot of stuff.

I was on the low end of the talent spectrum, I'm not arguing that, but I wasn't entirely alone at the bottom. Every once in a while someone who was worse than me wondered in and took the stage.

One of those was this hippie guy who called himself, Bread. Bread had Jesus stickers all over his guitar and case: "God is Love" and "Forgiven" and "One Way" the whole bit. His songs were kind of sermons, kind of propaganda and awful. He managed to do what I could not accomplish at that friendly little bar: he got booed.

I liked him well enough, but he didn't really shut up about Jesus. Once I laid it out for him. I said, "Hey, look, Jaybird over there shoots heroin, and Christina snorts coke. You ask them, they'll tell you how great the shit is. I'm sure what you're hooked on does it for you just as good as theirs does it for them. But if somebody doesn't ask, they don't want you to tell them. If somebody doesn't ask, they're not shopping for a new drug, got it? Their old drug is still working for them."

The thing about those self-appointed evangelists is, they don't take 'shut the fuck up you stinking Jesus freak hippie' for an answer. They really won't stop until they get socked in the eye, which Bread did get one night. That only made him more self-righteous. Guys like that, they like to take one for God.

I should say that I was learning how to be cool there. The other guys, other than Bread I mean, were all cool. One wore a cowboy hat that he slunk down over his eyes, another flipped a half dollar around on his knuckles. Most of them smoked and smoked, dangling their lit cigarettes off the edge of their lips or fitting them between the nut and peg of their guitars while they sang. All of them, smokers and non, had brooding down. You walk in there and see musicians learning up against walls, perched on the side of stools, looking out from under hats or from behind bottles and all of them brooding.

I tried but just couldn't get it down. When I tried it, I felt silly and I think I looked silly too.

Oh, so, forget that. This is more important. That song I wrote after I got my job I did end up playing there at Speak Easy and it went over pretty well. Well enough even that when I got off the stage and went to the bar for some water a girl talked to me.

"That was a nice song," She said, just like that.

I was still trying to brood like the real musicians, so I answered her as if I was moody. I wanted to get all excited and say something like, "You really think so?" but I didn't. Instead I said, "It wasn't intended to be nice."

I played it up too. I mean, I pretended not to notice her or even to care what she thought.

Not Okay

Although the song wasn't nice. It was about how awful the world was and how life sucked. Now that I think about it, it was weird of her to say it was a nice song.

"It touched me," She said, "I know what it's like to be crying inside with nobody seeing."

I smiled. I couldn't believe it. She was quoting my song. Well, really, misquoting it. Well, butchering the hell out of it, but still, she heard something I'd said on the stage and remembered it. That was kind of amazing.

"I'm sorry. No one should have to feel that sad," I said, and she smiled.

You should have seen this girl. Her clothes were pieced together with patches and embroidery thread. Nothing matched. Her vest was blue velveteen and the buttons had been replaced with bottle caps. The lining was hand stitched by someone who shouldn't be allowed to hand stitch anything. And there were things woven into her hair too. Seashells and beads, I guess, all different colors.

A thick, macramé rope served as a belt holding everything around her little waist and there were more beads on strings around her neck. She had so many metal bracelets on one wrist that she clinked whenever she moved. I don't think I have to tell you that I liked her.

"I'm Peter," I offered.

"Peter Wilson, yeah, I know," She replied.

I must have made a confused face.

"They said so, when they called you to the stage," She added, then said, "I'm Robin. Robin Blue."

I smiled some more.

Robin had two drinks that I paid for while we talked through everyone else on stage. I think someone shushed us once, but we didn't pay much attention to that either. Don't ask what we talked about; it was dumb stuff. What bands we liked, what movies we had seen, what movie star had signed my soda cart, that sort of thing.

And as much as I was smiling, she smiled more.

All of this was because of my song. And right then I thought it was the greatest song that had ever been written. I know it wasn't, but right then I thought it was.

Oh shit, you should hear it. Yeah, I should sing it for you. Come on, please, it's short. Let me sing it for you! It's called 'Dark Sunglasses' get ready.

I put my new sunglasses on
and walk along the subway platform
crying, behind the dark black glass.
Crying, but hiding it with class
So, no one can see I'm crying, crying,
no one can see my heart is dying,
all of my crying, nobody can see. Nobody but me.

No wait, that's not all. That's only the first verse. Three. There are three verses. The next two are just as good as the first one. Listen.

I wonder what it's all about,
I rush and scream, go in and out
trailing behind but covering my ass.
Trying to keep within my class
So no one can hear my screaming, screaming,
no one can see these tears are streaming,
all of this lonely, nobody can be nobody but me.

There's a little bridge here, where I do the chords like in the chorus but then I juxtapose the C with the E minor, you just have to hear it. When I can get to a guitar I'll play it for you, and you can hear it. Anyway, the last verse is a little slower and darker. It's great.

I fall into my quiet bed
and fight with dancers in my head,

Not Okay

I ask myself, do I want sleep or death.
Crying, but under my breath.
And no one can see I'm crying, crying,
no one can see my heart is dying,
all of my crying, nobody can see
nobody but me.

Fuck you, you don't have to like it. You're a lawyer, you don't know anything about music. It's a great song. Every time I ever played it someone liked it and said so, and this girl, Robin Blue, she asked me to walk her home. That says something pretty good about my song, I think.

6.

Robin Blue and I left Speak Easy at two in the morning, or a few minutes after. Last call got called, they announced closing time from the stage and just as we were leaving they were flicking the house lights on and off again. I usually stayed until after the front door was locked and most of the chairs were put up on the tables, since there is a lot more night after the end, talking with the other hangers on, we left at the early part of end, eager to get to know each other. At this point I was pretty sure I liked guys rather than girls, but I wanted to have sex with a girl to be sure and Robin Blue seemed to be as good a prospect as any.

People treat gay guys like shit in this world. If there was any chance that I wasn't gay and didn't have to go through life being treated like shit, I owed it to myself to try to find that out.

We walked across Washington Square Park, which was kind of neat at night, although this was a little too late. An hour or so ago there might have been jugglers, a fire breather, and all kinds of music going on.

It was still nice. It was one of those rare New York City nights when the stars managed to battle their way through the thick fog that blew in from Newark New Jersey.

Those stars made sparkles on the cobblestones, on Robin's blue velveteen vest and on my already sparkly black shirt. They were the kind of stars songwriters turned into metaphors. Since I was a songwriter just then, I tried to think of metaphors, but the ones that came to me were pretty lame. Waltzing fairies choreographed by God, and other stupid shit like that. I didn't write any down.

I reached out a little and Robin took my hand. We walked across the park holding hands like young lovers while those fairies waltzed on the cobblestones under our feet. At one point someone asked if we wanted to buy drugs. Robin said no right away or I would have asked him if he had some pot. It wasn't that important, and it didn't take anything away from the moment.

"I don't remember ever seeing you in Speak Easy before," I said.

"I haven't been here very long," She answered.

It didn't matter what she said, I just liked the way she said stuff. That's the only reason I asked her questions. I just liked to hear her voice.

My next question was, "Where did you come from?"

"I'm not sure I should tell you; I mean, people just don't take some things well," She hedged.

"I understand, hey, I don't like to talk about my past either. The past is over anyway. It's what happened to you, it isn't who you are."

And I got the biggest smile yet for saying that. It was one of the things people said in Day Treatment that I wanted to believe but didn't really.

She held my hand, not exactly tighter, but more completely, if that makes any sense to you. I started to worry because things were going so well with her. I mean, if I fucked up then and ruined it, I'd be really sorry. But I didn't know what would be fucking up. Just the thought of it all made me afraid my hands would get sweaty and then I thought about that.

I didn't know if it would be worse to pull my hand away or to let her keep on holding it and sweat all over her. I needed to get my mind off of it so I asked her another stupid question.

"What kind of work do you do?"

She looked embarrassed.

"Is that a sensitive subject too?" I asked.

"Yeah, kind of," She answered.

"That's alright. What you do isn't who you are," Now I was improvising.

"I think I want to tell you, but I don't think you'll be happy," She said, looking as nervous as I was.

I didn't answer.

"I'm an escort," She said.

"What's that?" I asked, really not knowing.

"I date men for money, only they never take me anywhere, not like a real date," She told me.

Robin looked like she was about to cry.

"You sleep with them?" I asked. I pretty much knew the answer by then, but I just wanted to be sure.

"Yes," She said softly.

She wouldn't look at me now. Actually, she pulled at her hand, but I wouldn't let it go.

I wasn't disgusted or anything. Really, I was happy. It meant she probably put out. I couldn't say that, so I tried to play like it didn't mean anything to me.

"I sell soda myself."

"That's nice," She said, a little taken aback that I didn't react more severely.

"How do you get into that kind of work?" I asked.

"I ended up with it by the process of elimination. There aren't a lot of opportunities for a girl like me."

"Like you, how?" I asked.

"No birth certificate, no school records, no identification," She answered.

"Why don't you have those things?" I asked.

After I asked that I started thinking that I was asking

her too many questions. I didn't want her to think I was grilling her or something, so I told myself I wouldn't ask any more.

"We don't have any of those things where I come from," She answered.

I thought that was weird, but I'd already decided I wasn't going to ask any more questions, so I let it go.

"We're here, this is my building," Robin said, saving me from having to think of what to say next that wouldn't be a question.

"Would you like to come in?"

I nodded. We went in and up the stairs without saying much. I don't know why she wasn't saying much. I wasn't because I was worried that she would see I had a hard- on. I was doing math in my head to make it go down.

Did I tell you the building was beautiful? Lots of old buildings in New York City are beautiful. I mean, not that they are trying to be, they just are. It was kind of run down but that was part of its charm. It is the way old buildings run down that are beautiful.

Old chipping paint, little cracks in the wall, all of it. If you had only ever lived in the suburbs you would think it was poverty. But apartments in the West Village like this were expensive as shit. Everything in New York was run down other than midtown.

Inside Robin's apartment was nice, but it wasn't normal. She had silky scarves over lights, a bookshelf made out of branches tied together with strips of fabric and burned up incense sticks stuck in candles all over the place with little trails of ash leading to them.

She didn't look as weird inside her apartment. Here, she just fit in and I looked weird.

I might not even have to say she was an artist, but

she was. Her paintings weren't very good, but they were original, and none of them were on framed canvases or anything remotely normal like that. The surfaces for all of Robin's artworks were essentially trash.

The biggest of them was a window with twelve medium sized glass panels, two cracked, one broken, and nine whole. This one, like most of the others, was roped to the wall through heavy duty eye hooks that were screwed directly into the art.

Each panel was a separate painting with a scene and each scene was stranger than all of the others. One was a bush with women's shoes growing on it as if they were fruit. Another had several animals standing in midair over a gorge in the land. Still another had horses with human busts. These I recognized as centaurs. I don't mean I had ever seen a centaur, but I recognized them from what little I knew of mythology.

"Do you like it?" Robin asked.

"I've never seen anything like it," I answered.

"I found it on the street."

"Really?" I asked surprised, "I just assumed you painted it."

"Oh, silly, I decorated it with pictures. When I found it, it was grey and plain."

"What does it mean?" I asked.

"It's a window," she replied. I gave her a look, but she must get that look so often she'd immune to it.

"I painted it with pictures from my home, so when I miss the place I can see it by looking through the window. Then it doesn't seem so far away. Here, this is a cherry tree. They aren't like cherry trees here; you can't eat the cherries there.

"Are they poisonous?" I asked.

"No, they explode," She answered.

I was coming to expect weird answers from her. She acted as though it were normal, so I thought I'd best do the same.

"Where is this place?" I asked.

"Peter, really, if I knew how to get back do you think I'd still be here?"

"I don't understand," I told her.

"It gets complicated. You wouldn't believe me anyway."

"I didn't say that. Go ahead," I encouraged her.

"Don't say I didn't warn you," Robin said, then she started explaining. And I hope you didn't expect her explanation to explain anything. I did and it didn't.

"Everything is mundane here because magic doesn't work. Where I come from there is magic and everything is magical. I wandered away from my nest and accidentally flew into the peephole of a large gourd. I searched through the nightmare worlds inside the gourd for days trying to find my way back to my own world and ended up here. Do you understand now?" Robin asked.

I had a million questions, the first should have been how long it has been since she took her medication, but I didn't even think of that.

"You could fly?"

"I was half bird. Here I'm all human," She answered.

"Yeah, you looked human to me. A gourd?"

"Where bad dreams are made," She told me.

"So why don't you climb back into the gourd that you came out of and retrace your steps?"

"It's one-way: there's no gourd on this side."

"Naturally," I said.

I started out confused, went from there to amused but now that it was getting to me that she wasn't kidding, I was starting to worry.

"You don't believe me do you?" She asked, looking like she might cry.

"I have no reason to think you would be lying," I said, and that was the truth. I didn't think she was lying, I just thought she was nuts.

Then I added, "There are professionals here who would know better than I do. Maybe we should ask one of them what they think."

Now she didn't seem to understand. I told her these were people who listened to people's unusual stories and answered questions about them.

"That sounds like people we have at home. But they are very expensive. A year's labor for answering just one question," She said.

She had a point. They were expensive.

Robin offered to make us some noodles, which sounded like a good idea to me. They were Chinese bean threads, which I hadn't ever seen before, so I wondered if she had brought them with her from her fantasies. She topped them off with slices of kiwifruit, which I had also never seen before, and which no one should ever serve on hot noodles.

Other than waiting for the water to boil, the whole thing took practically no time. I was fairly impressed, I'll tell you. And she did all of this without a kitchen.

This apartment was smaller than mine. It was the one room I told you about and the bathroom. She made a counter of sorts in the bathroom where she had a hot plate plugged in and that's what she did all her cooking on.

Not Okay

To eat, we sat on the floor and used a wooden milk crate as a table. She mixed some kind of drink with powder and water and gave us each a glass. I took a drink of it but it tasted like dirt and weeds, so I didn't drink any more of it. She finished hers.

We didn't talk while we were eating but every time I looked up at her there she was looking back at me and smiling. I didn't care if she was crazy. I really liked her. And she was already a hooker so banging her wouldn't be taking advantage of the mentally ill I told myself.

When we were done eating I scooped up the plates and took them into the bathroom.

"You don't have to do that," She said, and it had been so long since one of us spoke that it startled me.

"Let me, I like it," I said as I went.

Her bathroom sink already had the pot she had boiled our noodles in, filled with water. I added our plates and turned on the water, watching it splashing down. Robin was right behind me.

She took a bottle of dish soap from the back of the toilet and squeezed a thin stream of pink the liquid in a circular motion, creating a spiral on the top plate and part way up my arm.

I picked up the sponge and started to wipe the top dish. Robin put her hand over mine and helped guide it around.

I let my head fall back onto her chest. Her arms were around me, as if I were pinned to the sink by her delicate body. I was enjoying it until I started to feel trapped, then my heart quickened. It wasn't that I didn't want to do it, but I needed to be in control for a change. I turned around and put a hand on the back of her head. Foamy soap water dribbled down her hair onto her back.

Pulling her face up to mine I kissed her a firm, hard kiss on the lips. I used my tongue to pry her lips open and licked inside her mouth. The sweet taste of kiwi fruit was still there.

At first she tensed up, the way I had, but then she relaxed, allowing me to lower her to the floor. Her hair floated on the black and white tiles as the water continued to pour from the faucet.

I liked the water sound. It was like the ocean; it was like rain.

I pulled the knot in her rope belt free. That seemed to be the one thing that kept all of her clothes together. Once it was open everything was open and her naked body was exposed.

She looked much older naked, especially in the breasts. I mean, she looked like she had bigger ones once, and now there were a dozen lighter colored lines like rivers all over them. Not only that, but she had a big ugly scar that ran from her side to down under her gut. If I had seen her naked first, I wouldn't have even wanted to bang her, but I was too into it at this point for much of anything to have turned me off.

I opened my pants and pulled my cock out but didn't take them down or anything. Holding her strongly with both hands, I thrust deep and hard up inside her.

This was wonderful. I felt empowered for the first time in my life and she yelled out, "Stop!"

Confused, I moved off of her.

"What's wrong baby?" I asked.

She righted herself saying something about not being anyone's baby. She looked mad.

"I have to take this shit when I'm working, but I expect better on my personal time!" she yelled, and now she seemed as much hurt as angry.

"I don't understand, I thought you wanted to," I started.

"I wanted to make love," She said, still loudly.

"I thought that was what we were doing," I said, still confused.

"No! You were fucking me, and I was getting fucked. That isn't the same thing. Not at all."

She stared at me.

It was my turn to say something, but I didn't know what to say. My mouth hung open, wordlessly.

I left her in the bathroom, found my jacket in the living room and looked in it for my cigarettes. I found the pack without a cigarette in it.

"Fucking perfect," I said, crumbling the empty pack in my hand.

Robin followed me. In half a minute I had gotten fully dressed and she had gotten completely naked.

She touched my arm. When I looked at her she was looking straight into my eyes.

"We don't have to stop. Let's try again, just, be gentle this time, let me get wet, that's all. Treat me nice."

"I'm sorry," I told her, "I just got scared."

"You got scared? Fuck boy, you scared the shit out of me."

She wasn't angry anymore.

"I don't know what the hell I'm doing. I don't know how to do it with a girl. I better go," I said.

I took my jacket and walked out the door. As I got to the bottom of the stairs, I could hear her at the top, but I didn't turn around. I couldn't look at her.

I took a right at the street, not even knowing which way we had come from, and I started walking.

I pretended I couldn't hear her crying, up in her apartment. I couldn't have heard her; it was too far away.

When I was four or five blocks away I started yelling, "Shit! Shit! Shit!" which made me more upset.

I kicked a garbage can, which started a dog barking.

I went over everything I was mad at myself for, and it was plenty. I was mad at myself for trying to bang Robin, for stopping when she told me to stop, for what a horrible person it made me that I could have even thought about not stopping when she told me to stop, and most of all, for leaving my guitar at Speak Easy.

I knew I was walking in the wrong direction now: away from the club, away from the subway. It didn't matter. Speak Easy was long closed. I wasn't going to be able to get my guitar anyway.

I walked all the way to Canal Street before I found a store that was open and bought a pack of cigarettes. Two heavy drags on the first one and I started to relax.

"Fuck me," I said. I don't know for sure if I said it aloud or not.

When I saw a subway entrance I walked toward it. When I got to the entrance I saw, a few blocks further up, a triple x store with those twenty-five cent peep shows. I still had a hard-on or had it again anyway. Since I didn't have to get on the subway with it, I decided not to.

It was scarier than you might think. There are rows of red booths and guys just standing next to some of them looking at you as you walk in. I was expecting someone to see me and tell me I was being bad. I guess I did that to myself. I wanted to walk right out of there, run even.

I did it though.

I picked one of the booths that wasn't too close to one of those guys and walked into it.

I came back out again to get quarters from a guy and went back into the same booth again.

It wasn't a complex mechanism and I got it figured out right away. There were dozens of movies to pick from and a dial to flip from one to the next. None of the girls in these movies had gross stretch marks or shriveled up tits like Robin.

"Fuck Robin!" I said, I think to myself. I hope to myself.

Usually, I can't jerk off without some lubrication or something, but I was so worked up at this point that I had no problem.

I started with guy on girl stuff, but it wasn't working for me. I flipped around until I found two hot guys fucking and that worked.

Three quarters, twenty minutes and most of my dignity later I was on the A train heading for home. I'd like to tell you I was feeling a little better. And I was for a few minutes, but overall, I guess I was feeling even worse.

7.

The Wednesday after I met Robin Blue, I was working on Park Avenue, near 47th Street. This was a pretty ritzy area with an upscale pedestrian population. That was good in that nobody thought a dollar was too much for a bottle of soda, but not so good in that some of these people were too snooty for soda.

Most of my customers were either yuppies on their way up one corporate ladder or another, or older executives on their way back down.

Halfway into the day I had sold a little more than half of the sodas in my cart. I might have done better still if it weren't for the competition from a frozen lemonade cart and a cookie ice cream sandwich vendor. Both of these were recent additions to the street level marketplace. They were growing in popularity all over the city and the boss was worried about them, but I still sold more soda than they sold ice cream or frozen lemonade.

I'd say seven feet separated each of our carts. That was far enough not to be claustrophobic, but not so far that we weren't interfering with each other's business.

I was in the center.

I might have done better if I had moved up to the next block, but I had been there first. Fuck, I was selling there all March when it was cold and not nearly as many sodas would sell. The only reason the other carts came there was that I had cultivated the spot. Someone should have moved, but I didn't think it should be me.

If I didn't tell you it was a warm day for April, I'll tell you now. It was. Early afternoon the sun moved behind some clouds but before that it could have been summer.

Not Okay

When the boss came with her truck to restock me she said that everyone was doing well. I needed seven cases though, nobody had done quite that well.

When she drove off, leaving me restocked, I had a wad full of singles in my pockets. Normally she'd change our extra singles to twenties, but everyone had done so well that she was out of 20's, even 10's and 5's.

It was good she had come when she did. I might have had three cases of soda left, but I was out of cola and root beer, my two best sellers. Another hour and all I would have had left were fruit punch, and you can't sell a whole lot of fruit punch soda, not even if it is the only soda you have.

I continued to sell well after she restocked me too and was well on my way to having the best non-summer, non-parade sales day ever. And you know when things are going really well like things were going, something has to happen to fuck it all up.

The something that happened was an overnight delivery truck. It slowed down and drove passed where I was set up, stopped, and tried to back up into the parking space right behind me.

This was a parking space that might have been big enough for a regular car, but it was a pretty tight squeeze for a van. It could have been done, like, if one of the other cars moved out of the way until the van drove in and then went back, or if a helicopter airlifted the van or something, but the way the van was doing it, I don't think so.

The driver was determined though and drove up onto the sidewalk in the effort to make it happen.

The frozen lemonade vendor saw it coming and scrambled her cart out of the way in time. I had been taking care of a customer when all of this was happening so I didn't notice the van until it hit my soda cart.

I noticed then though. The cart made a loud scratching noise as it was pushed a foot or so up the sidewalk.

The cookie ice cream sandwich vendor yelled to the driver, "Hey! Watch out!" but the warning came too late if the driver noticed it at all.

I was trapped between my pushcart and the back of the van.

I hadn't exactly been hit yet, but I couldn't move until the van stopped.

Now I yelled, "Hey, Jerk off! Stop!" but the van kept coming.

Both of the van's back tires climbed up onto the sidewalk and still the van didn't stop.

My pushcart tilted, then turned over, being pulled slowly under the rear bumper of the van and taking me along with it.

My sodas went rolling down the sidewalk, crashing into signposts and a mailbox.

After the van stopped, my rival vendors unwedged the pushcart from under the van, otherwise I wouldn't have been able to get out at all.

The driver went right on about his business. He dashed into the building with his delivery without even glancing back at the damage he had done.

When he returned I yelled at him, but he acted as if I wasn't there. He got in his van and started it up. I went to his window and he reached over and locked his door.

"Who the fuck's going to pay for this?" I called out to him as he pulled out and drove away.

"Hey, you better sit down," The frozen lemonade girl said.

I didn't see the other vendor anywhere. He just left, leaving his pushcart unattended.

I didn't sit down, but I did feel a familiar warm trickle down my leg. I looked down and saw a big rip in both my pants and my leg. It was really gross. I mean, there was a flap of bloody skin the size of a pear right there under my hip, where the van had pinned me.

I touched my palm to the wound. I really did. I couldn't tell you why I needed proof that I was really hurt. I could see it you know. That should have been proof enough, right.

"Oh great! Fucking great!" I yelled.

I tried to pace, but now that I knew how bad my injury looked, it hurt too.

I stumbled forward and the frozen lemonade girl caught me. In her arms, I saw she had an Adam's apple. This was a pretty girl with boobs and a dick. The best of both worlds and I was too injured to enjoy it.

She lowered me to the sidewalk and got her shirt and denim jacket bloody for her trouble.

I rubbed my eyes, which was a really bad thing to do when you have blood on your fingers.

Looking up, I realized I was lying on the cement of the sidewalk with my head resting in the lap of a pretty girl with a dick that I didn't even know.

I could see her lips moving but I couldn't hear what she was saying to me, if she was talking to me at all. She might have been singing for all I knew.

"Oh, your clothes," I said, or I think I said. She didn't hear me either, but she was taking care of me.

This was a bad time to get a hard-on but I'm pretty sure I did as the building swirled out of focus and modulated into strange shapes that looked kind of human but faceless.

I tried to close my eyes, but it didn't work, or if it did, it didn't matter. There was just as much light under my eyelids as there was on them.

I turned away and tried to lift my hand to block it out, but I was too weak.

"What's your name?" A voice asked.

"Peter. Peter Wilson," I answered groggily.

"Well, Petey, my boy, you just relax. Do you know where you are?" The voice asked me.

"That's not fair," I answered, "That was going to be my question."

You might think that I wasn't really that funny in a situation like this. It's a crisis, there's fear, there's adrenaline, or there would be if I had the energy, and I don't know, maybe I'm actually just stupid in a crisis, but later, after it's over, when I am looking back on it, the way I remember it, I am way cooler. I can't tell you my story any way other than the way I remember it, so you need to know that maybe I wasn't really as cool as I remember.

Then we caught each other up. I was at Roosevelt Hospital; I wasn't severely hurt which was good. The pretty little frozen lemonade girl wasn't with me, which was bad. I tried to reach down to see if I still had a hard-on, but I was too groggy.

The doctor asked me the kind they ask you to find out if your eggs got scrambled.

"Do you know how you got here?"

"God planted a seed in my mother's belly and nine months later the stork came and put me under a cabbage," I answered. Maybe. Like I said, I remember myself being way cooler and way funnier than I think I actually am.

"What is today's date?" Was another question.

Not Okay

"Friday, April 20, um, 20 something, fuck, I don't know that when I haven't been in an accident."

"How about the year?" He asks.

"1983. 1984. 86. Something like that,"

"Who is the president?"

"Ronald Dickhead Reagan. No offensive if you're a stupid Republican" I answered.

"Don't worry about that, I voted for Anderson," The doctor said.

"Really?" I replied, "I had heard that someone had. So, you were the one huh?"

I opened my eyes and looked at the face that went with the voice.

"Hey, you're black," I said.

"I know," He replied.

"I'm sorry. I mean, I don't care that you are, I just didn't think you were. Oh shit, does that make me a racist? I don't want to be a racist, am I a racist for thinking you were white?"

"No, it's fine," The doctor, who clearly wasn't a doctor, replied.

I don't mean he clearly wasn't a doctor because he was black, there are plenty of black doctors, I just mean that when I saw him, I could see he wasn't dressed like a doctor. He was like an intern or an orderly or something.

I don't want you thinking I'm a racist either. I'm not. I hope I'm not.

I got a good bump on my head and a gash in my leg that needed fifteen stitches and that was the worst of it. I didn't have to stay in the hospital overnight, but there was a police officer waiting to ask me questions.

"What the fuck for? I didn't do anything," I responded, getting upset.

"They arrested the driver. Hit and run," He said.

It turned out that the cookie ice cream sandwich guy, when he took off, had called the police. He took down the van's license plate and the guy didn't make it very far before he got pulled over.

My blood was on his bumper, too, so he wasn't going to get out of it.

I agreed to come down to the police station to fill out some paperwork in order to press charges, and I took the officer's business card.

The most fucked up thing was that the hospital gave me my pants back. They were cut up and bloody and had to be a biohazard, plus, I was hanging out of them, but I put them back on and walked out of the hospital.

I checked and there was still a wad of money in the pockets. Oh yeah, the money was damp with blood too.

I didn't bother to count it. Since I didn't know how much was supposed to be there I wouldn't have been able to know if any was missing.

Outside the hospital I waved down a cab and took it all the way home. I felt that I had been through enough for a day and didn't need to deal with the subway too.

I paid the fare with nine bloody one-dollar bills and dragged myself up the stairs to my apartment.

That poor cab driver must have thought I was a psychotic killer or something, with those bloody bills I had. And I hadn't even killed anybody yet.

I took my pants off and put them in the trash after emptying the pockets. I didn't count the money. A little blood mark stayed on Uncle Will's dresser from that money and never came off no matter what I washed it with.

I washed up and went to bed without even turning the television on.

Not Okay

Most nights, even when I went out to a club or something, when I came home at three or four in the morning, I still turned the television on for a few minutes just to mellow out.

I had my video tape recorder programmed to record the shows I liked during prime time, so I didn't miss anything.

I recorded more than I had time to watch, really, and some shows I ended up recording over without ever watching. BJ and the Bear was like that, and Hart to Hart. But M*A*S*H* and Lou Grant I always caught up on. I wouldn't say I came to like M*A*S*H* but something kept me watching it.

I must have had three episodes of M*A*S*H* and two of Lou Grant waiting for me to watch, and some other stuff too, but I just went to bed.

I remember thinking, just as I was falling asleep, that I'd never ridden in an ambulance before, and the one time I did I was unconscious for the whole thing. And then wondering, did I imagine it, or did that pretty frozen lemonade girl have a dick?

109

8.

Thursday morning, I woke up late. I felt pretty sore, so I decided to take the day off from the world. I watched some of the shows I had recorded on my VCR until three or so in the afternoon then went back to sleep. Two hours later I was up again but I still didn't get dressed.

I jerked off thinking about the frozen lemonade girl who may, or may not have had a dick, but in my fantasy she had a big one and knew how to use it.

I was going to go down the police station to fill out paperwork like I told the officer I would, but it seemed like such an ordeal just to get dressed, let alone go outside.

Anything that I could do on Thursday I could do on Friday I rationalized and went back to doing nothing.

You know, before I got involved in psychiatrists I never said things like 'rationalized' I just didn't. Now I think about that stuff. I'm not sure if that's bad or good, but it is different, I'm just saying.

I didn't think of this, but I feel like saying it anyway, I read this somewhere: the trouble with doing nothing is that it is hard to know when you are done. It's true. Thursday blended into Friday blended into Saturday blended into Sunday and I was still doing nothing.

Sunday morning, I had read at least the first two pages of every paperback book I owned. After that I read I'm OK You're OK all the way through again. It made just as much sense to me as it did the first time I read it. I could have been sucked back into it but I had to assure myself.: "I'm not OK. Uncle Will was not OK. Sharon was not OK. Robin is not OK. The only reason I think the frozen lemonade girl who may, or may not, have a dick is OK is because I don't know her well enough to know differently. No one is actually OK."

Sunday mid-day, I tried to write a new song. I got through the chorus and a dozen lines and then went for my guitar which, of course, wasn't there because I never got it back from Speak Easy.

I tried to finish the song anyway but then I was thinking about if I'd ever see my guitar again more than whatever it was I was writing the song about. So, the notepad and half written song went on a growing pile of things I'd almost done that day.

I didn't even take the song out of the notepad and put it in the box I kept half written songs in, although I think I ended up doing it later. I thought I'd get back to it later in the day, but I didn't.

I had a lot of half written songs. Sometimes when I wanted to write a song and I couldn't think of something, I'd read through those partial songs and some new ideas for them came to me. When the song is half written already all you need is some ideas. It has ideas already you know, a few more and just like that the song is finished.

I don't know if that is how it works for famous songwriters, but that is it for me. I wondered sometimes if I was like famous songwriters, only not famous. I especially wondered that then. I really wanted to be a songwriter then. Sometimes anyway. More than I do now.

Oh, but that wasn't what got me out of the apartment and back in life. What did that was that I'd run out of food.

Well, I didn't totally run out of food. I had oatmeal but no milk, peanut butter but no bread. You know, like that. I needed to shop in order to eat anything, so I needed to face the city.

I hadn't really thought that I was avoiding going out because I was scared or anything, but once I was dressed and locking my apartment door I realized that I was. I was only going to the corner store, but I was scared.

It was like the city itself had hurt me. I was just doing my thing, not bothering anyone and wham! The city knocked me down. Safety was inside my apartment, danger was outside. I know it sounds stupid, but that was how I was feeling right then, and I totally gave in to it.

I unlocked my door again and went back in. I had a box of pancake mix that I had bought on a whim, but never used. Instead of milk, I used some flat Coke. I didn't have eggs either, but I did have some raisins, so I threw them in. And a sprinkle of powdered cinnamon and a half a bottle of vanilla extract.

I didn't have any syrup but, as it turned out, it totally didn't need any. Really, what it needed was to be disposed of in a safe way, so that it could not endanger any wildlife. I wrapped them up in newspaper, tied then in two separate plastic bags and buried them in the bottom of my trash. I was afraid, if I didn't hide them well enough, a neighbor would find them and know what I had done.

I didn't eat anything Sunday night. Monday morning, I reached for a cigarette and only had one left. I checked my carton and it was empty. That was it. I could go without food awhile, but I needed my fucking cigarettes.

Once I got out there I felt like I'd been retraining myself, locked in like Uncle Will had done. Like getting injured was bad and I needed to be punished. I should have hated being locked in like that again, but I didn't. It felt comforting. Weird as it sounds, it felt safe.

My hands were sweating, and my heart was beating harder, but I didn't panic. I told myself that I'd done this a thousand times before, and I had. I told myself that I was fine, and I was.

Really, you don't know how close I had come to turning into a total nutcase or something. Well, I was for a little while. People were looking at me as I was walking on Broadway in Washington Heights. As soon as I noticed they were doing it I stopped talking to myself though. I needed to attract less attention.

The first person I noticed I may have yelled at. I may have yelled, "This is a private conversation, mind your business" or something like that. But I did that as much to fuck with him as because I was weirding out.

Once I had a fresh carton of cigarettes I felt much better. Maybe I wasn't back to my abnormal, but I was good enough. I didn't even open a pack and smoke one right away. Just knowing I had them relaxed me.

I ended up not going back to the apartment at all. Since I was out anyway, and since the bag I got my carton of cigarettes with had handles, I decided to go down to the police station and take care of that report.

I grabbed the A train at 168th and Broadway and took it to The Port Authority where I switched to the Shuttle. Let me tell you, when you switch to the Shuttle at Port Authority 42nd street, you have to walk a fuck of a long way. It feels like further than the train even goes, you just walk and walk and turn and twist and go upstairs and then downstairs and then up other stairs. And that's when you don't make a wrong turn, which I always do. It is a stupid system, and somebody should do something about it. I mean, you pay sixty cents for a fucking ride you shouldn't have to walk half of the way yourself; you know I'm right.

It didn't bother me as much before I had a fucked-up leg but being hurt and sore it bothered me a lot. Usually there were people playing guitar there at least. Not this time though. When something sucks, let me tell you, it goes ahead and sucks all the way around.

Unlike any of the other trains in the New York City subway system, the shuttle only makes two stops. One here, the other there. Once there, it comes right back here, and that's all.

It has to suck to be the driver of that train, or conductor, or whatever the hell they call them. Monotonous, you know, having to constantly go back to where you just were with no variation at all. If I were the Shuttle driver I'd kill myself. I really would. Or quit. I guess quitting would work too.

Sisyphus has it easy I think, compared to the Shuttle driver. But that was his problem. Or hers. There's nothing to say a Shuttle driver couldn't be a woman. Still, I had my own problems. Like that I didn't bring the card with me and didn't know exactly where the police station I was going to was.

I could have gotten in a cab and just said bring me to the nearest police station I suppose, but I walked toward where I got hit instead, hoping I'd just find it. You may not think that doing things like that would work but let me tell you, it does, and it did. There was a police station only a few blocks from Grand Central Station and easy to spot because there are patrol cars all around it.

Inside, everything looked like I expected a police station to look from TV shows, only not as busy. The clerk was separated from me by a plexiglass shield that I figured was bullet proof, I mean, it wasn't there to be a sneeze guard, right. There were a couple of wooden benches, a cylindrical black and silver ashtray and some posters stapled to the wall.

Oh, one was pretty cool. It has a cop in uniform carrying an injured little boy out of some kind of an accident right, and the caption said, 'Some people call us pigs' or something like that. I don't know if it made me really think that cops didn't throw kids off of roofs or shoot them in the back or hassle them over a little pot or any of that other shit that got them to be called pigs in the first place, but it was a good poster.

I had to wait for over an hour to see the cop that I needed to see. He wasn't expecting me on Monday. I suppose I could have called first, but I was just making it up as I went along then. I didn't know I was coming until I was already out of my apartment and away from my phone, so I waited for him, that's all.

They called him on his radio and told him I was there, and he said to wait. If I had known it was going to be so long I'd have gotten something to eat and come back.

I passed the time looking at all of the posters, even the dumb ones. One was for a family violence support center. I know what they meant, but I still thought it was funny, I mean, family violence should be discouraged rather than supported. I told the guy on the other side of the bullet proof plexiglass, but he didn't think it was anywhere near as funny as I did.

There was a ten most wanted poster too. There really was. But only five of them were wanted. Four of the black and white photos had 'Apprehended' red magic markered across them in bold, block letters. Well, technically, one was spelled with only one 'p' but that was what they meant. A fifth was also crossed out but that one said, 'deceased.'

"That'll learn him," I said loud enough for the guy behind the bullet proof plexiglass to hear, but he just ignored me.

That didn't stop me from finishing my thought as if he were listening though, "He'll never do it again."

The five that remained fugitives were all black men in their 20's wanted for things like kidnaping and assault, robbery, and escape. Four of those five were armed and dangerous, and one had shot a police officer.

"Hopefully one of the ones that throws kids off of roofs rather than one that carries injured children out of the wreckage of accidents," I thought aloud.

I had so much time to wait that I got to thinking about what a guy had to do to make the top ten list. I mean, if I was going to be a criminal, I'd like to be a good one, I'd like to at least aspire to get on that list, you know, be one of the top ten. It isn't like they tell you the criteria for making the list though. It is a legitimate question, isn't it? What sets these ten apart from the hundreds or maybe even thousands of other criminals and suspects at large? Especially the one of them who isn't armed and dangerous.

I wondered what made him so special that he should make the list, knocking down some armed and dangerous felon to being the eleventh most wanted person instead, which sucks. I mean, you might as well be the one millionth if you aren't on that top ten. If you don't get to be on the cool poster, you might as well not be wanted at all.

I started to think that maybe the eleventh man was white and that was why he wasn't as important to the police as a black fugitive, even one that isn't armed or dangerous. Think about it. Unarmed but still dangerous could be a big deal, but if he isn't even dangerous why not leave him be, that's what I'm thinking.

But the important thing is that none of these wanted people were really good criminals. I mean, not like movie criminals. There wasn't anyone who was suspected of making a super laser to hold the planet for ransom or something like that. Really, after I thought about it, the field is wide open. The competition to be a top criminal just isn't that great. One, really motivated person could knock the shit out of those top ten, hell, maybe make the top ten of the year or even of the decade. At least, that was what I was thinking when the officer I was waiting for finally got there.

Oh, I guess I should have told you from the start, but the cop had me wait there all that time for no reason. When he finally got there, he told me he put the paperwork in that morning without my statement. The guy was ticketed for leaving the scene of an accident, that's all. If he pleaded guilty he'd pay a little fine and be on his way. No lawyers, no trial, no jail, fuck, he wouldn't even get his license taken away from him.

My statement meant nothing now.

The whole experience made me think about how really useless everything I did was. I could have dragged myself down there Thursday like I said I would. I could have blown it off and never gone. No difference.

That's the fucking worst thing, let me tell you, to realize nothing you do really matters. Man, I left that police station thinking I'd like to start doing things that matter. Or at least work toward doing things that matter one day.

I was going to go to Speak Easy next, but once I was out there, near where the accident happened and all, I decided I wanted to go see if I had left a blood stain or something. I guess I was hoping to see the frozen lemonade girl, the one who held me.

I wasn't planning on asking her if she had a dick, but I thought, If I looked at her really well, I could see. If it turned out she didn't, she wouldn't have been so pretty after all, but if she did, I would ask her on a date or something.

I wanted to thank her. Really I did. I wanted to see if there was any chance she might hold me like that again. When I'm not bleeding I mean. I got a hard-on just thinking about her. If I had been the romantic type I would have thought I was in love.

I wasn't about to ask her to hold me or to have sex with me though. I thought I'd just thank her and see where things went from there. Still, it was possible that right when I was talking to her a cement truck could come by and mow me down, twisting up and breaking a dozen of my bones right in front of her. For damage like that, maybe she'd have to fall in love with me.

When I got close enough to see I could only see one cart there. At first I didn't see which cart it was, but I hoped it was the frozen lemonade cart. As I got closer I could tell it wasn't one of my boss's soda carts. That didn't surprise me. I had picked that spot. If I wasn't there, there was no reason to think someone else would give up their own spot for mine. It wasn't like it was one of the best spots in the city.

It wasn't the cookie ice cream sandwich guy either. Maybe he moved on. More likely though, he got fired for leaving his pushcart unattended when he went to call an ambulance for me. Either way I caught a break. The one cart that was still setting up at my spot was the frozen lemonade cart. By the time I got all the way up to it I was smiling much bigger than I really wanted to be smiling when I saw her again. I wanted to play it cool. Do that cool brooding musician thing.

Not Okay

She didn't see though because the cart was attended by a grungy looking middle-aged man who needed a shave really bad.

"Where is the girl who works here?" I asked him, lighting a cigarette.

"I work here, this is my spot," He said.

"It is not. You weren't here last week, or all month before that for that matter, I was here alone" I told him.

"What about this girl?" He asked.

I knew he meant I wasn't there alone if the girl was there, but I decided to pretend I misunderstood him and describe the girl instead. I can do that. It's my right.

"She was about five foot five, blonde, denim jacket."

"What's her name?" He asked.

"God, I don't know, I never asked her, but I bled on her clothes, that should make me stand out for her,"

He told me he goes south for the winters and just returned from New Orleans, that none of the girls he had seen at work had blood on them, and that was something he would have noticed, that street vendors are transient, they move on with no warning. That part I knew.

"I see" I said, trying to hide my disappointment, if you do see her, thank her for me, tell her I really appreciate what she did for me."

"You want some slushy lemon juice?" He asked.

"Nah, that stuff's really expensive."

"Oh, on me" he says, so I take it.

"Lemon juice doesn't like to freeze you know," He starts telling me.

"Really? I didn't know," I said, not caring.

119

"No, that's what makes this stuff so special. It has some special chemicals that make it freeze like this. It is quite revolutionary."

"Experimental chemicals huh? That's got to be good for your body. I said, still not caring, but all of a sudden thinking that maybe I should."

I looked around the ground for some sign of the accident but there wasn't any. No blood. No glass from a broken soda bottle, nothing at all. It was as if the accident had never happened.

"Hey, this shit isn't half bad," I called over my shoulder to the guy as I walked away.

It really was good too. I couldn't think of any reason someone might buy a stupid soda when they could have some of this stuff, even if it was twice the price.

I was still thinking about that when I got on the subway, heading for West 4th street and McDougall. Once on the subway I thought of the idea of giving the frozen lemonade guy my number for her and saying that I'd replace her ruined clothes for her. That would have been a great way to see her again, but I didn't think of it in time. I said fuck and hit myself in the head really hard, but I didn't realize I'd actually done it until I saw how many people were staring at me on the subway. I thought I had only thought it.

By the time I thought about what I was doing again West 4th street was already behind me and I had missed it. I wasn't planning on going to work yet, but since I was halfway there already I figured I was supposed to, so I went there first.

I guess I should have called first. Everybody always wants you to call first. I never think of it, but I bet if I learned to I'd be better off. In this case though, I should have called Wednesday night or Thursday. Here it was the

Monday after and I hadn't made any contact with work. Just then it occurred to me that that was a kind of bad thing.

"What the hell happened to you?" The boss lady asked loudly when she saw me.

"Van hit me," I said, "didn't anybody tell you?"

"We came to get you at eight and found your cart empty and abandoned," She said.

I remembered then that I always got picked up well after the cookie ice cream sandwich cart and the frozen lemonade cart did.

"I was in the hospital."

"Where's the money for all those sodas?" She demanded, "You should have one hundred and eighty dollars for me."

I knew it wasn't nearly that much, even though I hadn't counted it. Then I realized, of course, the sodas that were left alone in and around the cart would have been taken. She was going to charge me for every soda that had been left on the street too, and what was worse, I'd only gotten restocked a little before the accident, that was a practically full cart.

Rather than fighting over that, I decided to say there wasn't any money. I don't know why; it was just what I thought of right there.

"I was unconscious when they brought me in. The hospital must have thrown out the money along with my bloody pants when they cut them off of me," I said.

I thought she was going to say something about the accident, maybe ask if I was OK now that she knew it was serious. No fucking way though.

"How are you going to pay me back?" She asked.

"I don't know," I said, looking at my feet like a scolded child.

121

"I do. You are going to work it off," She said.

"Work it off?" I said surprised, "I'll have to sell a thousand sodas to cover all of that, it'll take a week, what am I supposed to live on in the meantime?"

"Oh, you aren't taking another one of my carts out, not after leaving one on the street. Those are expensive. You're just lucky the cart wasn't stolen. You don't want to know how much you would owe me then."

"What about me? I could have been killed!" I yelled. That was scary. I'd never yelled at my boss before. It was almost like yelling at Uncle Will.

I went on to say that her insurance should cover the sodas and my medical bills too.

"Maybe, if I wanted to put in a claim and make my premiums go up, fuck if I'm going to do that," She says, just like that. Then she says I'll clean the warehouse and work off my debt at five bucks an hour.

"After that, we can talk about putting you back on a route, on probation," She says. I was getting mad now.

"Does that sound like a fair deal to you? It sounds like a big fuck job to me," I say, stiffening my body.

"Fair or not, it's the only deal you've got," She replies.

"Keep it," I said, turning to walk out the door.

"You're gonna pay me the money you owe me!" She yells after me.

"Sue me!" I yell back, walking away from her an unemployed man.

"Bitch!" I said next. I meant it just to myself, you know, a general 'bitch' about the situation, but I know she heard me and figured it was for her. I wasn't about to go back and correct her.

Not Okay

Back on the subway platform I was really mad. I knew I was kind of wrong, but she didn't know that, and she sure didn't try to find out, that made her more wrong than I was as far as I'm concerned. Regardless of who was wrong, I was the one out a job.

For a second, in the middle of being angry, I laughed. I laughed because I remembered something Sharon said a time or two. She would say, "It's the story of the pitcher and the stone," Which must have been a Grimm fairy tale or an Aesop fable or something, but not one I knew. It went like this: It doesn't matter if the pitcher hits the stone or the stone hits the pitcher, the pitcher is the one that is going to be broken. I think she meant it to say that when you have the most to lose you should just suck it up and take it even if you are right. You can bet I didn't believe that shit, but the story still holds. I am the pitcher and the world is fucking full of stones.

I did have a few hundred dollars and my rent was paid up, so things could have been worse. When I looked up I saw that the train was just pulling into the West 4th Street stop.

"My Guitar!" I said aloud, remembering that I wanted to get off there.

Walking out of the train and up the platform toward the 3rd street exit I noticed a man in a suit and tie looking at me. I know for sure I hadn't yelled something out at that very moment, so it wasn't that. This guy was checking me out. He really was.

I glared at him.

Right then, I felt like a little boy again. I wasn't, but I felt like I was. I felt like I was twelve or something and this guy was cruising me.

"Keep your eyes to yourself fuck face," I yelled.

123

He looked surprised, like maybe he hadn't been looking at me at all.

"Bastard!" I yelled at him, "You fucking monster bastard!" I yelled and kept yelling as I walked out the turnstile and up toward the street.

9.

City wind is nothing like country wind. I guess it is something like country wind, but it is very different too. Country wind warns you. It starts out gently and works itself into a big deal. City wind prefers to hide and wait until you are completely off guard, the day appears to be calm, then it strikes, whipping around buildings and smacking you hard, in the face.

Catching you when you aren't expecting it is wind's best weapon. I mean, it's just air, really. But that is one fuck of a weapon. The wind's other weapon is grit. If it is light enough, like sand and dirt, a good gust of wind can pick that shit up and leave your face pockmarked with it.

The day hadn't gone well so far, so it only seemed to reason that my day would get punctuated by a face full of New York City's grime when I got out on the street.

I thought about just going home and giving up on the rest of the day, since I knew it was going to suck. I'll tell you why, and I'll tell you what, you can call it Peter Wilson's law of Hell's momentum. I just thought of that. Here it is: A bad day in motion tends to stay in motion.

Friedrich Nietzsche has nothing on me.

Speak Easy was closed, but I'd gone too early before and there are always people in there cleaning up from the night before and getting the place ready for opening at six. It was close enough to six that all of the staff were either there or just coming in.

I pushed the door, it was unlocked, so I went in.

The old man who owned the place was right there. I don't remember his name or anything, but I'll call him Bunny because I've seen him eating carrot cake a few times.

125

So anyway, Bunny says to me, "We're not open yet, son, give us another twenty minutes."

He must have needed glasses because he was really squinting to try and make out my face. Still, I hadn't ever seen him with glasses on.

"I was just hoping to pick up my guitar. I left it here last week."

"Oh, you're that Peter fellow," Bunny said.

"Yeah," I answered.

The old man brought me to a little area behind the stage. A black curtain held up with push pins substituted for a door on a closet that was large, but overstuffed. A metal step ladder had to be moved to get at my guitar, which was leaning against a stack of boxes of glasses. Well, I didn't know for sure if they had glasses in them, but they started out as glasses boxes. You can bet that none of the boxes in my apartment have the things they say they are supposed to have in them. But that's my apartment. A bar might be different.

There were two guitars back there. The other one was much nicer than mine, but I still took mine. I must not be too honest though, because I thought about taking the other one, and I thought it was really good of me not to, rather than that I was supposed not to, I hope you know what I mean.

Cheap piece of shit it was, I'd still have missed my own guitar. It was mine; you know. I wrote some good songs on it. Not what you would think are good songs I guess, but good for me.

"Everyone, they talk of you," Bunny said.

You know, right up until then, I hadn't ever listened to the old guy enough to even notice he had an accent. Polish or Jewish or maybe Polish Jew or something.

Not Okay

"They do?" I asked, thinking maybe everyone had liked my last song.

"Why do you hurt that poor little girl?" He asked.

"What, Robin Blue? I didn't do shit to her! What did she say I did?" I asked with emphasis on the last 'I..'

"What they are calling it, date raping I think. This is not good for a young man to be doing," He said.

"Oh, for shit's fucking sake, is that what she said? It isn't true, she's fucking nuts!" I started to explain, as if his fucking opinion of anything mattered.

"You must only know," Bunny said with finality.

"What are you, fucking Yoda?" I replied kind of under my breath. I mean, I said it loud enough for him to hear, but low enough so it sounded like I didn't expect him to hear. I don't think he heard though. The deaf old bastard.

I left after that. I mean, there wasn't anything else I could do other than smash my guitar or knock over a garbage can. I thought about smashing my guitar or knocking over a garbage can, I really did, but I couldn't come up with a way doing that could have helped, so I walked to Washington Square Park instead. On the way, I did shoot a look at a garbage can or two, just so they knew I could have knocked them over at any time.

I feel like an artist when I'm walking in Washington Square Park. There's a cool arch there, that was on the cover of a book by some beatnik poet. I bet it has been on lots of covers, but this one sticks out in my mind because it sold like a cabillion copies and it was called Coney Island of the Mind or something like that. Really, when you think about it, the picture on the cover of a book called Coney Island of the Mind ought to be of Coney Island. Washington Square Park isn't even near Coney Island. It was stupid. I don't even know why I had thought it was cool up until now.

127

Coney Island of the Mind might have been a different book by the same author, now that I think about. Now that I think about it, I just don't know.

So, Washington Square Park was another great thing that was shot to fuck. Speak Easy was shot to fuck, with Robin telling people I raped her and shit, and now Washington Square Park was shot to fuck, because the picture from it on the cover of a book called Coney Island of the Mind or something completely different, should have been called Washington Square Park of the Mind, or something else like that. If I was a writer I would have written a book and called it Washington Square Park of the Mind, and then put a fucking picture of Coney Island on the cover just to spite that stupid beatnik poet.

Now that I think about it, it could have been a different book with the arch on the cover. The Coney Island of the Mind book might have had Coney Island on the cover. That would make sense and mean I was getting angry about it for nothing.

I sat down on a round stone of one of the stone walls and pulled my guitar out of its case. Two people stopped to listen while I positioned it, but quickly moved on when I started strumming a little rhythm that I just pulled out of the air on it.

"Fuck you, you shit piles!" I yelled after them, but they didn't even turn around.

My guitar was out of tune and I never figured out how to tune it myself. I had always counted on one of the real musicians to tune my guitar for me when I was at Speak Easy. I started thinking then about how I couldn't go back there. About how Robin fucked that good and now my guitar would never be in tune again. It kind of made me want to smash the guitar right then, but I also wanted to write some good lyrics that would tell my side of what happened so well that I'd win my friends back, so well even, that Robin's friends would turn on her and even spit on her when she walked by. Not that I wanted people to spit on her, just that I wanted the song to be that good.

Most likely, I wasn't ever going to come up with those lyrics, but the idea that I could kept me from smashing the guitar. As long as the guitar wasn't smashed, there was a chance I would write those lyrics.

Oh shit, let me tell you the fucked-up thing I saw in Washington Square Park then. Well, first of all, people are always doing strange and fucked up things in Washington Square Park, like breathing fucking fire and riding a unicycle while balancing two other unicycles on each shoulder. Once, I saw some kids dancing to boombox music on a big piece of cardboard on the ground, you know, like the kind a washing machine would come in, flattened out, and in the middle of it they'd end up on the cardboard gyrating flat on the ground, and spinning around and all kinds of shit, then popping up again. A week later there were kids doing that all over the place. Black kids doing this and getting a crowd and people dropping money right and left for them.

But now I'm telling you about this game someone invented, kind of like soccer I guess, because you don't touch the ball with your hands. You can touch it with your feet or your back or your knee or even your head, but not your hands, and you pass it around in a circle. I guess that isn't too strange, but the strange part is that they weren't using a ball. Instead they had kind of a round bean bag, small enough to fit in a fist, and that is what they bounced between each other. When they did drop it on the ground, which they were really trying hard not to do, the thing just flopped there. It didn't bounce or anything.

Part of the time I watched them I thought it was the dumbest thing I had ever seen. Another part of the time I wanted to go over and see if I could do it. I think the part of the time that I wanted to smash my guitar was the part that I wanted to go over and try it, and the part of the time that I wanted to write a great song for Robin was when I thought the game was stupid as shit. You would think it would be the other way around, wouldn't you, like that I'd be all hateful of everything and want to smash my guitar and think new games were dumb or I'd be all open and optimistic about trying something new or writing something new, but no, it wasn't like that. I guess I'm more different than you are. Smashing my guitar wouldn't be because I was angry, it would just be because I was done with it. Sure, I could give it to someone or sell it, but I need something definitive, a symbol to mark the completion of something, and smashing my guitar, oh boy, that would be a symbol, right. Then, if I had completed something it must mean I need to start something else. Do you see where the new game would come in then. Shit, I better give this game a name. I can't keep calling it just the new game you know. It is foot bag. Like football only a bag instead of a ball.

Where did I leave myself then, oh right, if I had smashed my guitar right then and started playing foot bag I could have made it famous. That dumb game could have caught on. By now people all over the world could have been playing foot bag, having fun in parks and on street corners, staying out of trouble and off of drugs, and they aren't all because I wasn't ready to smash my guitar right then and give up writing songs. If I didn't tell you before, I'll tell you know. I never did write that great song that would have fixed everything. I tried, but I never did.

Not Okay

I almost wrote a song about not writing that song. I did have a pretty good verse.

What made me think I could win you with a song
No words could be right enough
to fix everything that's wrong.

It wasn't bad and the melody for it wasn't bad either, but that was all I ever came up with for that song.

I had a crumpled dollar bill with dried blood on it that I was ready to put in a donation hat for a cardboard on the ground dancer or a fire breather or something, but there weren't any out right then, so I bought a fifty cent soda and stuffed the change in my pocket. Up town I sold fancy ass sodas for a buck. Here in Washington Square Park there was regular soda for fifty cents. I don't think the fancy ass soda tasted any better.

Walking out of the park on West 4th street, I told my guitar that it was time to blow this stupid city. If it had any reservations, it didn't share them with me.

At 7th Avenue there was a table with pamphlets and a very enthusiastic guy approaching people. I was curious so I got closer and listened to his spiel.

He was going on about a mysterious illness that was afflicting gay people, and people were dying from it. His group was The Gay Men's Health Crisis, or something like that that didn't make for a good acronym at all.

You know this as AIDS now, but I don't think it even had a name then and I didn't see anything about it on the news so I didn't even believe it was a real thing.

The guy was urging me to use a condom when having gay sex to keep from getting or spreading the disease.

"Do I look gay to you?" I asked indigently.

"Yeah, actually, you look really gay to me. Straight people don't wear black satin shirts with shell buttons."

"Well, I'm not!" I told him, "I am totally into girls," I said, leaving off the part where the girls I am really into have dicks.

"Sorry," He said, not sounding sorry at all, and moved on to the next gay on the street.

When I got back to my apartment I packed some things into an old army duffle bag. Just the things I wanted to keep so no shiny shirts with mother of pearl buttons. Fuck those. I never wore one of those again.

I took everything I'd written, both in notebooks and on floppy disks. I didn't bring my computer or my video recorder, or any of my tapes because they would have been too heavy to carry.

Extra strings and guitar picks were light so I brought them even though I couldn't tune my guitar, and a glass pipe with enough pot resin in it to get a little buzz on just by scraping it out and eating it, I would think, and a Coke bottle filled with water.

I wanted to put ice in the bottle, but the cubes wouldn't fit in the little opening of the bottle. I hit a cube with the handle end of a butter knife, but the cube shot across the room instead of breaking. I hit another cube with the heel of my shoe, which did break it up, but it also made the pieces of ice dirty. I washed off a couple of pieces of ice in the sink and put them in the bottle, but they were so small after I had washed them that they dissolved right away when I got them in the bottle. I tried a larger piece and went back and forth from bottle to the running water until it was small enough to fit. It was a lot of work, but I did get the one shard of ice into my water bottle. After thinking about it a minute I decided one ice cube shard would be enough. It might have been nice to have had a whole lot of ice in my water bottle, but it was just too much work. Instead, I decided to leave in the morning, you know, after a good sleep. That way, I could leave my water bottle in the freezer all night and get it good and cold. So that is what I did.

I used the opportunity to watch some videotaped TV shows one more time before I went to sleep. I slept right through until like eight thirty in the morning too, which was pretty good for me. Hell, if my bladder didn't wake me up I might have gone on sleeping another two hours. That's the way it is with me. The thing that'll wake me up is my bladder. I'll wake up after nine hours or so, even if I piss right before I go to sleep, because my bladder is full.

I pissed, tossed my duffle bag over one shoulder, my guitar in its case over the other then unlocked the door. I was halfway out the door when I remembered my water bottle and went back in for it.

I bet you don't want to guess who didn't have a bottle of water for his fucking exodus from New York Shitty, but I'll tell you, it was me. The water in my Coke bottle froze solid while I slept and broke the bottle open. The tube of ice was frozen to the floor and a side of the freezer. Putting it in there was a dumb idea. For a little right then I started the wonder if leaving like this was a dumb idea too. I kind of knew it was, but it wasn't dumb enough for me not to do it. I went out the door, locked it behind me and started on my way.

I waited until I was over the George Washington Bridge before I put my thumb out to hitch a ride, and then I got one right away, but only for a short distance. That was how I ended up on the Palisades Parkway heading north though. I don't know if I would have had better luck with rides on a different road or going in a different direction. After the first ride there wasn't another for a long time.

It wasn't people's fault. Most of the Palisades Parkway doesn't have much in the way of shoulder for a car to pull over and pick somebody up. I walked a lot and felt the cars whizz by me.

Every so often a car with teenagers in it would yell something at me from their car window as they passed. I'm sure it was very amusing for them, but I couldn't ever hear what the hell they even said. Every time it was always like, "bishleezipootrouuuuuukrrr" or something like that. The first few times it happened I thought the joke was on them, since I didn't even know what stupid thing they had said, but after a while I thought about them having rides and me not having a ride and so I guessed they were right in the first place. The joke was on me.

Hey, that reminds me. In my personal effects locked up here at the jail is a little plastic dog that smokes cigarettes, or kind of looks like it does. They aren't real cigarettes, just little toy things, but it is a little nifty to look at. I just thought about that. I bought that thing out of a vending machine at a gas station on the Palisades Parkway. No shit, I did. It was a buck fifty I'm pretty sure. I bought it and a can of Coke and a Snickers bar and that was my breakfast at like noon on the Palisades Parkway. The dog wasn't breakfast. It was just a cute thing that caught my eye. But I kept it in my pocket most of the time after that. It really is cute. If I ever get it again I'd love to show it to you. If that isn't too trivial a thing I mean. Hey, now that I think about it, you could get it from them if you tried. I would love to have it in here if you could do that. If you could do that I'd show you how it works too.

But I was on the Palisades Parkway heading North.

You know, I was on there all morning and afternoon, walking mostly, but getting a few short rides here and there. The whole time it didn't occur to me where I was heading until I saw a sign that said, "Spring Valley, Nanuet."

Without even thinking, I had gone back to the place I had escaped from. I put it out of my mind because I had to, but if I had stopped to think about it I might have turned around right then and gone in another direction.

Rockland County hadn't changed much at all. The Red and Tan bus still took you from just about anywhere in the County to just about anywhere else. The fare was cheap enough and I still had some blood-soaked dollar bills so I got on the bus and took it to the Summit Park mental health complex. The very same place I had gone to day treatment. It was as good a place as any to go.

I was thinking about signing up for more of that day treatment program, even though that doctor was such an idiot. I never would have thought I would have done that then, but since being in New York City I discovered that most people are idiots. You can't avoid them all. But I had another problem that I hadn't considered until I was already inside. That was that I had no place to stay at night.

I thought I was doing OK right up until then but when it crossed my mind that I had forgotten to think about where I would live I started getting confused. It was bad luck more than anything else that I was confused right when the intake worker was talking to me. I'm not confused most of the time but right then, oh boy I sure was. Right then I didn't really know what I was doing or why I was doing it and that's what I told the intake worker.

You would be surprised how quickly they move when they have an extra bed in a mental hospital. In under an hour I had my own room and I was a real, genuine mental patient. Let me tell you, it was long overdue.

They locked my guitar in a closet to keep it safe but said I would be able to ask for it and get it during approved times as long as I gave it back to be put back in the closet as soon as I was done with it. The thing wasn't in tune anyway so that was just fine with me.

Had I known about the strip search I might not have gone there. I understand why they need to keep drugs and weapons and shit out of the nut house, but it was really unpleasant and shit, having my naked body fucked with was what made me crazy in the first place. Maybe. I don't fucking know. That is how it felt right then though. That I had been violated and here I was getting violated again for fuck's shit.

The good thing was they did it quickly.

Oh, and they never looked at the bottoms of my feet. If I was going to smuggle something in, I could have used double-sided tape and had it on the sole of a foot.

The social worker I talked to made arrangements to have my apartment in New York City emptied into a self-storage room that would be paid for by the Rockland County Department of Social Services as long as I was in the hospital, but when I got out I would be responsible for the bill, which seemed more than fair to me. I thought I was just abandoning everything I had left behind. It turns out, if you are crazy enough, New York State has you covered.

All of the paperwork was easier because I had been on public assistance there less than two years before, so they still had my old files.

Not only that, but the food was pretty good.

At my first meal I sat next to a scrawny, fifteen year old red haired girl named Adrian who had a couple dozen pairs of pin sized holes in her arms, like little snake bites, from sitting in high school study hall going to town with a stapler The teacher noticed eventually and she ended up getting committed.

I was really interested in her story. Not just the stapling her arms part, but study hall too. I had never gone to high school so didn't know any of what she knew.

Later that night in my room she was giving me a blow job. The first one I ever had from a girl. I'd love to tell you it was the start of a loving relationship, but she told her therapist the next day and we were kept pretty far from each other after that.

It was still a great way to welcome me to my next new life.

10.

The White House Hotel was not at all presidential. Actually, it was what people in Rockland County called a 'flop house.' Well, I'm sure people called it that other places too, but the first place I heard of such a thing was in Rockland County. It kind of sounds cool, like a gritty street movie from the fifties, but the reality was it stunk.

No, I mean, really. It smelled like urine and mold. It has to be easier for places like flop houses to seem cool in old movies because, in old movies, you don't have to smell them. In the hospital, they told me I was lucky to be getting into this place because it had a pool and the other hotels that Welfare might put a person like me up in don't have pools.

The pool, I have to tell you, didn't have any water in it, was growing a green and yellow film on its walls, and had a fucking tree breaking up from a crack in its floor. A small tree, but a tree all the same. Even when rain filled the thing part way with water, I promise you, you wouldn't want to wade in that pool.

My room had fleas, cockroaches, and dark brown, hard shelled beetle like things that lived in the seams of the old mattress and bit me while I was trying to sleep. I just called them bedbugs, since they were in the bed and mothers told children not to let bed bugs bite, so we can assume that bed bugs, if allowed to, absolutely do bite.

I hadn't realized until just then how cruel mothers were to tell children not to let the bedbugs bite. I was an adult and I didn't know how to stop them, so children couldn't have put up much of a fight against them. How are you supposed to complain about the bedbugs biting when it is up to you not to let them, I mean, like, it is your own fault if you do let them. It just isn't fair, and mothers, if anything, should know that.

I bought insect killer from the nearest supermarket, but these bedbugs laughed at that stuff. As far as they were concerned, it was their room and I was an unwelcome intruder to be disposed of, one bug sized bite at a time.

Three weeks from the day I had returned to Rockland County I had run out of the money I had from the soda cart. I would have gone through it much quicker, but I was in the mental hospital for two and a half of those three weeks.

I really liked being in the nut house. It was much better than my apartment in New York City, and I didn't have to hold down a job or wash my own dishes or much of anything. But it made staying in the White House Hotel even worse.

Most of the people in the hospital were committed against their will, which I thought was just ridiculous. I don't get why someone would want to be anywhere other than in a nut house, it is so nice in there. I mean, an art room to paint in and no one telling you not to do this or to use tools like that, nothing. There was music, TV, food, and lots of talking and being listened to. Check that shit out! There were people who listened to what you had to say about your life and weren't trying to tell you about theirs. You don't ever find that outside the nut house.

And there was fucking. Lots of fucking and sucking and kissing and licking. It was all hetero as far as I know. Maybe other stuff was going on but they kept it quiet and I wasn't in the loop. I wasn't a participant in much of it but I could get as much as I wanted. It was like all of the girls that really liked sex were put into mental hospitals just for that. For a guy to get into a mental hospital he has to be really fucked up in the head, like me, but for a girl, really liking sex was enough.

I enjoyed that place more than I should have let on and not because of all of the fucking if you think that. At this point I realized I wasn't attracted to guys and I wasn't attracted to girls either, unless they had a dick. I did it with a few girls in the nut house, but it wasn't satisfying. I wished it was the frozen lemonade girl instead of a nut house girl with a vagina.

When they kicked me out they actually said the hospital wasn't my own personal resort vacation. But it had been just that for me.

When I was leaving I wanted to stay so bad that I almost told them about Uncle Will and Robin and the frozen lemonade girl. I mean, they were saying that the hospital was for sick people and that I wasn't sick at all. If I had told them everything there was to tell they would have known I was sick enough to stay there. But I didn't know how bad the White House Hotel was going to be. If I had known, I would have told them everything. I bet I'd still be in there today if I told them everything I could have told them. I just bet.

But I didn't so I was staying at The White House Hotel, getting just enough money for cigarettes and movies as long as I went in the afternoon and paid the afternoon price. I should have used some of that money to wash my clothes, but then I wouldn't have been able to go to the movies at all, and I really liked going to the movies.

It wasn't so bad, washing my clothes in the shower and hanging them to dry on one of the water pipes that ran along my ceiling.

I wasn't expected to go out and look for work, which worked for me. Really, all The Department of Social

Services wanted from me was to stay out sight until those bedbugs ate me.

I guess I got a little depressed.

I had gotten away from Uncle Will and struck out on my own and ended up right where Uncle Will said I would be without him. Nowhere, a failure, broke, useless, what else should I say, what can I say that he hadn't already. And it was all true.

Once, at the mall, I saw Sharon in the food court while I was killing time before going to see a movie with Daryl Hannah as a mermaid and Tom Hanks fucking her, or something like that. I don't remember exactly but I know I liked it at the time. At one point the mermaid screamed and broke all the TV sets in a store or something like that and it was very funny. Not now, but then, it was funny when it happened in the movie if you know what I mean. But this was before the movie and there was Sharon, who I wanted to see and didn't want to see both at the same time. A part of me wanted to walk up to her, but the part of me that controlled my legs had me duck behind a pillar and sneak away so she didn't see me. I don't know if that was the part of me that wanted to play with the foot bag or smash my guitar or what. I haven't gotten a handle on the different parts of me and how they can disagree with each other and all.

Sharon didn't see me.

Did I tell you I hadn't taken my guitar out of the case this whole time I was at the White House Hotel, because I didn't. I wasn't going to be able to play it out of tune and I didn't know anyone who could tune it for me, so it just sat in its case.

I didn't write any songs during this period either, because I kind of need to strum on the guitar to get lyrics to come to me. But I did go see a bunch of movies.

I didn't shave the whole time I stayed there so Sharon might not have recognized me anyway. But I didn't take the chance. I didn't have to go to work so why should I groom, I thought. I could always fix my hair and shave if I needed to. That is, if it ever became Monday morning. And it just kept not becoming Monday morning if you know what I mean.

It wasn't much different from being trapped with Uncle Will, now that I think about it. Two questions stopped me from running away and trying to make it on my own again. They were 'how do I start?' and 'how do I succeed?'

I had no answer for the first question and fewer for the second because I had a list of ways not to. Really, I hadn't gotten away the first time. Sharon got me away.

Now I had a shaggy beard, dirty old clothes, bugs, and body odor. Getting a spoiled daughter of privilege to fall in love with me and save me wasn't likely anymore. So, I stayed at the White House Hotel for months. I stayed long enough that it felt normal. I stayed long enough that what I did was routine. I stayed long enough that I was the kind of person that stayed at the White House Hotel.

In time I figured out that I could put the plastic shower curtain between the top sheet and the bed and sleep on that. As long as I washed both of them in between I hardly got bitten by the bedbugs at all.

When I first moved in, I mean, when I was first complaining about how bad it smelled there, people would tell me that was nothing. People would tell me to wait until summer and see how bad it smells in the summer heat. But by the time summer came around something inside me had adjusted to the White House Hotel. Mid-day of the July 4th that I stayed there was so hot the road steamed. It was so hot and steamy that I heard people who had been staying there since long before me complain about the smell, and if you want to know, I didn't notice it.

There was a copy of the day before's newspaper on the creaky old porch where the creaky old guys sat complaining about the heat and the smell and other things beyond our control. I picked it up and found the listings of where all of the Independence Day firework shows were going to be. I almost said something about wanting some of that independence, but it was another one of those things that were beyond our control. Instead, I read the listings and thought about going to see the fireworks.

A lot of the things I thought about doing I ended up not doing. But not this. This time, I thought about going to see fireworks for the 4th of July and I actually did it too.

There were shows in Suffern and Piermount that were closer to me in Spring Valley than the one I went to, but I didn't go to those closer shows.

Instead, I took the Red and Tan bus to Suffern and walked from there, a good six miles to Ramsey, New Jersey to see the show at Don Boscoe Prep School.

I wanted to be sure I saw a good firework show and I didn't know if the one in Suffern or the one in Piermount were going to be good. Maybe they were good. Maybe they were better than the one I went to; I don't even know, but I didn't want to take a chance at being disappointed.

I'd seen Don Boscoe's before and knew it was great. I had seen it and really enjoyed it, even if I was with Uncle Will at the time. It was the 4th of July 1984 and I was going to enjoy some fireworks.

It must have taken me three hours to get from Suffern New York to Don Boscoe, which was across the border in New Jersey and it was getting pretty dark by the time I got to the gate. I was lucky I hadn't gotten there any later because when I did get there, they were about to start. I was lucky I didn't get there any earlier too and I'll tell you why right now.

There was a $2.00 charge to get inside the gate and I didn't have it. If the newspaper had said anything about that charge I didn't see it, but I saw it on the big sign as I was walking up to the gate. It was big as shit, painted red on a white board wired to the gate.

I'll tell you what I did and then you'll know how it was that I was lucky I got there so late. I walked in the gate like I owned the place, looking straight ahead. When the kid at the gate said something, touching my shoulder, I told him I had just gone out to put a bag in my car.

"Didn't you just see me come out?" I asked kind of indignantly. He apologized right away and let me in.

There weren't any spots left to sit on the bleachers, so I stood. At first I tried to sit on the ground, but the grass was kind of damp. It must have rained in New Jersey even though it hadn't rained on the New York side of the border. That happens down there.

In the short time that I tried to sit on the ground people walked by me way too close and sometimes even bumped me with their feet as they walked by. It wasn't so crowded that they needed to walk that close, and it wasn't unreasonable to expect people might be sitting on the ground so people should have looked where they were walking. After it happened a few times I gave up on sitting on the ground. They knew I was there, I'm sure of it. They were just being fuck stains. There are a lot of fuck stains in the world and even more of them in New Jersey. That's why New Jersey gets rained on more than New York. Because they deserve it for being fuck stains.

The fireworks started just about the same time I stood up. People should have settled down then and watched but just the opposite happened. People were rushing around then, trying to get back to wherever they were with their paper cups of sodas and shit from the concession stand and shit like that. Now they were bumping into me even when I was standing. They were bumping into me like I was invisible, and I guess I was now. That's what happens when you don't shave for a long time or get new clothes or live in a home that doesn't smell bad. You become invisible. It isn't the worst thing that can happen. I mean, if you watch out for people who might bump into you. Being invisible could have its uses.

At first I was watching the sky like everybody else was, but after a while I was looking at the faces of the people in the crowd. It was neat the way the fireworks reflected off of their faces and they were all looking up at the sky so I could look at their faces really well without them noticing. At first I thought about writing a song about it, which was neat because I hadn't thought about writing a song for a really long time. But then I thought that it was beautiful just as what it was. A song wasn't going to be better than the real thing, so I didn't bother.

There was something else too, about all those people. They were all doing a better job at living than I was. They had reasons to exist, goals they strived for, goals they didn't have to strive for because some things were just handed to them. They had cars and houses and jobs and clothes and everything. Well, they didn't all have everything. Some people had some things and other people had other things but all of them together had everything and none of them had as much nothing as me.

These people were OK, the people they knew were OK. It was possible. You just had to start out not being me.

I don't want to be the kind of person who is jealous of other people, but I guess I was kind of jealous. And mad at them too. I wasn't mad at them for having stuff as much as I was mad at them for not knowing they were OK. For needing a stupid book to tell them they were OK. I was mad at them for having all kinds of bullshit complaints that I didn't know they had, but thought they had, because people who have stuff don't appreciate it and complain about what they don't have and that is just the way it is and that is what I was mad at them about. Plus, I was mad at them for not being able to see me.

Let me put it another way if I can. You see, successful people have all sorts of people to thank for helping them to become successful. You know, people that they owe their success too. These successful people wouldn't have become successful, or wouldn't have become as successful, if it were not for these people. If they thank them or not, successful people owe lots of people thanks.

So, every failure must be a failure because one or more of those people that they would have owed thanks to for their success just didn't hold up their end. I was a big failure because someone I should have been owing thanks to didn't bother to help me and that is the truth.

Now I was bumping into things.

I walked right into the side of the concession stand while looking at people's firework covered faces and being angry at people that I didn't owe any success to. The guy behind the concession stand was really nice about it. He could have called me an idiot, but he didn't. Instead he asked me what I would like.

"I'll have what you're having," I said.

"I'm not having anything right at the moment," the guy answered.

"Life man. You are having a life," I said back.

I wasn't really paying him much attention until he answered me, and what he said was pretty shitty. What he said made me notice that he looked down on me.

"You should try working for a living," He said. He said it just that way too. That shitty, looking down on me way, the fucker.

"I did that," I told him, "I worked for a living and I didn't get one."

It was a good thing I was invisible. If everybody could have seen me they would have thought I was pretty strange.

I lit up a cigarette and let the smoke swirl around me before going back to looking at the fireworks on the faces of the crowd. Smoking was more fun than feeling like a worthless piece of shit. So was watching fireworks. Two or three fireworks later the concession stand asshole was completely out of my mind. I enjoyed 20 minutes of fireworks before my heart just stopped beating.

Maybe my heart didn't stop beating but it sure as shit felt like it had.

"What the fuck?" I asked aloud, and two people near me turned in my direction.

Something had set off alarms in my head even before what it was had fully registered.

I looked back at the faces of the people I had just seen and there I saw Uncle Will watching the fireworks with a boy who looked like he was 12.

He didn't see me but even if he had I don't think he would have recognized me, between the beard and me being invisible.

That's another thing I should have mentioned. I never shaved when I was with Uncle Will. Not ever. But I didn't have any beard. It is kind of strange how not changing something makes you change, because you change anyway, and if you want to stay the same you have to change. Like, if you want to keep a hair free face you don't have to do anything at first, and then when you get older you have to shave. I guess that isn't as strange as I thought it was before I said it. Maybe I just needed to reason things through, and now I have.

I was going to turn away, but I looked right at Uncle Will instead. I couldn't believe he was there even though the last time I was there I was there with him. Somehow, I had convinced myself that the Spring Valley police had locked him away after I was gone. That the Spring Valley Police had locked him up over a year ago and that for the longest time he was locked up in a jail cell where he would never see a firework or a star or a moon again.

I was angry at myself for a very short period of time, for thinking that the police were going to take care of Uncle Will. I didn't stay angry because I was a dumb kid then and I was smarter now. Back then I didn't know anything about the police. But now I knew that they don't take care of things. And then I started feeling pretty good.

I wanted to matter and there was a reason to matter right in front of me. I had plenty of free time, I was invisible, and Uncle Will needed to be killed.

You know, he was still driving the same car.

It was a somewhat light green, mid-seventies Lincoln. Distinctive and easy to spot in the parking lot. I went out looking for it when the fireworks were well underway.

"Now, don't forget me this time," I said to the kid at the gate as I walked out.

"Oh, I won't," He replied.

And then I was in the parking lot looking for Uncle Will's car. And then I was trying the door to see if it was unlocked, which it was.

I could have taken the hubcaps off of twenty cars in that parking lot without anyone noticing what I was doing what with all the attention being on the sky. Remember that, if you ever need to rob someone's car or pick someone's pocket or something. The time to do it is on the 4th of July during the fireworks when everyone is looking at the sky, I'm telling you.

I got in Uncle Will's car and started snooping.

There wasn't anything on the seat or dashboard or on the floor up front. On the seat in the back was a white and blue plastic windbreaker. Not Uncle Will's style and too small for him. It had to belong to the kid. On the floor of the back seat was a can of oil, which actually wasn't special either. There was one of those air fresheners that are usually shaped like pine trees hanging off of a radio knob, but this one was shaped like Garfield, the cat and smelled like vanilla instead of pine. That might have been special under some different circumstances, but it was so not what I was looking for that it wasn't at all. Oh, and there was an almost empty candy bag. Almost empty because it had one little red Skittle left in it. I had seen Skittles around, but I had never tasted one before, so I ate it, and it was gross.

I checked the pockets of the wind breaker and there was nothing in them.

I chucked it back on the back seat and then looked back to see if it would look like it had been moved. I was already disappointed that there wasn't something good in a pocket.

Looking back though, I saw something obvious that I had missed.

"Donny Roche."

This was the kid's name.

His mother must have ironed the name label onto the inside of his collar, the way good mothers do before sending their kids off to be miserable at summer camps. Maybe something she did right after tucking Donny into bed one night. Maybe right after telling him that he would be responsible for the impossible task of not letting the bedbugs bite. But at least I knew the kid's name.

I should tell you that I was having a really good time. It was like I had found my calling. Right then, I wasn't a bum anymore. I was a spy. Really. Staying at the White House Hotel was just a cover. I was on a noble mission for the good of all of kidkind. I was going to kill a monster.

Did I tell you Uncle Will was monster? I think I did, but if I did, it was a long time ago so let me tell you again. Uncle Will was a monster. The real kind. Fuck fangs and claws and turning into a wolf or a bat. Uncle Will was a monster that preyed on innocent young people, infected them with his sickness and made them fucked in the head for the rest of their lives, like I was.

I was still searching inside Uncle Will's car, and even though I had found Donny's name, I hadn't found everything I was looking for.

I hadn't found what I was looking for mostly because I didn't know what I was looking for. But I don't think you need to know what you are looking for to find it, so long as you will know it when you see it. I thought I would. I mean, I did find the kid's name.

Most of everything I found worth mentioning I found in the glove compartment. It was an unusual glove compartment because Uncle Will kept a pair of gloves in there. In case you don't know, I'll tell you, no one keeps gloves in a glove compartment. They just don't.

Another thing that Uncle Will kept in his glove compartment that most people don't is his spare set of car keys. Uncle Will is not stupid about a lot of things, but he was sure stupid about where to hide his extra set of car keys, I'll tell you that.

Oh, the important thing I found was some of his recent mail, including an electric bill and a bill from the Columbia Record Club.

To elude the Spring Valley, Police, Uncle Will had moved all of twenty miles away, to Ridgewood, New Jersey.

"I got you," I told him, even though he wasn't there to hear it.

Uncle Will was sitting on the bleachers watching the end of the firework show with his little boy, completely oblivious to the fact that I had gotten him.

I kept the Columbia Record Club bill and put the rest of them back in the glove compartment. At first I was going to write the address down, but I didn't have a pen and the only thing I could have used to write something down on was the back of the Columbia Record Club envelope, so I just took it. In the future, I decided, I mean, if I was going to do this often and I hoped I would, I would bring a little notepad and pen with me.

I closed the glove compartment and then the car, leaving it pretty close to the way I had found it, then headed back inside the gate.

Walking past the kid who had almost become my friend, I nodded to him and he waved to me.

Inside, I kept a good distance from Uncle Will and Donny and watched them, so I didn't lose track of where they were. What I didn't want now was for Uncle Will to see me and have some warning that trouble was coming.

I hadn't missed the grand finale of the fireworks, although it wasn't quite as grand as I remembered it being a couple years ago.

The last thing that went off was a big American Flag on a twenty-foot-tall pole, which burst into red white and blue flames as the band played The Star-Spangled Banner. A few seconds later, the stars started spinning in different directions and then the whole thing exploded into sparkling, flaming words that read, "LET REEDOM RING."

It was very impressive aside from the letter F not going off.

I stayed, alternately watching the crowds leaving and the fizzling out of the last few sparkles on the sign. For ten minutes or so, the parking area was as much fun to watch as fireworks. People beeping and starting and stopping as they tried to negotiate terms with each other's vehicles where there was no clear rules follow. Looking at that, in my mind, I imagined cockroaches scurrying around my room's floor when I would come in at night and turn the light on.

I heard a pop and looked back at the sign, but all I saw was the tiny glow of two embers that hadn't quite gone out yet.

I looked back at the parking area which was mostly empty now and Uncle Will's Lincoln was gone. That wasn't a problem for me. I knew where to find him, after all.

The bleachers were completely empty at this point. Looked them over too, just to make sure. There were paper cups, cigarette butts and empty packages, paper hot dog plates, you know, the kind that are kind of shaped like a hot dog, oh, and napkins and straws. No one was cleaning up, like you would think. I guess they had left it to clean up in the morning. That is what I would do.

There were people working on the ground, collecting power lines and loading pyrotechnic equipment onto a couple of trucks, but that was it. Even the guy who was at the gate and the concession stand guy had left.

I was right at the gate when I heard another pop from the darkened sign. This one sounded even more like a spark. I turned back to look and there it was.

A bright, sparkling red "F" appeared on the sign that was up on that pole. While I was walking out of the gate and down the hill the "F" lit up the empty field behind me. I don't know why it made me smile but it did. Other people's fuck ups almost always made me smile. It made me feel better about my own fuck ups. That one, right then, made me feel better about the big fuck up I had done in not killing Uncle Will back when it would have been easy for me to. I mean, the "F" lit up eventually. So, what if it was a little late as long as it gets done. That's the important thing.

11.

Two sharp raps on my room door loosened a few flakes of once white paint that floated like a feather to my floor. I think that the news that lead paint causes brain damage never got to this landlord. Not that I knew it was lead paint or that it wasn't, but if it was, I knew the landlord didn't care and saw no reason to correct it. Anyone poor enough to live here had to be stupid already. A few more or less brain cells weren't going to make much of a difference.

I was in bed, still wearing the pants and shirt I had been wearing the day before, and the day before that too. In fact, I had been wearing that shirt and that pair of pants for five days, if you must know. The 4th day that I had been wearing those clothes was the 4th of July, which I just told you about, but I think I had taken them off to sleep one or two of those five nights and put them back on the next morning.

I looked on my nightstand to see what time it was. This was a reflex kind of thing to do, I didn't have a clock there. I did own one, but it was in storage in New York City along with almost everything I owned.

Whatever time it was, I was sure it wasn't noon and when I had called Sharon, I had said to let me sleep and come at noon. I called Sharon when I got to Suffern at about two in the morning. The Buses weren't running that late and I had actually thought I was going to ask her to come pick me up and drive me back to the White House Hotel, but once I got her on the phone I decided it would be better if the first time she saw me again I was clean and shaved. So, I just arranged for the meeting and walked the remaining ten miles back to my flop. I got to bed at seven in the morning.

I opened the door with a fresh, unlit cigarette stuck in my mouth.

"Mr. Mustafa!"

"You are surprised?" he asked.

Mustafa was Jewish, but not like Bunny, the owner of Speak Easy might have been. Mustafa dressed like someone would if they were going out for Halloween as a Jew, with a black suit, a black skull cap that he told me the name of but I forgot, a frilly dish towel kind of thing that had a name too, and all that other stuff. But this wasn't a gag, it was the real deal. He really looked like a regular person making a joke though, at least to me.

His accent seemed more like a joke than real too. Sometimes I was almost sure that he wasn't a Jew at all, but an Italian mobster hiding out from the law, pretending to be an Orthodox Jew, or maybe a member of a hippie group from the sixties that blew up a college ROTC or something like that and was on the lam. It was a great cover. It really was. No one but me would ever suspect anything.

I hadn't heard the word antisemitic before so I didn't know that I was, but now I know that I must have been antisemitic something awful because I heard people say things and I didn't know not to believe them so I really did look at this guy differently than I looked at other guys.

"I was expecting someone else," I said.

"Like this you are having company?" He asked.

"Oh, yeah, I don't think she is due for a while, what do you want? I was sleeping," I mumbled from behind my cigarette.

"A lady friend you have?" Mr. Mustafa said. Well, asked, but really it wasn't a question. I don't know if it was a rhetorical question, you know, like I ask all the time, because he just always talks like that.

I guess they were rhetorical questions because I never got to answer them. When I started to, he would lift a hand, shrug and say, "Is this my concern? I should say not," Or something like that.

If I didn't tell you Mr. Mustafa was the landlord, he was. I don't know if he owned the place or just worked for whoever did, but he was the only landlord I ever saw, and I only ever saw him when he wanted to be seen. He had this great way of not being around when you wanted to ask him a question or complain about something.

He always made me nervous when he came to the door. Rockland County's Department of Social Services paid the rent directly, and I didn't make any loud noises at night, so there wasn't any reason he ever had to bother me as far as I could think.

I couldn't have been asleep more than two hours before he came to my door and that isn't enough sleep to be able to think before I talk, so instead of asking why he was there I asked if he fucked through a hole in a sheet. Someone else who lived at the hotel said that Orthodox Jews did that and someone else said that Mr. Mustafa was an Orthodox Jew. I didn't believe it but I wanted to know for sure and he was standing right there.

He just ignored the question. Now that I think about it, I might not have asked aloud. It is hard to know, but now I am thinking that I didn't because if I did, I think he would have reacted in some way.

"You should want to wash up for this lady caller, I should think?" Mr. Mustafa asked, or said. Shit, I just couldn't tell what was a question and what was a statement with him.

"When I wake up, yes," I'm sure I said that aloud.

"Later you cannot, but now you can. My brother is

coming from Long Island to work on the pipe and the water will be off after nine. You can take a shower now."

"What, nine? It isn't even nine yet?" I asked.

"It is seven thirty."

"Fuck, I haven't even slept at all," I said, and then I asked, "How long will the water be off?"

"I should know how long this will be taking? My brother, we should be grateful if he gets the pipes back together at all when he is done."

"He is a plumber?" I asked.

"No, but he knows a few things about old pipes, he said he would take a look and I said, what will it hurt? But now I wonder," Mr. Mustafa answered.

I hadn't even closed my door before he was pounding on the next one, and I did get into the shower knowing the hot water wouldn't last for all of us.

I left my cigarette, still unlit, on the edge of the sink, hoping to smoke it after my shower, but wouldn't you know, I must have splashed water on it when I got out, and now I wouldn't be able to smoke it until it had dried out.

I only had one towel and it wasn't even mine. I had borrowed it from a woman who lived two doors down my second day there and she moved out before I could give it back to her. Since I only had one, I did my best to keep it off of the bathroom floor.

There was always a little leak under the bathroom sink. It wasn't so bad that it covered the entire bathroom floor with a sheet of water or anything, but it seemed that no matter where on the floor my towel got thrown, it always ended up right in the wet area.

Going into the shower, I put my towel on the toilet seat where it would stay safe and dry. Coming out though, you better believe it was not just on the floor instead of the seat, but right in the wettest part of the floor and I knew I hadn't put it there.

I picked up my wet towel and tried to find a dry part of it to use, cursing the cockroaches and bedbugs for pushing my towel into the water. Oh, and that was when I noticed that my cigarette was wet too.

"You bugs suck!" I yelled, even though I didn't have any proof that the bugs had anything to do with it.

I dried off with my dirty shirt then hung it on the shower rod to dry a little before putting it back on. I was going to shave, but I didn't have a razor yet. That was one of the things I had asked Sharon to bring me. Really, I didn't look or smell any better than I did before I got into the shower. It really made me feel stupid to bother doing what little I could.

Sharon was happy to hear from me, and I didn't know that she would be. Even if she would have been happy just to hear from me, I didn't know that she'd be happy to hear from me at two in the morning asking her for a bunch of stuff.

Most of the stuff I was asking her for she could just steal from her father. Her father, unlike me, had lots of stuff. He had so much stuff that I didn't think he would be able to keep track of it all, so he would never even know if some of his stuff went missing.

I was going to go back to sleep after I took that shower, but then it was so hot that I knew I wouldn't be able to get to sleep. I opened the door so there would be a little breeze, and sat, wet, on the bed, digging the dirt out from under my fingernails with a plastic fork.

When I was done with my fingernails I moved on to my toenails. I don't know, I was enjoying it so much I didn't want to stop. I was especially enjoying seeing the little pile of dirt grow larger as I pulled more out and piled it on top. When I was done with all of my fingernails and toenails, I started rolling all of the dirt into one ball. It seemed like a perfectly normal thing to do right up until Sharon got there. Then it seemed like something I should be embarrassed about, so I hid the ball under the bed sheet and pretended I hadn't been doing anything.

Sharon arrived a good half hour early. The door was wide open, but she knocked on the door frame.

"Be careful of that thing, it has some kind of a prayer inside it," I told Sharon, because she was knocking really close to this thing that was nailed up to ward off evil spirits or something. To tell you the truth, I don't know what it was, but Mr. Mustafa said it was important. It was Jewish too, whatever it was. And since it was important to him, I thought it should be important to me too.

"Oh, Peter, what happened to you?" Sharon asked.

I grimaced at her as a reply.

"I brought you the things you asked me for," She said, coming in, "What are you going to do with them?"

I was going to tell her that it was better if she didn't know, but even as I thought it I thought it sounded like something stupid that someone would say on a stupid TV show, so I grimaced again.

"Black clothes, crowbar, rope, flashlight... you are going to rob someone aren't you? Ooh, it's so sexy. Can I help."

"I'm not going to rob anybody. I haven't turned into a bad person, is that what you think?" I replied.

"What then, what are you going to do with all of this stuff that isn't bad?" Sharon asked.

"If you must know, I came back to kill Uncle Will. Are you satisfied now, you know?" I fired back at her.

159

"Oh, Peter. Be careful. It could be dangerous," Sharon said.

"Hey, Sharon, you know, I'm going out of my way not to sound like a Hardy Boys Adventure, I'd appreciate it if you do the same."

She looked back at me like I had hit her, which made me feel guilty, so, without even thinking about it I gave her what she wanted, I kissed her on the lips. It was stupid of me. And cruel too, because I was setting her up for me to hurt her worse later.

That's right when I knew I was using Sharon. I was using her before but that moment at the White House Hotel was when I knew that I was. I needed to, in order to kill Uncle Will, which was a really important thing to do, but I had to go over it in my head. You know, ask myself if the ends justify the means kind of thing. Right there, while Sharon stood next to me, I had that argument with myself and she lost. I kissed her again and held it longer. I closed my eyes and pretended it was the frozen lemonade girl, and when Sharon opened her mouth, I really did it. I gave her the tongue.

When I pulled my face away she was red.

"I know you don't love me," She said.

"Sorry," I said, and I really meant it.

"You're still going to fuck me," She said back.

"So, I'm a whore," I said, finally lighting the cigarette that had been wet and taking a drag off of it.

She pulled back a little.

"No. It's OK. I'll be a whore. But if I'm a whore I'm not a cheap one. Clothes and a flashlight I can get anywhere,"

"What do you want?" She asked.

"I'm going to be putting myself into a really

dangerous space, you know? It could get really messy and not only that, Uncle Will could kill me while I'm trying to kill him. I could use an edge."

"My father keeps a gun in his study desk. I could get it for you, but I would have to bring it right back," Sharon told me.

"That's fair," I said.

"My parents are going to Lake George for the weekend. I can bring it to you Friday night, but you have to give it back to me Saturday night."

I agreed and she lunged for me, connecting our lips together and grabbing both sides of my head in her hands.

"Friday," I told her, pulling away.

"May I at least have a glass of water?" She asked.

"There's a deli across the street," I said without even flinching.

I could have told her that the water was off, and I really should have, but I was kind of mad at her for making me a whore. Before, when I kissed her, I was mad at myself for using her, but it was different now. That's the thing with me and Sharon. One minute she's the victim, the next I am, the next she is again, then I am again. We are always being each other's victim: Sharon and I.

"Friday, then," I said, nodding toward the door.

When she was gone I looked through the things she brought. Little of it was exactly what I asked for, but it would all do.

The black jogging suit was too heavy for the weather, but if it was a cooler night as some are, it might turn out to be perfect.

I took out a three pack of disposable razors and a travel size can of shaving cream from Sharon's package, went into the bathroom and turned on the water faucet.

"Shit," I said when nothing came out, remembering the water was off.

"This is the girl you are to like?" I heard from outside the open bathroom door.

Mr. Mustafa stood in my doorway.

"She's just a friend who brought me some things," I replied.

"Is it my concern?" Mr. Mustafa said, hand up, face turning away as he does.

"No. Not at all," I said.

"It is just the tears she drives off with, she could hit a tree not able to see where she is going, this friend of yours."

"It's a painful world, Mr. Mustafa, crying just means you are smart enough to notice."

12.

The few days before Friday were spent well enough, practicing, doing pushups, shaving and trying to keep shaved, and buying clean clothes with some of the money Sharon left me. I hardly noticed the time go by until Sharon was back at my door. Then I knew it was Friday.

"You get it?" I asked.

"Not exactly, Peter, I was afraid too. If the cops traced the gun to my father they could catch you."

"That's just great," I started, not yelling, but raising my voice. Reached for a cigarette but ended up not taking one out.

"Wait," Sharon interrupted.

"What?" I asked.

"How about this?" Sharon offered, bringing out a ten-inch-long, black bladed hunting knife with an equally black handle and an even blacker leather sheath.

"I bought it for you, it's dark. Will it work?"

I always used to talk before, but I'd gotten started telling Sharon things by grimacing at her, so I kept on, and that's what I did then. I grimaced at her.

"It's the best I could do," Sharon explained.

"I could use a ride to New Jersey," I said, putting the knife in the bag she had brought me before.

"I better not," Sharon replied.

"I thought you wanted to help," I said.

"If you need an alibi, I should be far away from the crime, you know," Sharon said.

"What crime?" I asked.

"You know, killing Uncle Will. It is murder."

"No, it isn't," I told her, "Murder only applies to

killing human beings. Uncle Will is a monster. By fucking little boys, he gives up his humanity, you said so. He's a monster, not a person, so it isn't murder. The worst I'll be guilty of is cruelty to animals."

That's what I told Sharon, or something like it, and I think that's what you should say in court too. That's how I'd like you to defend me now that I think of it. I can't be guilty of murder if the person I killed wasn't human, and he wasn't, he was a monster. You know he was too, a predatory monster.

So anyway, Sharon actually thought I was going to fuck her for the knife. Well, the knife and the money and everything else she gave me.

"I paid forty bucks for that knife," Sharon protested when I didn't.

"Not enough, the deal was for a gun," I said.

"Then I'll just take it all back, how about that," Sharon said.

I wanted to push her but I needed the stuff in order to kill Uncle Will so I didn't. Instead I gave a little.

"Let's see if it is good enough. If it does the job, you'll get what you want."

"How will I know if it did the job?" Sharon asked.

"Next time you see me, if I'm alive, that'll be your sign," I told her, and did that nodding thing I had done before, toward the door, telling Sharon to leave.

"Wait, I have something else," Sharon said.

"What?" I asked.

"This," She said, and she pulled a smooth, flat, yellowish brown stone from a front pocket and put it in the center of my hand.

"It's a petrified garlic. In Egypt, they used to put these with the mummies of the worst people. It was supposed to keep the evil spirits from escaping the dead body and going into someone who was still alive."

"What am I supposed to do with that?" I asked.

"Peter, don't you understand? This is a tool of the monster slayer. Real ones. The legend of vampires being afraid of garlic comes from this. It could be true, and if it is, you've got to leave the petrified garlic with the monster's body to keep the evil spirits from escaping, oh Peter, if they escape, you'll be the closest person, they could turn you into a monster."

She made me promise to leave the garlic stone with Uncle Will, I put it in my pocket. Then she left.

Since I didn't have a ride and it was already after ten, I decided to wait until Saturday night to go kill Uncle Will. Had everything I needed to do it too. Well, everything but a ride to New Jersey, oh, and a gun. I had a nifty ass black knife which wasn't too bad, but I would have rather had a gun. It wasn't that bad. At least I didn't have to sleep with Sharon.

I didn't want to, and at the same time it kind of turned me on that she wanted to sleep with me so badly, if you know what I mean.

Hiding in the bushes outside of Uncle Will's apartment complex, staking it out, watching and waiting for hours, I got a hard-on thinking about it. If Sharon had been there right then I'd have let her blow me. I would have, right there in the bushes.

Uncle Will's car wasn't there all night and after a few hours I was so bored of waiting outside in the bushes for him that I decided to break into his apartment and wait for him in there.

Black clothes really aren't the best thing to be wearing for this sort of thing. They should have been, but they really aren't. If I had been wearing normal street clothes I would have been more inconspicuous, but I didn't know yet. I hadn't ever killed anyone before, you understand.

My best shot at not getting spotted was to do it quickly, so that is what I prepared to do. I looked at my wrist and, if I had had a watch there, I would have known what time it was. I looked across at the door to Uncle Will's apartment, the balcony, and sliding glass doors. My plan was to pry the sliding glass doors open with the crowbar and get inside as quickly as I could.

When I did run for the balcony, I ran in a snake pattern rather than straight, to keep from being directly under any of the lights. I climbed on the balcony and pulled out the crowbar, but when I went to put the crowbar's flat side between the door and the door frame it fit too easily.

Uncle Will's sliding glass door was open a couple of inches, which was kind of disappointing. If I had asked Sharon for binoculars too, I might have known that. I had even thought about asking for binoculars, but I didn't, figuring that I wouldn't really need them.

So, then I was inside Uncle Will's new apartment. The whole trip, from bushes to inside took a minute.

I looked out the sliding glass doors for any signs that someone saw me. There weren't any. It looked like I had done pretty well so far.

I wanted to snoop around but another thing I had forgotten to ask for was gloves, and once I was inside I was really worried about leaving fingerprints.

I took a washcloth from the bathroom and used it to wipe the sliding glass door where I might have touched it. Then I wasn't really sure where I had touched it and I was wiping all over it. I must have wiped a third of those sliding glass doors, but I was sure that I had somehow missed the precise spot where I left an incriminating fingerprint. I knew what I was doing wasn't wrong, but that didn't mean the police wouldn't arrest me if I made it too easy for them.

I went away from the sliding glass doors and then back to them a few times, being satisfied that I hadn't left any prints and then later being worried that maybe I had after all. In between wiping the sliding glass doors, I did snoop around, carefully. I took a piss first and was careful not to touch anything other than my cock as I did. It was still kind of hard, even while I was pissing. It might not have been Sharon. It could have been the excitement of planning on killing Uncle Will. It could even have been that I was involved with Uncle Will again. I did have a lot of hard-ons with Uncle Will in the years I was with him. He did make me cum a lot of times. It is weird how you can like something physically but not emotionally at the same time. When it comes to Uncle Will, I don't understand what all my feelings are. Still, being that close to killing him was a super turn on.

Uncle Will had a lot of new electronics. That wasn't unexpected. He always liked the latest gizmos and gadgets. He had two VCRs hooked up to each other so he could rent movies and make copies of them, or maybe so he could make copies of porn or something. He also had a home computer and a bunch of shit for it. I made a note to myself, to take some of that stuff with me after I killed Uncle Will, but I didn't inventory it all right then. I was more interested in what he prized the most, which was his kiddie porn photos.

They weren't hard to find under his bed, but there were more than two shoe boxes full now. In the time I had been away from Uncle Will he managed to collect enough of that shit to fill up six shoe boxes, some to overflowing.

All those kids he had fucked after me. Every one of them my fault, because if I had killed Uncle Will before I left none of those kids would have been fucked.

I looked at some of the pictures.

"Oh, Donny Roche. You poor dumb kid," I said, finding a stack that were of the kid I saw with Uncle Will at the fireworks show.

Just then I heard the sound of running water.

Turning around, I dashed for the bathroom and jiggled the handle of Uncle Will's toilet. Then I wiped the handle with the washcloth I was carrying. I wiped it a few times and was thinking about going back into the living room to wipe the sliding glass door down again when I heard another noise.

This time it was the cylinders of the lock on Uncle Will's front door.

"Fuck fuck fuck," I said fast because everything got a thousand times more real in an instant. He could have had a little boy with him right then, on the spot, and then I would have to decide if I could trust him not to give me up or if I would have to kill him too, and if I killed the victim along with the monster I wouldn't be much of a hero.

"Fuck fuck fuck," I said again.

I had about a second to run for that sliding glass door, go out and get away. A second that came and went without me moving.

Uncle Will was in the apartment and on his way down the short hall toward his bedroom and the bathroom. Uncle Will was about to catch me in his apartment and no part of my plan covered what to say when we saw each other again.

I pulled the black hunting knife out of its sheath and held the handle of it inside my bag.

Not Okay

I heard each of Uncle Will's steps as he got closer to me. Four would do it, and I had heard four.

I backed up just enough to hit the heel of my shoe on the base of the toilet. I thought about my shoe leaving a traceable scuff mark and hoped that I would remember to wipe it after I killed Uncle Will.

At the last possible moment, as Uncle Will turned to walk into the bathroom that I was also in, I pushed the knife up into my sweatshirt sleeve so that the tip of the blade was under the cuff, pressed against my wrist.

He had turned the corner in a hurry, apparently heading for the toilet with some urgency.

When he saw me, I had a foot up on that toilet and my arms folded.

"Hiya Uncle Will," I remember saying, cocky as I could sticking a cigarette in my mouth, but not lighting it.

Maybe I didn't say that. Maybe I said that but not so well. Now I remember my being super cool, but I think I told you before, I'm not always as super cool as I remember being when I think about it later.

Either way, I know he gasped in surprise and jumped back.

"Wha, you!" I think he said, and then he said, "What are you doing here?"

"Oh, I thought I'd stop by for a visit, catch up on old times, what's wrong, didn't you miss me?"

"You were an idiot to come looking for me!" Uncle Will said.

"I'm an idiot anyway. What difference does it make?" I fired back.

"Should have killed you when I had the chance," Uncle Will told me, which was really pretty funny, since that was what I had been thinking about him since I left.

"Peter, Peter, Peter..," Uncle Will started, walking toward me, "You think you can get the best of me, you foolish little boy."

As he spoke, he reached into his jacket. As his hand was coming out again I saw the glint of something metal.

What's going on in my head is, 'he's got a fucking gun and I don't! What the fuck?' and while that was in my head my arm was moving. I slid that hunting knife out of my sleeve and had a fist around its handle before Uncle Will could get his hand all the way out of his jacket. I squeezed the handle hard as I swung it in Uncle Will's direction. What was going on in my head too, was that right now, either he was dead, or I was, and it was all going to depend on which one of us moved faster.

I had a lot going on in my head. I was bitching out Sharon for not getting me a gun and I was squeezing the handle of my knife so tightly because I thought I would drop it from fear if I didn't.

He saw the knife when it was maybe two feet from him, and I was swinging fast. I came at him kind of sideways because of how I was standing with one foot on his toilet.

I may have looked like a fighting crab, but it worked. When I let go of the knife it was sticking all the way in his chest. It pinned his jacket to him like a note to a cork board, and he looked at it instead of me.

His hands were empty now, both of them, and one of his hands felt behind him for balance as the other moved to his wound.

"But I, but I, I, loved you," He said as his ass hit the floor just outside the bathroom door.

That should have been the end of it right there, but it wasn't. He kept on talking, if you could call it that, even as blood came out of his mouth. That part was gross. There wasn't much blood coming from the knife, but there was more than just some coming out of his mouth.

"I knew it. I knew it was going to... be... I knew," he said, or something like that.

I didn't blink, but I did pull the knife out of him.

That turned out to be a little bit of a mistake.

You know how I told you that Uncle Will's wound didn't really bleed much, well, that was because the knife was holding the blood inside him. Once the knife was out of his chest he bled like a motherfucker. It didn't exactly spurt, but it did get on me.

This hunting knife had a really jagged edge with the thick end much thicker than the blade end, so it left a triangular shaped hole rather than a neat slit. With all of his bleeding now he sure should have been dead, but he kept on babbling.

"Turn on... light... I want to get a look... look at you... oh Peter, oh boy, you got big didn't flew, flew glot blidder ten shee worsh worshu shlee..."

"Shut up!" I yelled, and rammed the knife back into him, this time, closer to where I believed his heart to be. I hadn't ever looked at an anatomy book at this point. I really didn't know that hearts are much closer to the center than off to one side, but whatever my blade went through it took care of the babbling. Uncle Will's head fell limp and he didn't move or speak again.

I looked at his limp, rag doll body and couldn't believe I had ever been afraid of him.

Then I looked on the floor for what he had taken out of his pocket. I wanted it to be a gun now because I really needed one. It wasn't though.

I didn't know what it was, but it wasn't a gun.

It was rectangular, larger and thicker than a pocket calculator, with a cover on a hinge like a woman's compact or a communicator from Star Trek. I knew what it was as soon as I opened it. It was a wireless telephone.

"Neat Uncle Will, how long has this been on the market?" I asked. I didn't get mad at Uncle Will for not answering me, since he had a really good excuse.

I'd like to tell you he was dead, and he sure should have been, but I checked a little after that and he still had a fucking pulse if you can believe that. People are much harder to kill than you ever would think. But don't worry. He died eventually. I didn't leave until I knew he was good and dead.

The thing was that I didn't really have to stab him right then, since he didn't have a gun at all. He was just going to call the police and have me arrested for breaking into his apartment or something like that. More likely he was only going to threaten too, since he tried to keep a low profile when it came to police, and I would be a little hard to explain.

The point is though, that there's no way to say it was self-defense, and even if you could, that would only explain the first stab. It was the second one that really did Uncle Will in, and I stabbed him the second time because he was annoying me with his babbling.

I went there with the intention of killing him to keep him from making any more victims like Donny Roche and me, but once I was there, I ended up killing him because he was annoying the fuck out of me.

But don't tell a jury that.

I succeeded and that was the important thing. Uncle Will was not a threat to anyone now and every little boy that Uncle Will didn't fuck up the ass from that moment on, if they know it or not, has me to thank for it. And everyone on the Jury who has a kid who hasn't been fucked up the ass by Uncle Will has me to thank for it too, and that's the truth.

I told you I didn't leave right away, although I really should have. The longer I was there the more likely I would have been caught with Uncle Will all bloody on the floor in front of his bathroom door. And we weren't exactly quiet just before I killed him. But like I said, I didn't know better, so I took my time.

I wiped the knife clean and washed the blood spots off of my clothes as best I could. I kept the phone rather than try to wipe my fingerprints off of it, and I filled my bag with things that looked easy to carry and expensive.

I checked Uncle Will's pulse and he was still alive, then I wiped his wrist because I didn't know if you can leave fingerprints on someone's skin. I still don't. If you know, I'd sure appreciate if you would tell me. I'll feel pretty silly, having done all that wiping, but I'll know not to do it again.

Oh, I cleaned him out too. I checked Uncle Will's pockets and his wallet, and I took all of the paper money he had, which was pretty close to $200.00. It wasn't stealing so much as it was recouping expenses.

It was only right that Uncle Will should pay for his own execution. You can't exactly get his future victims that now won't be victims thanks to me to pay up. You don't even know who they aren't. No, monsters need to pay the expenses and wages of the monster killer, that's just the way it is.

That meant I had a job again, which made me feel much better than a mentally ill bum in a welfare flop house. Hell. I wasn't a bum in a welfare flop house at all. I was just what I said. I was a monster slayer using a mentally ill bum staying in a welfare flop house as my cover.

By the time I got to the Atari 5200 video game machine, my bag was already too full to put it in. I took the games but left the machine, which sucked later, because I would have enjoyed playing those games back at the White House Hotel if I had the machine too.

One more experience to hopefully learn from.

The next time I checked Uncle Will he really was dead. I checked him good, too. I checked his pulse and I checked his breathing and I looked at his eyes. In the movies, you always see people closing dead people's eyes. I didn't do that. I kind of liked seeing Uncle Will staring off into hell with his dead eyes.

I remembered Sharon's garlic stone and took it out of my pocket and wiped it off with a fresh washcloth. I then used the washcloth to put the stone in Uncle Will's hand and to close his fingers around it.

Right then I decided that this garlic stone would be my calling card. They might not know my real name, but they'll know that Uncle Will was a monster and he was killed by a real live monster slayer.

I left through the front door and locked it behind me with Uncle Will's own house key. I walked as casually down the street as I could and made it the equivalent of three city blocks before ducking into the woods and cutting over to the next street.

While I was in the woods I wiped the key clean and stuck it into the dirt.

It was just about midnight when I got to a strip mall in Upper Saddle River. That was the first I knew that I had been walking in the wrong direction for a couple of hours. That was also the first I knew, when under the lights of the closed strip mall, that I still had some of Uncle Will's blood on my sweatshirt.

I should have turn it inside out and worn it that way, but what I did was I took a hand full of dirt and rubbed it into the blood mark. Now it looked like it could have been anything.

In front of the closed laundromat was a free courtesy phone for a taxi service. On a lark, I picked it up and asked how much the fare would be to Spring Valley. They told me fifteen dollars, which sounded worth it to me, considering I was making a get away from a murder and all, so I said yes and had the cab come and take me home.

Well, not home, but 2 miles away. I walked the rest of the way to the White House hotel. I didn't have a clock, but I think it was close to one in the morning, which was earlier than I expected I was going to be.

Once in my room, I took the sweatshirt with the dirt and blood mark and held it in the bathroom sink, turning the faucet on. Nothing came out.

"Fuck," I said. The water was off again. But at least I had gotten something productive done. I killed Uncle Will. Not bad for a day's work.

175

13.

Sabrina has got a last name. I know she told it to me right when we met, but I'll be soaked in propane and set on fire if I could remember what it was five minutes later, and now it was five hours later.

I think we could have gone on another five too, if she hadn't run out of cigarettes.

She said two hours and she let me talk on and on for five hours.

She looked pretty beaten.

Not as beaten as fucking Uncle Will looked half out of his bathroom doorway, but pretty close.

The floor of the room we were in looked bad too, with an entire pack of cigarettes butts stamped out on the floor around us.

She rubbed her eyes with a finger from each hand.

Hearing my life must have been as exhausting for her as living it had been for me.

"They say killing someone in cold blood and I was all about that, but really, blood is warm, and when you are actually killing someone you feel hot, even if an air conditioner is running, that's the truth, no matter what they say about cold blood."

Sabrina interrupted me right here. It was a shock because for all the hours I had been talking, she didn't say anything, she just let me go on, but now that I got to killing Uncle Will, she had something to say.

"This is..," Sabrina flipped through her file folders, looking at papers, "William Forester Buckner, yes, so this Uncle Will is the man you are charged with murdering?"

"I can't believe you haven't been paying attention," I replied, "Uncle Will wasn't even really named Will. Buckner is my freshest kill. Five days ago, shit, his blood is still tacky. Uncle Will was July 1984, six years ago. Uncle Will was the first monster I killed. He was the messiest, I got much better after the first few."

Sabrina didn't show much emotion, but she swallowed when there was nothing to swallow and that was as telling as a grimace.

"How many people have you killed, Peter?"

"Oh God, I'm not sure. Five definitely. Sometimes I don't know if I killed someone or just thought about how I would do it enough that I started believing I actually had. Some I remember going really smoothly. Like, I was a superhero and they were completely out matched by my greatness. I'm pretty sure I only imaged those. The real ones were much harder, messier. The real ones didn't go as smoothly as the ones I think I only imagined doing."

"So, what do you think? Can you tell the jury that I don't kill people, I kill monsters, can you get me out of here so I can go back to work?"

"I think you are fucked," Sabrina said.

I bet it was true, but I was still pretty surprised that she said it.

"Are you that direct with all your clients?" I asked.

"So far, but you are the first," She answered.

I fucking knew it!

"I hope you are as good first time at bat as I was. But anyway, the next morning the water was running again in my room and I…"

"Hold on," Sabrina interrupted again.

177

"It is midnight, I've been here too long, let's stop here and pick it up tomorrow. Shit, not tomorrow, I forgot, the day after tomorrow."

"Why not tomorrow?" I asked.

"I have a birthday party to host," She replied.

"Yours?"

"My son's."

"How old is he?" I asked, mostly because I didn't think she was old enough to have a child.

"Seven," She told me.

"That's plenty old enough to be molested," I said.

"That's not going to happen!" Sabrina answered, standing up.

"Why not? Have you taught him what to watch out for? Have you taught him what to tell you about?" I pressed.

"I will tomorrow," She said, sweeping her files and things back into her black leather portfolio.

"That might reduce his risk but that's all," I said, baiting her.

"It won't happen."

"You don't know that miss mommy, you don't. You have to get me off. I am the only line of defense your child has against monsters and you know it."

We didn't shake hands or anything, but we didn't need to. I knew I got under her skin.

Back in my cell I regretted smoking so many of her cigarettes. All that night my whole body hurt when I breathed, and the next day, when I was used to it, I didn't have any at all.

I did get to make a phone call, which was nice. I was given an hour outside of my cell every day in a little area with a payphone, but every time I had been there before someone was on the phone. It wasn't that I wanted to make a call especially or I would have asked for a turn or something before, but this time there was no one on the phone anyway so I went ahead and used it.

Of course, I called you, Sharon. Yours was the only phone number I knew from memory and you were the only person I knew who would accept a collect call from me.

"Where are you now?" you asked.

"Jail," I answered.

"Which one?"

"Orange County, Goshen New York. I killed a priest," I told her.

"Was he a..," you started to ask.

"You know it."

"How much is your bail?" You asked. That was you. Always down to business.

"I don't know: lots. You'd never have enough."

"Do they have a good case?"

"I don't know, my lawyer says I'm fucked," I said.

"In those words?" you asked.

"Exactly those words."

"That is not a good sign," you said.

"Will you come visit me?" I asked.

"I'll think about it," Which meant you would.

Tuesday morning came early.

Sabrina was there to see me at seven in the morning and I wasn't even out of bed yet. Which was something for a place that forces everyone to wake up shit fucking early every day. Breakfast was at a quarter to Eight. I had fifteen minutes of sleep due me and I wasn't going to get it now.

She must have been into my story, to get there so early. Which was kind of neat considering that I was a failure as a serial killer. I mean, I killed people plenty well, but I never got the recognition for it. I didn't tell Sabrina, but I'll

179

tell you. I was going to leave a garlic stone on the body of every monster I slew, you know, as a calling card. If I had done that I might have had big headlines as The Monster Slayer or something neat like that. I might have been a real folk hero. But I never could find another one of those stones.

I went to stores that sold precious stones and semi-precious stones. Lapidaries, I found out they were called, and I went to a bunch of them. Not one of them had heard of a garlic stone or the legends of Egyptian people using them in tombs or any of that stuff you told me.

One of them said that a petrified bit of garlic was an oddity, but that it wasn't worth anything, so they didn't sell them. But it was worth plenty to me. It would have let everyone know that there was a monster slayer in town.

Sabrina was right to be surprised that I was a mass murderer. She thought I had just killed this one guy. That was what she had been told and that's what the authorities thought. A fine serial killer I am. Five kills for sure and no one even knows my kills were connected. That is pretty pathetic for a serial killer, and it was all because of your stupid garlic stone.

I was getting kind of pissed off at you as I was walking the corridors of the jail down to the conference room where my lawyer was waiting for me. I had been in jail a few days now and had gotten pretty good at keeping my eyes forward and feet on the right part of the floor in relationship to the painted line and all that stuff.

It was a long walk, so I had plenty of time to think about you and your stupid garlic stone and how badly it messed me up. You have to understand that this was when it really counted to be famous. Sure, some people would think I was a bastard, especially the child fuckers, but other people would consider me a folk hero, and one of them could be inspired by me to continue the work I had started.

I thought could be in jail for twenty years and if I was in jail I couldn't be out killing monsters. If I didn't inspire someone else to start there might not be anyone doing it at all, and that would be awful. These are also things I decided I wouldn't tell my lawyer, at least not right now. I mean, they aren't really facts about the case, they are kind of opinions, you know, like that, and everybody has the right to come up with their own opinions. I can just tell Sabrina the rest of what happened, and she can decide if I'm a folk hero or a bastard, or if I should have thought about my image more than I did.

When I got to the conference room, I didn't get right down to telling my story again. First, Sabrina gave me a bunch of stuff. She gave me a carton of cigarettes, which was really nice of her. They were Winston and they weren't menthol. Not just was that great because it was what I wanted; it was great because it meant she had been listening to me.

She also gave me a paperback book.

She told me that this particular book had a little something to do with me, so I should be especially interested in it. She showed it to me and asked if I recognized it and I said I did not.

"The author's name is Piers Anthony, and it is part of a series of books called, Xanth. Cherry bomb trees, gourds with magic peep holes, centaurs, they are all in these books. Your friend, Robin, she must have taken her past from these books. She was either pulling your leg or out of touch with reality."

"Oh. I wanted to believe her," I said. I pushed the book away as I said it, but then I pulled it back. The biggest problem with being in jail was boredom and a book was a way to get away.

"So, you are giving me something I can use to escape with," I said.

"Something like that," Sabrina replied with half a smile.

"Have you ever lost yourself in a book like this?" I asked.

"Not as fully as your friend Robin Blue had, but when I was a little girl I read C. S. Lewis until the pages fell out."

"I think I've heard of him, The Hobbit and The Rings and stuff," I said.

"That was J. R. R. Tolkien, also very good. The Lewis books were The Chronicles of Narnia."

You know, we must have talked about stupid fantasy books for twenty minutes before we got down to anything important and I couldn't stop her because she was enjoying it so much. Me, I could take or leave unicorns and fairies, but she was all over that stuff. But after that, we got down to it.

"I should say, some of it gets nasty after here," I warned her.

"I think I can handle it," Sabrina said back.

"I don't remember the last thing I said," I said.

"Well, you told me you had killed five people."

"Oh. Yeah. Five for sure. Maybe more, maybe a bunch more, but definitely five," I replied.

"I didn't kill anyone for a year after Uncle Will," I started, "For a while I thought I got it out of my system, especially the next day back at the White House Hotel"

"I was feeling pretty good. Relieved, really. I thought I had done what needed to be done and now I could get back to my life, or back to getting a life, or something. I didn't know that later down the road I was going to go into killing monsters full time. I thought about it, but there is a lot of difference between thinking about it and doing it. It is a big commitment, becoming a monster slayer. Or serial killer if you like that better. It isn't a decision you make quickly, not if you are really serious about what you are doing."

14.

You can't find a much nicer place to live in Rockland County than Nyack. The town sits right on the Hudson River and looks out onto water so sparkling; you wouldn't even know that the fish were so polluted they'd kill you to eat them.

My house wasn't along the river, but the river was a close enough walk and that was good enough for me. I couldn't afford to buy it, I rented, but I was doing much better than I had been when I was at the White House Hotel.

Sharon helped me get into the place and got me a lawyer to sue the delivery van company that hit me. We settled out of court and I got seventeen thousand dollars after the scum sucking lawyers, no offense, took their share and then some.

You might think there was a story there, but really, there wasn't. The lawyers did everything lawyerly between them, calling me once in a while saying something about the process that didn't involve me. Then they told me I had to be around for a deposition, whatever that was, then they told me there was an offer on the table and I said just take it, and that was the whole story, really.

When I got the check was a little more of a story because I bought a few things I always wanted. I wanted to buy a car, but Sharon started telling me about everything I would need to do to get a driver's license and it just seemed like too much for me at the time.

I picked up a better condition copy used copy of *I'm OK You're OK* and started reading it as if for the first time. I learned more in the first few chapters than I had in all of my time in day treatment and in the nuthouse. I didn't know why I had ever doubted it. This book says, hey man, everyone's fucked up, everyone's life is fucked up, there's nothing different about you. We're all just OK. The whole psychiatric profession is a waste of time. This is all you need to know to be sane.

I was feeling saner then. Some things are outside of your control but can make you feel like there's something wrong with you. Things like having to wipe your ass with your hand and wash the poop off in a sink. That kind of thing chips away at you. Now I always had toilet paper. I bought a new pack before the old pack was half empty. The good stuff too. It helped me to really feel like I was OK to have plenty of extra toilet paper.

I did get home delivery of the newspaper. That might not seem like a big deal to you but man, it made me feel like a real person. On TV, real people read the newspaper.

I didn't read much other than the bold print, but I looked at the pictures and the captions that went with the pictures and that gave me a pretty good idea about what was going on in the world around me.

There might have been a lesson to be learned by my experience the last time, in New York City, about waiting until the money had run dry before looking for work, but whatever that lesson was, I didn't learn it.

In May of 1985 I spent my days sitting on the rocks near an expensive, riverside restaurant watching boats break slits into the water that spread out, dancing the colors of the sky like a liquid kaleidoscope.

Obviously, I didn't come up with that cool a way to describe it right away. It took a lot of hours out there to come up with that. I thought it would be for a song, but it was yet another song I never wrote. Just because nothing productive ever came out of the hours I spent by the river doesn't mean it was wasted time. The sound of the waves relaxed me, the picture of the boats did too, even before I had a nifty way of describing it. You can't just dismiss something that helps you to relax. Plenty of people take medication for that. I got it from the Hudson river.

The thing was though, that I spent a lot of time in town, just out and around, so I got to know people who were out and about too, and I knew Suz and Reba.

I wouldn't say I knew them well, but I knew them. When they were ditching school, sometimes they would come down to the river where I spent so much time.

Reba was the older of the two of them and she carried a sketch book if it were a part of her. It is gone now, but back then, there was an old lighthouse out on a small, manmade island, and Reba must have sketched it fifty times.

It wasn't a real lighthouse, I don't think, it was more of a decorative thing, 20 feet tall I guess, but people didn't care. The liked it and they liked sketches of it too.

Suz talked more than Reba, so the couple of times I talked to them I mostly talked to her. Reba would be drawing and Suz and I would watch her draw, and maybe I'd say something like, "your sister's work is really good," and then she'd say, "Do you really think so?" or maybe she'd say, "Do you like this one?" and then I'd say, "Yeah, it is really good," or something like that.

Once I thought about teaching her some stuff about art, but I didn't really know anything about art, so I didn't. It doesn't help someone to teach them things when you don't know them yourself, even if you kind of think you might know, and that was where I was.

Not Okay

If I was going to teach her something, it would be that there is more to art than reproducing what you see. I mean, there are cameras for that, you really don't need an artist to do it. Art, I would have taught, if I was teaching, has to be more than that. Art is looking at something everyone else has looked at and seeing what no one else saw, and then making it possible for other people to see it. Or at least I thought that right at the time and pretty much believed I was right, but not knowing for sure that I was right, I didn't try to teach Reba anything.

I did ask her what artists she really liked. Of course, she said Edward Hopper. Hopper was from Nyack I think. There was a whole museum in Nyack dedicated to him and his work, if you were a young artist in Nyack, you'd damned well better like Edward Hopper.

She also said she liked Wyeth, but when I asked her which one she said she didn't know.

"There were two, or maybe three of them. To tell you the truth, I don't know which one is which either," I told her.

From there I think we talked a little bit about Vincent Van Gogh, who she knew about, and then Robert Motherwell and Mark Rothko, artists I really liked who she didn't know of. At the end, it made me want to learn more about art myself, but I didn't end up following up with it.

So that was as much as I knew of Suz and Reba when I saw a little poster on the telephone pole outside of my apartment building stoop with their pictures on them, saying they were missing.

In real life, Reba was six inches taller than Suz easy, and had redder hair that Suz. In the black and white picture though, they looked like they were both the same age, the same height, and had the same color hair.

My first theory was that they tried to get a better view of the lighthouse, by climbing on the moss slippery rock ledge, and maybe fell. It wasn't a good theory. If one of them fell, the other would have gone to get help, and what were the odds that they'd both fall, but I went down to the river to look anyway. I thought, if Reba's pencils were there, or her sketch pad, it might mean something, but I went and looked there was nothing like that.

That night, they made the news. The local news anyway. They kind of played it down, like they were most likely going to turn up of their own accord after a little running away stunt. The police officer heading up the investigation told the TV reporter, "These young ladies have a history of getting into trouble," It sounded to me like the entire investigation was going to be the posters and pictures on the news, asking people who might have seen them to call. It didn't seem like enough to me, but I knew less about investigating missing people than I did about art.

I wouldn't have done anything else but for a strange coincidence that was more likely to mean nothing than anything, and that happened the next day.

I had gone into the Stop and Cop a few blocks up the road from me for cigarettes and a magazine. The place wasn't really called the Stop and Cop, that was just what I called it. I think it was called Shop and Go, or something like that. Anyway, the guy that was checking out right when I was ready and was going up to the counter gave me a bad feeling. He looked like a bad person, and even though I couldn't place him, just outside of my memory I thought I knew him in a really bad way.

I'm going to tell you now, even though I didn't figure it out yet, that where I thought I had seen him before was in a couple of the pictures in Uncle Will's collection.

"That thar's a twenty," the man said to the guy behind the counter.

"...and eleven forty-two is your change," The guy behind the counter said, counting his change out to him.

He took his bag and walked out the door.

"What an ass," The guy behind the counter said.

"How so?" I asked.

"I'm sorry, I didn't mean for you to hear that."

"Ok, but I did hear it so tell me. I don't like him either, what makes him an asshole to you?" I asked.

"Nothing I guess. About a year ago that guy tried to say he gave me a twenty when it was a ten. I had to count out my entire drawer and it checked out perfect. He said I ripped him off after that, but he kept on coming in, and every time he hands me a bill he tells me how much it is, like I'm stupid or a criminal. I'm not either," He told me.

"He was a bitch before that too, and he's always complaining about how much cheaper the same things are in the supermarket. The supermarket is different from a little convenience store, and no convenience store anywhere is as cheap as a supermarket."

He mentioned supermarkets, which got me thinking that most people buy just a few items at the Stop and Cop, and he had a whole bag full. All of that must have cost him four bucks more than it would have been at the Shop Rite, which wasn't all that far away.

"That's a lot of junk food for one guy, don't you think?" I asked.

"He never used to buy that shit. Hell, he only ever bought diet soda even. Now he's been in here every day buying a six pack of Coke and Ring Dings and Twinkies and all of it."

"How long has that been going on?" I asked.

"Just a couple days, three or four," I was told.

He had bought Diet Coke too, and while maybe he just had family visiting, maybe his company was those two girls, so I waited until he was halfway down the block and I went after him.

"I'll buy something another day," I said to the guy leaving the magazine I had picked out on the counter.

I didn't really need it. I had lots of old magazines filled with articles I hadn't read yet.

You have no idea how easy it was to follow him either. The guy never looked behind him and lived close enough to me that I could see my stoop from his.

As soon as he was inside I walked right up to the door and pressed my head against it. I kind of thought I heard a female voice call someone a bastard, but it was faint, and I might have even imagined it. What he might have been doing to those two girls in there made me really mad. The name on his door was Maldonado, so now I was mad at Mr. Maldonado.

"Maldonado you Diet Coke guzzling fuck face, you just wait," I said.

That night I was on stake out.

I planned this one a little better than I had the last, bringing plenty of snacks and a drink with me as well as cigarettes, a lighter, and an empty screw on bottle if I needed to take a piss.

I couldn't buy a real gun without a permit, as it turned out, but I was able to buy a pellet gun without anything at all.

"Can this kill somebody?" I asked.

"Sure, if you are close enough and hit them enough times, it is possible, I suppose," The guy at the sporting goods store said.

"Well, that's good enough for me," I replied and bought one for seventy-seven dollars and fifty cents.

I wanted another Garlic Stone because I was pretty sure going in that I was going to kill this fucker, but like I told you, nobody sold garlic stones or even knew the legend of the garlic stone other than Sharon. If it wasn't for Sharon and her stupid Garlic Stone, I'd have come up with a better calling card and really left it every time I killed a monster, and then you would have heard of me. Damn, when I think about that, I feel like such a failure. I have to focus on what I did right, and I did murder the motherfucker. That's the important thing. I did kill the shit licker.

Don't let movies fool you. A stake out is just about the most boring thing in the world, next to episodes of Three's Company without Crissy.

I watched Maldonado's place from the park across the street from his house from ten in the morning until nine at night and that whole time, nothing happened.

Something might have happened when I was in Tony's Pizza getting two slices with mushrooms, but I didn't have my eye off his place more than fifteen minutes. That was about three. It wasn't that I hadn't brought enough food with me, but I could smell the pizza cooking and, if you like pizza, you can only smell pizza cooking for so long before you need to have some.

I did bring it back and eat it in the park, watching the house the whole rest of the time. But at nine at night or so, I was pretty sure I had missed the moment when something actually happened. It wasn't a big deal though, because another moment was coming.

This moment was the one when Maldonado showed up with a couple of shopping bags. One of them was plain and could have come from anywhere, the other was a blue and white, handled bag from Bouton's Camera store in the mall.

I'm sure you are going to say that there are plenty of reasons to go to a camera store, but you don't know what I know. Uncle Will was into camera stuff big time. I'm telling you; photography is a pedophile's hobby.

I had quite a pile of garbage around me at that point. There were candy wrappers and empty soda cans, a bottle half filled with pee, the plate from my pizza and a dozen cigarette butts. I didn't do the best job of scooping it all together, but I collected the most of it in my arms and brought it to the garbage can, which was closer to Maldonado's house than where I had been sitting. Mostly what I left was cigarette butts, and maybe one candy wrapper, which wasn't that bad.

It is important not to litter because it messes things up for everyone.

Oh, by the trash can was a pay phone and right then I got the idea of letting the police handle Maldonado. Yeah, I know they didn't do much of a job with Uncle Will, but I was tired after being on stake out all day and I thought they should have another chance, so I called, 9-1-1.

"Emergency operator, what is the nature of your emergency?"

"Give me the Nyack police," I said.

"Is this an emergency?" The operator asked.

"No, bitch, it's a chicken pot pie, what the fuck do you think it is damn it, put me through!"

"One minute please."

Not Okay

When you know how to talk to people, you can usually get what you want. Remember that.

"Nyack police, dispatch."

"Send a car over to 413 Larchmont road, this guy, Maldonado, I think he has those two missing girls in there, you know, Reba and Suz."

"What is your name, sir?"

"This is an anonymous tip. If I give you my name, I won't be an anonymous anymore, will I?"

"Could you tell me how you know?"

"Well, first, he went to Bouton's camera in the mall, and you know pedophiles are into photography. Not only that, but he bought Coke and Diet Coke at the same time, now what does that tell you?"

Even as I told him all of this I knew he was skeptical He just didn't know enough about this sort of thing to know how damning the evidence was.

"You aren't going to send someone to arrest this kid fucking bastard, are you?" I asked, and the dispatcher didn't say he was.

"Bitch!" I yelled, smashing the receiver against the side of the phone and kicking the trash can, which made something in the can, like maybe rotten melon rinds, smell really bad. I wasn't calling him a bitch. I was just saying the situation was a bitch.

I want to tell you what was happening inside Maldonado's house at this time. I guess it would be better if I tell you later, when I get to the point where Suz and Reba are telling me what happened, but two things.

One is that I think it would be better if you already knew before you hear what I do next, so you know that I wasn't wrong. The other is that Suz and Reba didn't actually tell me what happened down there.

I'm filling in this part of the story from what I think must have happened. Maybe you think I'm a sick fuck for even thinking up this stuff, but really, he was the sick fuck, I'm just seeing him for what he was.

But before I knew better, inside, I knew the evidence was shaky. Someone might have thought that I imagined the whole thing about Maldonado being the one and all. I might have too, if I didn't turn out to be right. But I did turn out to be right and that meant that I had some terrific power to figure out things that regular people just don't know. I was right about him being the one. Chances are, I was right about what he said and did as well.

Sometimes, you just have to trust your powers. Especially when the lives of children depend on it. So let me tell you.

Maldonado's first name was Calvin, and he was half Puerto Rican, half Irish. That didn't turn out to matter at all but for a while I was making note of what people were, thinking there might turn out to be a pattern. There wasn't, I mean, other than all of them being men.

Cal had a little bunker built into the cellar of his house, which he told Reba and Suz was where he kept his art studio. He met them on the street, as I had, and told them he was an artist too. He offered to let Reba use his studio once in a while, and that was how he got them to come into his house and down the stairs into his cellar.

Once there, he locked the door with a key so they couldn't get out and just overpowered them.

The cellar bunker smelled like dirt even though he had built cement blocks all around it and put down a wooden plank floor. The two beds were planks too, built right out of the walls kind of like a jail cell.

Not Okay

One of each of the girl's ankles were chained to different sides of the bunker with a small amount of lead, so they could hug each other, only in the middle of the room (which they spent a lot of time doing while they were his prisoners).

Right at the time I was outside deciding if I should go home or bust in and kill the fucker, Calvin Maldonado was down in his bunker toying with Suz and Reba.

"What are you going to do to us?" Reba cried while Suz, who used to be the talkative one, curled fetal in a corner.

"Why I'm not gonna do anythan ta you girlygirl. Anything you do for me, you do on your own, like, if you want to, you can suck my cock."

"Fuck you! I won't do shit! You can go to hell!" Reba yelled at him.

"That's just too bad girlygirl. Because if you don't make me happy, I'll take it out on your kid sister."

Both girls said, "Oh God" at the same time then, and then too, Calvin Maldonado unzipped his pants and showed them his cock for the first time since they had been his prisoner.

"See here? Big isn't it?" He asked. It wasn't really, but the girls didn't answer his question.

"The choice is completely yours," he said to Reba, walking toward her with his cock in his hand.

"You can put your mouth over it and suck till it squirts down yer purty little throat and slurp it on down if you want…"

"No fucking way!" Reba screamed.

"That's fine, just fine. You don't have to; I won't force you. But if you don't, I'll have to get my satisfaction somewhere else. Would you like to know where? See, I'll just

195

ram my big fat cock up your little sister's ass. It'll hurt, she'll bleed, she'll cry. She might even die and all because you wouldn't cooperate.

"You bastard!" Reba said, crying.

"Only you can save her, big sister. It won't hurt you, but it'll sure hurt her."

Like I said, I didn't know exactly what was said down there. What they did tell me was not words so much as whimpers, but this is how I remember it now.

As I picture him taking his first step away from Reba, toward Suz, his doorbell rang. It was me. That's how close it was. Maybe. I think.

I rang the doorbell again and started banging on the door with my first too.

"I'm a'comin, I'm a'comin, hold yer got dang horses," Calvin called from hallway up the cellar stairs.

"Who the hell are you?" I heard from the other side of the door.

I looked up and saw the peep hole, through which he was surely looking at me. My eyes widened with panic. I had to think of something to say and I had no time left to think with.

I thought of, then thought better of, several stupid ideas before I landed on the stupid idea that I ended up going with.

My first stupid idea was to tell him there was an accident and I needed to use his phone to call an ambulance. That had worked for Malcolm McDowell in A Clockwork Orange. But he could have made the call himself and not opened the door for me, and maybe he saw that movie and wasn't going to fall for it.

Not Okay

My next idea was just as lame. That was to tell him I had a package he needed to sign for. But I wasn't dressed like a delivery person.

I almost blurted out that his house was on fire. I'm glad I didn't because he would have smelled there wasn't smoke. Instead I stood there for more than a minute without saying anything while I thought.

"Well, what the hell do you want?" He yelled.

Even a stupid plan was better than no plan at all, so I resolved to go with the next idea that popped into my head, no matter how lame, and that was what I did.

"I live next door. Somebody is trying to break into your garage, man."

"What?" He yelled, swinging the door and screen door open and stepping a foot outside to look.

His pants were still unzipped.

The following two events, near as I can say, happened simultaneously. One was that Calvin Maldonado got a clear view of his garage, standing, unmolested, at the end of his driveway. The other was my pushing the large man back into his house, closing the door behind me.

"What tha hell is this?" He demanded.

He was taller and stronger than I was, but I had adrenalin working for me. I was so pumped up on the stuff I thought my blood vessels were going to rupture.

"Where are the girls?" I asked.

"Who the fuck are you?" Calvin demanded.

"I am the ghost of your old partner, Jacob Marley, waooohaaa," I chanted, waving my arms at him.

I think. That's what I remember saying now.

"You are fucking with the wrong guy, buddy," He responded, and I still didn't know myself if I even had the right guy.

"If I am, I'll be on my way. Just show me around to prove it," I said.

I'm not stupid. I know when he said he was the wrong guy he meant that I should be scared of him, not that he wasn't the monster that abducted those girls. I just pretended to misunderstand because I was more interested in the girls than if he was tough or not.

"Get a life," He told me.

"Ok," I replied, pulling my gun from between my pants and underwear, "I'll take yours."

I fired two shots at less than three feet away.

Bright red chunks of flesh splattered away in a cone of red glop.

"Holy shit," I said, looking at the gun, "I thought they said this gun wasn't very powerful."

I know I should have made sure he was the right guy before I shot him, but you have no idea how strong the compulsion is to shoot someone when they are right in front of you like that and you've been wanting to shoot them all day. Not only that, but it was so cool when he said to get a life to say, 'Ok, I'll take yours.' I only wish there was someone there to see it, I mean, to see how cool I was. Right then, I'm telling you, I was a really cool action hero.

He backed away, yelping like a puppy hit on the nose with a newspaper, which made a lot of noise. More than my shooting did even.

I held the barrel end of my pellet gun right to his body for my next shot and fired. The bullet must have stayed inside because there wasn't a splatter, only a thunk as he fell on his ass.

"Jesus H. Christ," I said, looking down at him.

"This was supposed to make less of a fuss than a knife. Fella, could you bleed a little quieter. Christ. Jesus H.

Christ," I said to Calvin. Calvin said nothing back, which would have been rude if he hadn't been indisposed.

"H, in case you didn't know, is God's middle initial," I told the former Calvin Maldonado, "that's why it is 'our father, who art in Heaven, *Howard* be thy name."

"That's alright. You don't have to laugh. You've had a hard day, getting yourself killed and all. Why not put your feet up and relax while I try to find those girls?"

I searched around and was down the stairs in the cellar pretty quickly. I could hear the girls on the other side of a thick metal door, but it was locked so I had to go back upstairs and find the key.

You don't even want to know where the key was, but I'll tell you. It was in the motherfucker's pocket, and I got blood on myself getting it out.

"Damn!" I said, "You'd think I could kill someone once in a while without getting messed up with his blood."

I saw the guy had a computer set up on a desk by the front window and I went to check it out. I'm not sure why, but I grabbed all of the disks and shoved them into my pockets, including the one that was in the machine.

I pulled the desk out to make sure I hadn't missed one that was hiding and when I pushed it back I knocked a picture off the wall. It fell and broke. It wasn't really a picture; it was a poster. I read it and it said, 'Equus, Plymouth Theater' in white letters on a black background.

I paid attention to the computer and the poster and a lot of other things too, because right then I was worried that I would unlock that door and there would be cleaning supplies on the other side. If I had killed this guy for no reason, I would have felt pretty bad.

But I didn't have to feel bad because he was the right guy. As I unlocked and opened the door I heard Suz's voice. It was raw from screaming, but I recognized it.

When Suz saw that it was me and not Calvin she looked relieved.

I was relieved too because right up until that point I was thinking that I just killed the guy because I wanted to kill a guy, that I was fooling myself into thinking, out of all of the people in the world, he was the one that abducted these two girls, or even that anyone had rather than that they had run away.

Now I knew though. He really was the guy.

"You are alright now," I said, but really they weren't alright yet. Not even close. For one thing, they were both chained to the walls and I didn't have the key to the chains. Reba was naked, Suz was half naked and Reba had dried blood on her face and a big purple bruise on one of her shoulders.

Both had dark red gashes in their ankles where they had fought the restraints that held them.

"Who are you?" Suz asked.

"That's Peter, you know, down by the river Peter," Reba filled in.

There was more joy in Reba's voice than there was in Suz's.

"The bastard," Suz said weakly.

"He can't hurt you now," I said.

"Is he going to jail?" Reba asked.

I laughed.

"Fuck, no. Bitch is going to the morgue."

"You killed him?"

"Shit, yeah. What do you think, I'm Spiderman? This hero don't take no prisoners," I said.

Not Okay

I hated leaving them alone, but I had to find something to cut their chains with, and there wasn't anything down there.

I found a toolbox in a room off of the kitchen that also had a washer and dryer and got a pair of bolt cutters and a hacksaw, hoping one would do the trick. I also looked around for money and valuables. He had about thirty bucks on him and there was another ten or so in change lying around but he really didn't have much, which sucked.

Another thing that sucked was that the bolt cutters were too small to work so I had to cut the girls out with the hacksaw, which took a little while. That was when I got what I got of their story from them. I filled in the rest with assumptions and imagination, but I wouldn't be able to tell you know what they told me and what my mind made up. I think my mind made up most of it. Maybe my mind made up all of it. Maybe I didn't get there in the nick of time. Maybe it was way past the last minute. I can't deal with that. I won't. I've decided it was in time and that's just that.

It took a while to get those chains off of them.

As soon as I did we went for the door.

Here's a bitch for you!

You know Calvin Maldonado, the dead guy, well he wasn't totally dead. I mean, he was limp enough when I was going through his pockets, but when we were all up there together you could hear him breathing.

"Damn, Shut up," I said, shooting him again in the mouth.

"Talk about biting the bullet," I said, but neither of the girls laughed.

Maybe I only remember saying that now.

He wasn't biting the bullet though. He was only biting a pellet. Maybe that was why Suz and Reba didn't laugh. I just didn't think jokes had to be so literal, but I'm not an expert on the subject.

"He doesn't look so good," Suz said.

"Must have been something he ate," I said, and still not so much as a giggle from either of them.

They were just not in a comedy mood.

I pointed my gun again, pulled the trigger and heard the click of an empty chamber.

"Did I really shoot him that many times?" I thought aloud as I reloaded.

"No problem. I've got plenty of these little fuckers," I said, shooting him twice again in the head.

This time there was blood and bits of skin.

"Now stay dead," I said, lighting up a cigarette.

Reba reached for one too. She had tried to get smokes from me before, down at the river, and I always said no, she was too young. This time, I didn't say anything, I just tapped the back of my pack and let one slide out enough for her to take it.

I lit her cigarette.

We both took deep drags on them as Calvin got up yet again.

It was like a stupid horror movie where the bad guy keeps falling down and getting back up. It was exactly like that even.

Suz picked up an end table and clobbered him over the head with it. I think that's what actually killed him.

Her ankle was worse than Reba's. She hobbled on it and winced every time she put her weight on it. Reba had a sheet wrapped around herself and Suz had one of Calvin's jackets over her in another minute and we were heading for the door when Reba stopped to thank me.

She put her arms around me and said, "You're my hero," then planted a little kiss on my cheek.

That was the first thing the two police officers saw when Suz opened the front door for us to walk out. They were coming up the steps.

Once at the doorway, they saw the big mess that was on the floor too.

"Are you all alright?" They asked.

"Well, he's not," I said motioning to the dead guy on the floor.

"I think he's never looked better," Suz said.

"I did call you guys first. You just weren't that interested in checking it out," I said as one of the cops took the pellet gun from my hand.

"Whose gun is this?" He asked.

"It isn't really a gun, see, it's just a toy," I said, handing it to the officer who had asked about it.

"Well, we will take care of things from here," That said, "You young ladies have been through enough and so have your parents,"

The other cop looked right at me and said, "You best get lost."

"What about all of this?" I asked surprised.

"All of what? He was so full of shame that he killed himself. That's how my report is gonna read, how about yours?" He turned to his partner.

The other cop nodded, "Suicide."

"I guess I'm out of here then," I gave Reba a big hug, reached for Suz to do the same but she recoiled, so I gave her a light, supportive touch on the shoulder instead.

15.

Sitting on the rock I usually sat on, down where you can see the old lighthouse, I thought I'd see Reba and Suz coming down toward me at any moment. Reba, with her sketch pad under her arm, a box of charcoal pencils in hand. I went down there more often but stayed for shorter times. I kept wanting to see that everything went back to normal for them, but of course it didn't. Just like there wasn't any normal for me after what Uncle Will had done, there will be no normal for them anymore.

I never saw either of those girls again, although I heard here and there that the family moved far away. One person said Vermont, another Montana. It kind of killed me not to know.

Heroes are supposed to arrive just in time. At the last possible second, maybe the one before that. Definitely not a second too late, or two seconds. The way Suz had acted when I tried to hug haunted me. It made me wish I had given her my old copy of I'm OK You're OK.

The news told of Reba and Suz's freedom, of Calvin Maldonado's suicide, and of a stockpile of child porn movies that were found in his garage. There were multiple copies of the same films so the authorities believed he was in the business of making and selling it, but they weren't able to find his customer list or records.

"Fuck!" I said, realizing that I had them.

I took the disks I stole from Calvin's house out and stacked them up in front of my computer. I put the first disk in the drive and typed the command to open it.

"Cannot access disk" came on the screen.

Calvin and I didn't have the same kind of computer, but I didn't remember what kind he had.

There were computer stores in Rockland County, but I really needed to go to a good one, in New York City, to find out what I would need to open the disks. That meant taking a bus ride that I could hardly afford and buying a computer I definitely couldn't afford.

I realized I was going to have to make some changes if I was going to be a monster killer full time, and that was the direction I was leaning.

First, I needed to make sure that I robbed the monsters well. Second, heroes don't ride the bus. I needed to learn how to drive, get a license and a car.

Even knowing that I wouldn't have the money left to buy what I needed, I bought the bus ticket and went into New York City. I kind of missed the place anyway. Once there I asked around until someone pointed me in the direction of a computer store. By mid-day I had a geekish kid putting my disks into a computer and scanning it with a utility program of some kind.

"It is WordStar documents, or DataStar, one of the two, running on CPM," The geek said after a few minutes.

"What kind of computer is that?" I asked.

"Any computer with a CPM card," He said.

He types something on the keyboard and pulled up a menu. He typed something else and the computer asked for a password.

"Well, that's it. You need a password to get in. Five to Twelve letters, no spaces."

"How do I find out what the password is?" I asked.

"You can ask the person who made it."

"He isn't very talkative anymore," I told him.

"Well, you can keep trying different possibilities until you hit the right one."

"Will that work?" I asked.

"Maybe. It's only letters, which is a plus. If it was letters and numbers it would be harder. Then again, if it was just numbers it would be easier. Most people use names of relatives. Almost no one uses a random sequence of letters. If that's it, you may never find it."

"Great, thanks."

I left with the information about the card I needed to buy for my computer in order to work on breaking into those disks.

It was early, so I took the subway downtown, to West 4th Street, where I used to spend a lot of time, and walked around.

It felt good and bad at the same time. I missed the place. I missed playing with my guitar all the time too, like I did when I lived in New York.

I missed Robin too, but I didn't miss her for long because there were posters on telephone poles up and down 8th Street with her name on them.

"Recent paintings and sculptures by Robin Blue" big and bold and the address of a gallery and other information in smaller type.

The picture was a black and white photograph of a color painting. Unmistakably hers, but not one I had seen before. This one had four figures with snakes for arms standing around a tree with human, women's legs.

The opening was a week away, which would give me plenty of time to decide if I should go or not. I took one of the posters down, folded it and put it in a back pocket.

Thinking about Robin and Speak Easy and being in that area made me feel creative again. I started thinking of new lyrics. So many that I wouldn't remember them all if I didn't write them down. I knew the neighborhood well though and headed right to the stationary store on 10th near 7th Avenue. I walked there as lyrics were boiling out of me.

But it was a jewelry store.

I walked in anyway and talked to the woman there.

"What happened to the stationary store?"

"Oh, that moved a year ago," She replied.

"How does a stationary store move?" I asked.

She stared at me blankly.

"I don't suppose I could buy a pad of paper from you, could I?"

But, I couldn't. She tried to tell me where the stationary store had moved but I would have none of that.

"A stationary store can't move!" I insisted and she still didn't have an inkling of what I was talking about.

It wouldn't have mattered if I had found the store a minute later. The lyrics were all gone. They do that. They appear in my head and then, if I don't write them down, they just leave.

I smoked a cigarette instead, and then another. I usually didn't do that, but I did this time.

I lit my next cigarette off of my last one and smoked it down to the filter. Then I called Sharon from a payphone in New York City before I took the subway back uptown to take the bus back to Nyack. Well, really, to Spring Valley where I could switch to a local bus home.

If I had thought it through, I would have known to call her from Spring Valley and have her pick me up, since I got back to Rockland County at nine fifteen and the buses stop running at nine. Instead, I was stuck in Spring Valley at nine fifteen and she was waiting for me outside my apartment, where I couldn't call her.

I hitchhiked up Route 59 to Nyack, which pretty much meant walked, only slower because I stopped and turned around with my thumb out every time another car passed.

I didn't blame them for not stopping.

I mean, you never know who you could be picking up, right. For all they knew, I was a murderer or something.

Do you think that's funny? I see you smiling. I hope you thought that was funny because I thought it was hilarious.

I laughed off and on all the way to Nyack. When I got to my apartment, Sharon was practically asleep on my stoop. It was near one in the morning.

"Meet you at nine hu?" She said.

"Whatever. Come sleep inside. We can talk in the morning," I said, unlocking the door, stripping off my sweaty pants and shirt and collapsing on my bed.

She might have taken her clothes off too and gotten in bed next to me. She might have even gotten cuddly with me, and I wouldn't have stopped her, but she didn't. I didn't know until the next morning that she slept out on the sofa while I was flopped across the bed.

Five hours later I was not quite awake enough to know that the buzzing sound I was hearing was not part of my dream, but I reached up and pushed the snooze button down on my alarm clock.

I didn't need to wake up at any specific time, but the alarm was still set from the morning before when I wanted to get an early start going into New York City.

The snooze button gives me ten more minutes to sleep. I never take it though, because pressing it wakes me up enough to not be able to go back to sleep.

Not Okay

My dream had been pretty good for a while, too. I was on a clean beach with shimmering blue-green water and mustard sand. It was a hot day but there was a cool breeze and a gentle mist from the ocean that smelled fresh and salty, not fishy like the Jersey Shore. Off in the distance, the top of a Ferris wheel could be seen, implying amusements and a boardwalk far down the beach.

Baked sand was running between my toes and between my feet and a pair of light blue, rubber flip-flops with a dragonfly motif. And there were lots of women. None of them were homely or fat either. These were all sexy women with tight bikinis and hard nipples and bulges in their bikini bottoms. It was a beach full of the right kind of women, the kind with bulges in their bikini bottoms. They were splashing each other in the shallow surf, jumping for volley balls and rubbing coconut smelly suntan lotion on each other's bodies.

It was a good dream until the mosquitoes came.

Ten thousand of them swarming like a seething mass of black and grey protoplasm on the horizon, buzzing with the buzz of twenty thousand tiny wings colliding into each other, becoming louder as they drew closer.

Even if I could have gotten back to sleep, the alarm clock's buzz had spoiled the whole day at the beach dream. Next, most likely, those mosquitoes would have been sinking their sharp proboscises into sexy, oiled woman flesh leaving ten thousand pointillist dots in their wake.

I dragged myself into the living room, saw Sharon waking up on my sofa and thought, had it not been for the mosquitoes turning me off at the end, I might have woken up with a hard-on and done her right there.

"Hey," She said, wiping an eye.

"Yeah," I replied, "hey."

In the kitchen, I pushed a testicle back into my jockey shorts and put four pop tarts in my toaster. two were for Sharon, which was pretty nice of me, I thought, but she didn't eat them. Something about breakfast needing to be more substantial than sugar.

I told her I was going into the monster killing business and that I needed a car and a license to do it properly. I knew it was a hassle and there was a lot to keep track of what with licenses and inspections and eye tests and all of that, but it had to be done.

I also told her about the disks and the CPM card I needed for my computer.

"What's on the disks?" She asked.

I sat down next to her on the sofa and tried my best to explain.

"I don't know for sure, but I'm hoping one of them has his customer mailing list on it. With that, I can find a shitpile of monsters to rob and kill."

She was kind of worried about me getting hurt but she agreed to help me, like she always did. She had to see how excited I was about the whole career choice and that had to be supported.

I was so excited talking about it that I got a hard-on right there in front of her. I was still in my underwear so if I had stepped away she would have seen it. She wasn't putting any pressure on me about sex either and that made it easier to think about fucking her too, so right then, in the middle of talking about killing guys, I just kissed her.

"Where did that come from?" She asked.

"Do you not want to?" I asked back.

"No, that's not it but..," She started to say.

"Shut up then," I said and kissed her again.

"Oh Peter," She said when I let up on her lips.

"What the fuck, girl?" I asked, starting to go down.

"No, really, I want to, it's just, um, bad timing."

I still didn't get it. I didn't have to say anything to let her know that. The dumb look on my face was enough.

"My monthly visitor," She finally said.

"You're on the rag? Really? Can I see?"

"No! What are you, sick?"

I backed off of her a little. It was OK to do it now. She'd managed to make my dick limp pretty fast with all that not responding shit.

"Oh Peter," She said again, which kind of bothered me because Uncle Will used to say that a lot, but it was sexier when Sharon said it. On top of that, as she said it she reached for me and ended up with a handful of cock. I was hard again real fast after that.

"Oh my god, is that all you?" She asked.

"I'm afraid so," I said embarrassed.

Then she was stroking it. Damn. Just like in a peep show movie, she was stroking it like she wanted it.

"I think you better blow me," I said, half expecting her to get insulted and stop.

"I think you may be right," She said, pulling my cock out of my underwear.

She didn't lean over and put her mouth on it though, so I figured it was up to me to bring my cock to her. I stood up off the sofa and pushed my cock in the direction of her mouth.

I still kind of expected to piss her off, hell, I was trying to piss her off, but she went for it and that was pretty cool. In a second she was slurping on my cock and I was pumping away at her mouth with my eyes closed.

Actually, Sharon's mouth felt better than Robin's pussy did. It was tighter and Sharon rolled her tongue around and shit. The only other mouth I had ever had around my cock was Uncle Will's and I was feeling pretty good about being able to do this at all without freaking out.

Thinking about Uncle Will made me limp again and even though I was still kind of enjoying it.

Sharon stopped.

"What happened?" She asked.

"Nothing happened, I'm just done, that's all. Thanks, it was great, come on, let's get to a computer store, and we can stop at a DMV on our way back. Maybe I can get a learner's permit or something. At least find out what I need."

I had my pants on before I was finished talking and Sharon just looked at me. I never would have thought that somebody other than Uncle Will would have wanted to have a mouth full of cum, but it sure seemed like Sharon did. That was pretty fucking weird, but neat too.

I don't need to tell you about the computer store or the Department of Motor Vehicles. That all was pretty normal stuff. I mean, exactly what you would expect from a trip to a computer store when you know exactly what you want and a trip to the DMV when you don't know much about what you need.

What really mattered was that after we got back to my apartment Sharon and I really fucked. We did it and I was OK with it too. We started out just making out and she kept bringing up that she was on her period and all, but I kept going at it, biting on her neck and ears and shit until she didn't even remember about the bleeding and all.

I rammed her good too and she liked the shit out of it. She was moaning like a motherfucker and I just rammed at her and rammed at her.

Not Okay

Everything I knew about having sex with a girl I learned from porn so if I got something wrong it was porn's fault. Right or wrong, it was right enough that she liked it.

Before I'd seen porn I thought girls didn't like sex. I still thought that all of this was fun for guys and girls just put up with it, and that porn was unrealistic, but in this case, damn, she was on board with whatever I did.

After a while of just going in and out and I was starting to feel sore so I tried making a circular motion, putting it in and out of her like a corkscrew, you know, and she just loved it.

At the end, when I was about to cum I remembered how she wanted my cum all in her mouth so I pulled out, swung around and shoved my cock in her mouth.

She didn't suck like she had before, and she tried to pull her head away but I got my hand behind her head and pushed so that I shot right on the back of her throat. It was so fucking hot the way she like struggled to get away from that, like in the porno movie in the peep show, I must have cum twice as hard as I had ever cum before. It was so hot that it still felt good after I was done so I just kept holding her head there with her mouth around my cock for a while.

I eased off gently and she looked up at me with her mouth half open and some of my cum dripping out of it.

Right then I was thinking that I wished I'd had a video camera running because the peep show people could have bought that from me.

"Why did you do that?" She asked quietly.

"I knew you'd like it," I said, getting out of bed.

"Like it? Why would you think I'd like that?" She asked.

Girls are so fucking confusing. They act like they are going to like something and then without any warning they turn out not to like it at all. In this case, she was fine with having my cum in her mouth but of all the stupid things, she didn't want her own period blood in her mouth.

If I was a girl and the kind that got periods, you would bet I would want to taste it.

"You were really repulsed?" I asked.

"Yes, damn it," She insisted.

"I really dug it. I think I kind of liked you being repulsed. Does that make me as bad as the shit fucking monsters? Do you think I should kill myself?"

I wasn't kidding.

That fixed her. She had her arm around me telling me not to think like that and shit and even said that she was going to teach me what is OK to do with a woman and what isn't. It wasn't long after that she started teaching me about things like objectification. I got it OK after a while, but it was confusing. I could objectify dicks but not pussies, men, but not women, but white women couldn't objectify black men. I didn't tell her how I had a thing for women with dicks. She didn't need to know that. I don't think she would have been able to tell me what was right or wrong there anyway and besides, I don't think this is all written down and agreed on anywhere, she just made these rules up.

Sometimes I see myself as a dark and brooding person. Other times, I know I just do that because it works on Sharon. Then I think I'm a manipulative fucker. Most of the time I just don't know. Whatever the why of it all is, I wanted to turn around and kiss at her and shit, but instead I pulled my jockey shorts on walked away from her all dark and brooding.

"What is a fucking garlic stone anyway? What kind of an asshole stone is that? I could have been famous; I could have been a legend and you blew it for me," I yelled.

Not Okay

"What?" Sharon asked.

"Never mind," I insisted.

I hadn't told her exactly that I had killed Uncle Will or Calvin either, for that matter. I hadn't told her that I didn't, I'd just kind of left it open ended. I figured, if she really wanted to know, she would ask, and then I'd decide if I should tell her or not.

I sat myself in front of my computer and tried to figure out how to take off the back to put in the CPM card we picked up.

You know how, if you focus your eyes on one little thing long enough it feels like you are drilling a hole right through it, well, that's what I was doing to the screwiemagiggers on the back of my computer.

They were like screws, but they didn't have any slots in them. I mean, nothing. No slit like a regular screwdriver, which I actually owned, and no crisscross for a Phillips head screwdriver either, which I thought I owned too, but if I did it was in the kitchen where I had used it and a hammer to poke open a can of Hawaiian Punch.

I've had a can opener for a couple of months, but I hadn't gotten around to putting my Phillip's head screwdriver back on the living room closet floor with the other tools I had.

Really, even if it had been a screwdriver type I had it most likely wouldn't have been the right size. My screw drivers were both kind of big and those screws were smallish.

Sharon came into the living room where I kept my computer and sat down quietly on the sofa right where she had been sitting when I had kissed her for the first time.

I acted like I didn't notice her.

After staring at the screwiemagiggers a while longer I just popped up, went into the bathroom and locked the door behind me.

I didn't have a stopper for the bathtub. Instead, I took a rolled-up washcloth and wadded it into the drain hole. That worked fine for now, but I made a mental note to take a drain stopper and some smaller screwdrivers from the next monster I killed.

Standing in front of the sink with hot water running into the bathtub, I pulled my cock out of my jockey shorts and washed what was left of Sharon's period blood off of it. There was a ring that was kind of dry and crusty now and even though I was about to step into my bathtub, I wanted to wash it off right then.

Sometimes I do things when I am alone, and I know no one can see me, that I wouldn't do if there was even a chance someone would see. I don't mean big things, but little, unimportant things. Here, in my bathroom with the door locked and the water running no one could see me.

I turned from the sink and walked a couple of steps to lean over and add more cold to the mix, you know, so I didn't burn myself when I got in. That in itself isn't different, but I didn't put my cock back in my underwear before I did it and that was kind of strange.

I mean, if I knew it was going to be as silly a thing to do as it turned out to be I might have been too embarrassed to do it in front of myself, but I didn't know. It was pretty silly though. My wet cock bouncing as I walked half out of my jockey shorts, leaning over the its edge like a periscope.

You don't have to tell anyone about that. It isn't important to my case and I don't think I needed to tell you but since I did could you just forget it now.

Not Okay

Anyway, I took a bath and let Sharon stew for a while. Really, she deserved it being so hard to figure out. I mean, I try to piss her off and she loves it, then I try to please her, and it pisses her off. Girls are fucked in the head. I'm glad I'm not one, no offense. I'm not perfect or anything, but you won't have any trouble figuring out what I will like or not like, you can bet on that.

I like a bathtub.

This was the only bathtub that was ever mine. When I first got the apartment, I was so happy that I was finally getting my own bathtub. Then, I expected the thrill of it would wear off, you know, that I'd just get used to having a bathtub. You know what though, I never did. It was always a thrill for me and whenever I needed to remind myself how good my life was, like now, I took a bath.

I stayed in there a long time and even washed my hair and shaved. I swished mouthwash in my mouth which was the closest I ever came to brushing my teeth. A few times, I listened to see if I could tell what Sharon was doing but she didn't make a sound. I thought maybe I'd hear her leave or something, but she didn't.

What she did do, was put the CPM card in my computer. She sure as shit did. She put the card in and she installed the driver for it too. Not only that, but she did all of that naked.

While I was flipping my dick around like a periscope, she was doing something useful. That's girls for you. Guys are dumbasses that swing their dicks around. Girls do useful shit.

When I came out of the bathroom wrapped in a towel with another one over my hair my computer was all ready for me to play with, with the screen asking for a password and everything.

That girl. I really owed her. I'd have gone down on her right there to show my appreciation, but she was on the rag and all. I did think about it, so I did look.

"What is that?" I asked pointing to her crotch.

"What? Oh, it's a tampon you idiot."

If I hadn't already pushed her so much I would have said something more. I would have said she looked like one of those jester toys where you pull the string between their legs and their arms and legs bounce up, you know, like that. I mean, you don't expect to see someone with a fucking string dangling down between their legs unless they are a toy like that. But like I said, I'd already pushed her pretty far and there was no telling if she'd take that as something not nice.

"Thanks for setting this all up," I said instead.

"Would you like to try a word?" She asked.

"What have you tried?" I asked back.

"Oh, I didn't try any passwords, how would that be, if I found it right away and took the fun away from you," She said, getting out of the seat and let me sit in it.

I looked at the screen and thought about Calvin Maldonado a little. I thought about Uncle Will and I thought about Calvin and then I thought about how cool I would be if I was so clever that I could deduce what Calvin's password was with just my cleverness.

I typed.

E - Q - U - U - S

I pressed enter with a smirk on my face.

"Invalid password" the computer answered.

I furrowed my brow. I smiled. I typed.

S - E - X -W-I-T-H-K-I-D-S

Enter.

"Invalid Password"

My lips puckered.

S - N - U - F - F
Enter.
"Invalid Password"
K - I - D - D - I - E
Enter.
"Invalid Password"
B - L - O - O - D
Enter.
"Invalid Password"
L - U - S - T - I - N -G
Enter. "Invalid Password" Enter. "Invalid
Password" Enter. "Invalid Password" Enter. "Invalid
Password" Enter. "Invalid Password" Enter. "Invalid
Password" Enter. "Invalid Password" Enter. "Invalid
Password" Enter. "Invalid Password" Enter. "Invalid
Password" Enter. "Invalid Password" Enter. "Invalid
Password"

"You did kiddie," Sharon said after half an hour of watching me.

"No, I did kiddy with a Y," I said.

"No, you did kiddie, I E, you didn't do kiddy Y at all," She insisted.

"Shut up, what difference does it make, it'll take more time to argue over it than it'll take to type a dozen new words,"

"Yeah, but you are already repeating words, Peter," Sharon pleaded.

"So, maybe it was the right password, and the computer made a mistake,"

"Computers don't make mistakes,"

"Do you think it's a mistake to piss me off? Because I think it's a big mistake and you're making it," I said, raising my voice but not yelling.

219

That shut her up.

I really didn't have to yell with Sharon. If I just started to raise my voice she got it and left me alone.

I knew I shouldn't smoke in front of computers, but I did anyway, because I was pissed at Sharon. I was in front of that computer for two more hours at least and went through three more cigarettes. When I got off she was dressed and in the kitchen making dinner for us.

"What's that smell?" I asked walking in on her.

"Swedish meatballs," She said, turning away from the stove.

"I had the stuff to make Swedish meatballs with?" I asked perplexed.

"You didn't have the stuff to make toast with. I went to the grocery store," She replied, motioning toward the little counter where there were two bags and a tossed salad in a bowl.

"The convenience store up the hill?" I asked.

"No, the real grocery store," She replied.

"Good. Don't go to that convenience store. Its fucking evil," I said.

She walked up to me and put a cherry tomato in my mouth. I wasn't really wanting a cherry tomato in my mouth right then, but instead of being a bitch about it I pretended I liked it, rolled it around in my mouth for a while and when she wasn't looking I spit it into my hand.

That was how she should have handled it when I put my period bloody cock in her mouth, I thought. That was the way to be polite. I didn't make a big deal about the cherry tomato to show Sharon how to be polite.

I don't think she learned it though. But I was more careful from then on about what I put in her mouth, so I didn't know. From then on, if I was putting my cock in her mouth I'd bring it up close first and wait and watch for her to open her mouth. We didn't talk it through and agree about that, I just started doing it and it worked. Sometimes you get lucky that way. Sometimes you just try something, and it works.

I brought my plate to the computer but before I tried more words I had a thought.

Wisecracks don't come easy. I can't think of something funny to say right on the spot all the time, especially not in the heat of battle. Adrenaline is pumping, panic is kicking in, if I didn't plan ahead I'd end up crying instead of saying something funny. And I had the dictionary right in front of me, so I went right to the back of it.

"Zygote, Zymogenesis, Zyranian" I said aloud.

"Zygote, Zymogenesis, Zyranian" I repeated a few times. I wrote it down to remind me to practice so if the time came, it would come naturally.

"Sharon, help me out here. Come here and act like you are about to kill me. Cool. OK now, ask me if I have any last words."

Sharon came over but only said, "hu?"

"Just point your figure at me like it's a gun and ask me if I have any last words."

She did, and I said, "Sure! "Zygote. Zymogenesis. Zyranian!"

"I don't get it," Sharon told me.

"Someone will get it," I responded.

I turned back to my computer and tried S - C - U - M - B - A - G and S - L - E - A - S - E and S - L - E - A - S - E - B - A - G and S - L - E - A - S - E - B - A - L - L and a bunch of other words that came to mind when thinking about Calvin and Uncle Will.

You want to bet what the computer said back, well,

you don't have to, it said what it had been saying so far, over and over, every time.

"Invalid Password"

At a quarter to five I noticed the green glow of my computer screen reflecting off of my front window and knew I had been asleep. I don't know for how long.

The last word I remembered trying was N - U - B - I - A - L but I had been winking on and off for a little while already. I could have tried words for hours in my sleep for all I knew.

I looked around for Sharon and didn't see her. My dishes were cleared. Most likely washed and put away too. I sat up in my chair and typed.

D - I - S - H -E - S
Enter.
"Invalid Password"
M - O - N - E - Y
Enter.
"Invalid Password"
P - U - B - E - R - T - Y
Enter.
"Invalid Password"

When I saw my computer screen again it was 6:30 and B - R - E was typed onto my screen I didn't know what word I was typing when I'd fallen asleep again.

I stared at the screen and I stared but I couldn't think of any words that started with B - R - E so I deleted the three letters and typed a new word.

U - N - D - E - R Enter.
"Invalid Password"

I got up, walked into the kitchen and splashed some water on my face.

Not Okay

That wasn't enough to I opened the refrigerator and then the little freezer door inside the refrigerator and pushed my face in as far as it would go.

This should have been farther than it was, but Sharon had stocked me up with food that I didn't know about.

I saw the loaf of bread on the counter and ran back to the computer.

B - R - E - A - D

Enter.

"Invalid password"

Enter. Enter. Enter. Enter.

I thought I was going to press the enter key fifteen thousand more times without typing in a new word, but I got bored after four.

Since I was still naked, other than the towel around my waist, I went into my bedroom and climbed into bed next to Sharon.

I ran my finger from an ear to her neck to the middle of her back which woke her up enough for her to make a purrish noise at me.

We rolled into sex the way I imagined an old steam train rolls into a station. Slower than most, gentler than most, but firm and solid and really really noisy.

I'm pretty sure I got my cock hard and inside her before I fell asleep.

In my dream, I fucked the shit out of her.

In my dream, she looked the same but that she had a big stiff dick between her legs instead of a dumb old pussy.

I don't remember cuming but I didn't have to. The whole thing was so good. Dreams are great that way. You never get real sex as good as the sex in a dream.

16.

Sometime in the night, when I wasn't paying any attention, my mind came up with an idea and just had it waiting for me when I woke up. It was a good idea too. So, the morning of June third, 1985, just like the morning of June second, I woke up alone and went out into my living room where Sharon was sleeping on my sofa.

I opened my dictionary to the first page of words and started typing:

A - A - C - H - E - N

Enter.

"Invalid Password"

A - A - L - B - O - R - G

Enter.

"Invalid Password"

Invalid passwords didn't get to me anymore. I had a whole book of words to try and I was trying them at a rate of 80 an hour.

When Sharon woke up I was typing A - B - S - T - A - I - N which I really didn't have any high hopes for.

After one more entering and one more invalid password message I turned to Sharon and gave her a good morning.

A - B - S - T - A - I - N was the last word on page four, so even though I'd been crossing out each word individually as I went, I put a big cross out on the entire page.

1546 pages of words to go.

I flipped the switch on the back of my computer and watched the green light fold in on itself and become a green dot in the middle of which lingered before fading to dark.

Not Okay

I'd kind of like to skip telling you about the driving lessons, since I yelled at Sharon a lot and got frustrated a lot and did a lot of stupid things like knocking into things and all. If you think it is important I'll tell you, but I'd rather not if it is all the same.

Not? Good. That is good because it really didn't cost much to replace a headlight and I didn't hurt anyone other than Sharon's feelings and nerves. All three days of mostly learning to drive and trying words were mostly the same other than the positions we tried and the things we did when we were fucking.

I was giving this vagina thing a real try and making a little headway. Some of the times I didn't even think about dicks. I decided that sex was actually pretty good no matter who it was with as long as no one was holding me down and forcing me.

On day four, I took and passed my driving test.

It was a really hot day. Sharon said we should celebrate by driving to the Jersey Shore for the weekend but I kind of wanted to go into New York City to see Robin's art show.

I didn't want to tell Sharon that so, instead I told her I couldn't go the beach without a pair of flip flops that had dragonflies on them.

We went to a dozen stores and no one had ever heard of flip flops with dragonflies on them, but I insisted that I had owned a pair once even though I may have only dreamed that I did.

"We are never going to find flip flops with dragonflies on them," Sharon finally said.

"OK. You can buy me a car instead," I said.

Would you believe, a car was too expensive, and she wouldn't do it.

That night we didn't have sex and the next morning, Saturday, she seemed ready to negotiate.

As with all of the previous mornings, I was up and trying words on the computer before she even woke up.

"I should go home at some point. My parents will be worried," She said.

"Let me use your car today. I'll drop you off at home," I said.

"Why do you want to do that?" She asked.

"I have a license now. I want to experience driving by myself. I want to go somewhere and back just to see if I can," I said.

It wasn't a lie, I did want that, but I also wanted to see Robin Blue without Sharon around, so it wasn't completely the truth either.

I don't think she would have agreed if not for that I was asking her to buy me a car and she wouldn't or couldn't. She did agree so I rewarded her with a kiss which turned into more and yeah, we were fucking yet again before we got under way. The fucking wasn't getting dull or anything, but the more I fucked Sharon the more I wanted to fuck someone else too. It sucked and I was a bastard for feeling like that, but I did, and I was stuck with it.

After I dropped Sharon off I started toward New York City and all the anticipation about seeing Robin gave me a hard-on even though Sharon and I had just fucked like an hour earlier.

I was almost going to stop and jerk off in a gas station bathroom, but I wasn't going to walk up to the attendant a big fucking hard-on poking in my pants so I tried to think of other things until it went down.

You want to know what will bring your cock down like nothing else, I'll tell you, it's rain. I mean you are driving, and it is hot as a motherfucker out there and then just like that it is crashing down rain on you.

If you still have a semi, try driving in a sudden rainstorm and having the windshield wipers work for only half a wipe because that's what happened.

I found the windshield wipers switch, which was no small task, and turned them on. The motor made noises, the wipers come out, they hit as far as they go, start to come back and then just stop with the blades right in front of my face I swear to God.

I've only driven a few hours in my whole life, I never drove in rain before and now I'm on the Palisades Parkway with rain smashing on my windshield in front of me, well, that is, Sharon's windshield in front of me, it is her car, and if I never told you before, there is no shoulder to pull over onto on for most of the Palisades Parkway. It really is dangerous, it really is.

It sucks if you are hitchhiking on it, it sucks even more if you are driving and it is raining hard and your windshield wipers stop working.

"Oh, fuck me!" I yelled, driving up on the bumpy grass and stopping.

I sat in the car asking myself what to do. The more I tried to clear my mind to think the more I kept seeing words that started with two A's or A then B in my head and that didn't help at all.

Once the air conditioner in Uncle Will's car stopped working. I remembered that he had pulled open a fuse box under the steering wheel and messed around with them, which got it to work.

I found the fuses in Sharon's car and gave it a try. I pulled each fuse out with my fingers, looked at it and put it back, hoping one had gotten loose or burned out or something. Some of the fuses were harder than others to pull out but I managed.

When I pulled out the 10th or 11th one, the rain stopped.

I looked at the fuse.

"Well," I said, "I don't need the windshield wipers to work if I pull out the fuse that runs the rain."

I tossed the rain fuse on the floor of the car and continued on my way.

After I had tossed it I thought about it. I really should keep track of it, I thought, and put it back in later. Sure, it was good for me that it wasn't raining, but at some point grass was going to need to water and stuff like that.

Sometimes you can go somewhere, and nothing happens at all. Nothing happens on your way there and nothing happens on your way back and maybe even nothing happens while you are there. That doesn't mean though, that if something happens on a trip you can be sure that nothing else will.

Sometimes something happens on a trip and then something else happens, and sometime was this time because between getting off of the Palisades Parkway and getting on the George W Bridge, I got a little lost and confused, I took a few more turns than I needed to and that isn't all. On top of that, on my very first drive by myself, of all the rotten luck, I got pulled over by a policeman.

When I saw the red lights reflecting off my windows and shit, I thought it was an ambulance or a fire truck or something.

I hadn't done anything wrong; I had no reason to think I was getting pulled over. But the lights were for me.

The police car was so close to the back of Sharon's car that if I had stopped as short as I could have, he would have smacked into me. If that had happened it would have been his own damn fault, but try explaining that to a cop.

I got over and waiting a long fucking time before the cop came up to my window.

"What did I do?" I asked the steering wheel.

The steering wheel didn't reply.

"Other than kill a couple of scumbags?" I added, "There isn't a law against that, is there?"

Once the cop was at my window I asked him the what the hell did I do question. I left out the part about killing scumbags, just in case that was illegal. I sure didn't want to be late for the opening of Robin's art show.

The officer told me I didn't signal for my turn, which I absolutely did, and I really hate being told that I didn't do something that I did do almost as much as I hate being told that I did do something that I didn't do, so I totally argued with him.

"I did, I did, I fucking did," I said, which may not have been the best way to talk to a police officer, but he didn't seem to mind.

"Turn your signal on now," He said calmly.

I did and he walked back and looked.

"Other direction" He shouted and I switched them.

"Apply brake," He said, and I did.

He walked back up to my window.

"Your brake lights work but your turn signals don't. It may just be a fuse, but you better get it fixed right away. In the meantime, use hand signals."

The officer was nice. I didn't know hand signals and he showed me. We had a little laugh about it being my second day with a driver's license.

Conveniently, I was white, so I drove on without getting a ticket.

I knew how to make turn signals by hand after that, which was pretty neat.

I looked down at the little red fuse on the passenger side floor of the front seat of the car and thought about putting it back in the fuse box. If I had just done that I was pretty sure, the turn signals would work again, and I wouldn't need to remember all the turn signals by hand and shit. But the windshield wipers still didn't work, and I didn't want it to start raining again so I left it out.

I took a cigarette out and put it in my mouth for a few minutes, but I put it back because I really didn't want it right then. It was just something I thought I should need after being pulled over by a cop, but it turned out that I didn't need it at all.

Parking in New York City turned out to be another hassle. It took me an hour driving around the same five or six blocks to get a space. Finally, the way I did it, was to double park at the mouth of a one-way street and watch people coming and going until somebody got into the driver's door of one of the parked cars. Then I drove up behind and waited.

The driver waited too, not knowing what I was doing. I could have let the guy know that I was waiting to take his parking space just by putting on my turn signal, but I didn't have one. I used a hand signal, but he didn't understand it. Apparently hand signals aren't nearly as common as my police officer friend would have had me believe. But the guy figured it out in a short while, or didn't give a fuck about the details, and pulled out his car out of the space.

His car was smaller than Sharon's and the space wasn't really big enough to get into, but I discovered that if you keep pushing forward after you hit another car's bumper you can move the other car a few inches and make room for yourself.

So, I mostly got into the space with only a little of an angle and not that much of the back-driver's side corner sticking out into the street, and both the car in front of me and the car behind me touching mine, or rather, Sharon's.

The gallery was on a side street and away from the main flow of foot traffic. It wasn't South of Houston either, which made it even less of an attraction to art buyers. On top of that it was a plain black building. The words, 'Exhibition Space' were painted in pastel green letters over the door, right on the wall.

One of Robin's paintings was on display in each of the two, large, plate glass windows on either side of the door. To see these paintings, you had to be standing outside. I wouldn't have done it that way.

Robin had improved on her skills and had gone beyond painting images from her fantasy home, but the work was absolutely the product of her imagination. The magical, fantasy aspect was there still, but darker, and mostly scenes of New York. New York, as she saw it.

Her New York City was magical, and frightening. The painting to the left of the door was of the Statue of Liberty, mouth curling into a grin, standing over the harbor filled with floating corpses. Her torch glows eerily.

The painting in the other window was smaller. It was a view of the entrance and inside of the Lincoln Tunnel. I suppose it could have been the Holland Tunnel, or any other tunnel for that matter, but the Lincoln Tunnel was the one I knew best so that was the one I thought it was.

Unlike any of those tunnels, this one appeared to be swallowing the cars that were entering it. The people in the cars farthest away from the tunnel appeared to be, if not happy, no more than a little worried. The closer they got to the mouth of the tunnel, the more panicked the drivers and passengers appeared to be.

Although grey and hard to make out, the people in the cars inside the tunnel looked like they were screaming and clawing at the back windows and things like that.

The one painting inside that really struck me was of a little boy. Eight or ten, I'd say, standing naked in a doorway. He's kind of backlit so you can't exactly see his business hanging between his legs, but within the shadow you can kind of make out that it is there. A large bladed kitchen knife in one hand and blood up both arms, dripping down. The expression on his face is somewhere between surprise and terror.

It kind of looked like I felt.

There were other paintings too. Subway trains, Central Park, Time Square. All twisted. They seemed so normal though. When you looked at Robin's paintings for a while, they seemed more like how things really are than how things really look if you can get that. It was like there was a spirit around the city that you could almost feel but not see, and then Robin's paintings made it so you could see it too, and then you'd be like, yeah, look at that, that's how it feels.

Her surfaces were all nicely stretched canvases now. No more of those found materials she was painting on when I had met her. That part was too bad. I liked the found materials. I think they looked good painted.

Not too far from the door was a desk with single sheets containing biographical information about Robin and a price list. I looked at her biography enough to see that it said nothing at all about her. Nothing about her being from another world but nothing about her being from anywhere else either. It was mostly about where her work had been shown before this show, all of which was in the last two years. The paintings were priced between $800.00 and $1200.00.

Oh yeah, too, there was a chair at the desk, but no one in it.

Looking around, it occurred to me that Robin's life story had gone on without me in it, just as mine had without her in it, neither of us knew how the other got from then to now. It was like skipping ahead in a book.

"Peter?" A voice from behind me spoke, "Peter, I thought it was you."

The soft, sweet sound of Robin's voice assured me that we not only could make up, but that it was very likely, despite what had happened before.

"Robin. Good to see you," I said.

If I had been angry at her before, the anger melted away looking at her.

"Long time," Robin said.

"Yeah," I answered.

"You look well," She said.

"So do you," I replied, and on and on like that.

It might have been a scene in soap opera if it hadn't been even too boring for that. One of us had to say something interesting fast or we were both going to drop dead right there of dullness. It was about to be me, but she beat me to it when she asked, "How's life treating you?"

"Life is purgatory and we are all plummeting toward hell on a mining cart of the cursed at such a speed that it flattens your lips, straightens your eyebrows, and forces your ears behind your head in a most unnatural way, which is all a distinct improvement over how things had been in the recent past, how about you?"

"I've gotten by, not nearly as well as it sounds you

have, but good enough for me," she replied.

I smiled.

"So how did you get to be selling paintings for a thousand dollars apiece and shit?" I asked.

"I'm not selling them; I'm trying to sell them. I haven't actually sold one yet.

"I don't get it, who would give you a show if you haven't even ever sold a painting?" I asked.

"I did. I gave myself this show. I rented the gallery and put up all the flyers and everything else too. I need to sell three of these paintings to cover the costs of the show. Four and I'll make some profit. I don't know if I'll even sell one though, with so few people here for the opening and all."

"Oh, I'm sure they'll come. It's just the rain," I said, even though it stopped raining hours earlier.

"I hope you are right. I had to screw a lot of jerks to pay for this," Robin said.

"You still doing that?" I asked.

"I'm still eating, so yeah, I still need to pay for food,"

"Maybe if you offered a free screw with every painting you sold," I suggested.

I was trying to be funny, but I think it came out as insulting. I didn't want to insult Robin at all either, but that was what came out.

"Might," She said, not giving me much of an indication if she was serious, offended, or amused.

I looked around the gallery floor at the twenty-five or so paintings and the ten or so people.

"There are some people here," I said.

"Four of them work here, the rest are my friends. There's no one here that's what you would call the public," She said.

"Sorry."

"I always have my ass to fall back on."

"Yeah," I answered, lighting a cigarette.

She lit one of her own. It was one of those stinky clove cigarettes that are so popular with artists like Robin.

"You want to have dinner with me, talk, you know, like, maybe?" I asked.

"We don't have to be eating to talk, Peter, we're talking now. Since you brought it up, I'd like to know what happened with you now. I thought I'd never get to ask you what happened, but here you are so please, tell me," Robin said. She was talking fast, kind of the way I do when I get the way I get, you know. Robin was a lot like me. Well, some ways anyway.

"Are you sure you want to do this here?" I asked.

"What I want is to just kiss you and roll all over the floor with you. If you don't watch yourself, I might do that yet. I'll settle for you telling me what your problem with me is, or your problem with sex, or your problem with sex with me is."

"Rolling around on the gallery floor, now that might draw a crowd," I said.

"You flatter me, and yourself," Robin replied.

"You are very pretty," I said.

"You are avoiding the question," She replied.

"God. The truth is I'd never done it before. I mean, not with a girl. I didn't know what to do so I just did what was done to me. I thought that was what I was supposed to do, and it turned out all wrong. I just got it all wrong."

You can bet Robin was taken aback then.

"I've done it with girls now. I kind of know what I'm doing. I think I could try again and not fuck it up so bad," I said.

Robin just looked at me. It was like part of her vocabulary.

"So, you wanna do that rolling around thing?" I asked.

"I don't think so. Not right now. The gallery closes at ten, we can go out for something late night and see what happens."

"Maybe I'll come back at ten then," I said, touching her hand.

She smiled.

"Excuse me, are you the artist?"

Robin turned away from me and to someone who looked like a real person, you know, the kind of person who buys art rather than the kind that makes it.

"I just love bla blablabla bla blabla bla" The woman said to Robin. I walked away but glanced back every few minutes to see that either the woman's or Robin's mouth was flapping away as they talked that very important art show talk that art show people talk with each other.

I left the gallery thinking I was going to be back at ten and fucking Robin by midnight and yet, I walked right to the parking space I had left Sharon's car in.

Both the car that was in front and the car that was in back were gone. There were new cars in their place, but neither were parked as close, which made it easy to pull out.

Pulling onto the Henry Hudson Parkway toward the George W. Bridge I knew that I was driving back to Rockland County, and not meeting Robin at ten.

I stared at the traffic light on the other side of the bridge as it turned from yellow to red and then green, but I still didn't go. I was thinking about how great traffic lights were and how there should be something similar for life. I never know for sure what I am supposed to do in life. I'm always going when I should be stopping, or being careful when I should be going, or not being careful at all when I should be.

Cars behind me honked their horns while I thought about it. Fuck the people behind me. They probably always know what they are supposed to do. Or just do whatever they want and don't care. I waited longer and got honked at more before I went.

At home, I saw that I had, like five newspapers that were still in their rubber bands. The newspaper was quite an expense if I wasn't going to open them, but rather than stop the subscription I sat down and looked at them all at once.

I even read some of the articles but none of them were interesting enough to remember. Mostly they kept me from thinking about ten o'clock when it came and passed.

I liked Sharon and I knew that she really liked me. If I spent time with Robin again all that could happen would be that I'd blow it with Sharon and end up blowing it with Robin too. By leaving it the way I did Robin and I could stay liking each other forever and that was what I wanted, so Robin and I never saw each other again after that.

17.

When I got to C - H - E - R - U - B in my dictionary that was it, I really thought I had it. I typed the word into the keyboard faster than the hundred or so words I'd typed before, I pressed the enter key hard and looked eagerly at the screen which popped up, "Invalid Password" just as every previous word had.

I wasn't scared that the one, valid password would turn out to be a proper name because if I got through the whole dictionary I'd have started on a twenty thousand names for baby book. I mean, I was a little scared of that because it would mean going through the entire dictionary before I got to even open the right book, but that was the kind of scared like thinking it might turn out to be Z - Y - M - O - S - C - O - P - E which, I knew now it wasn't.

There were a hundred words like Z - Y - M - O - S - C - O - P - E which I got so convinced would turn out to be the right words that I'd jumped ahead to try and crossed off individually. The nice thing about that was that wherever I was I could say I was really further because some of the words ahead were tried and crossed out too. But so far, I hadn't done that with any names.

I had 231 pages crossed off at this point. I resisted the temptation to waste time counting how many words that was, even though I really wanted to know. It would have taken a lot of time away from trying new words, which was more important than satisfying my curiosity.

There were many more letters and words ahead of me than there were behind me, and just getting to roughly the middle of the C words had taken me over two months.

Not Okay

The 4th of July, which was kind of an important day to me now, or should have been, came and went without my even noticing. I worked instead of going to see any fireworks.

I worked instead of doing much other than fucking Sharon and eating. When I did go outside, I just walked around for an hour or Two and then I went home again and got back on my computer.

This was a really dull time for me. Even the interesting things that happened weren't that interesting. Like trying anal sex with Sharon. I did Sharon in the ass just like I would have liked her to do to me if she'd had the equipment for it. It was tighter than her pussy and she squirmed more, but other than that it wasn't the big deal I thought it would be.

Another interesting thing was changing from thin spaghetti to angel hair spaghetti. I didn't like the regular stuff and thought that thin and regular was all there was, but Sharon bought a box of angel hair and cooked it one time and I liked it so from then on, I wasn't going to use thin anymore. This was pretty important because I really like spaghetti, but like I said, it was kind of boring too.

I had a cold at one point and was sniffling and wiping snot away with toilet paper for a few days. Halfway into that I walked into the bathroom and found a bunch of weeds hanging from the showerhead.

"Fuck is this shit?" I yelled to Sharon.

She came into the bathroom to see what I was referring to and she explained, "It's eucalyptus. It'll help clear your nose."

"Oh, no," I said, taking the stuff down and handing it to her. "Get rid of it, it'll attract koalas."

I don't think Sharon ever realized I was trying to be funny when I was. She always assumed I was serious, but no matter how crazy it seemed to me to say things like this seriously, she never acted like she thought I was crazy either.

Trying to be funny broke the monotony up a little, but only for the moment it was happening. The one thing that wasn't completely dull wasn't good, and it happened the day I had tried C - H - E - R - U - B on the computer and it turned out not to be right.

I typed two, maybe three more words after that, but my enthusiasm was low after feeling so sure that C - H - E - R - U - B was the one. I had felt really sure like that about a lot of words. Two or three a day I'd say. There was kind of a buildup of disappointment though, like the tenth was worse than the first, and the one hundredth was worse than the tenth and so on.

I walked downtown.

As I got closer to the river I felt like something was missing but I didn't get what it was right away. When I was much closer than before I knew that I should have been able to see the top of the lighthouse and I didn't.

I walked faster, got closer, and still nothing.

When I got to the rocks and saw over them I could see the island where the lighthouse had been, and still no light house. There weren't remains of a fire or anything like that either. The old lighthouse was just gone.

"Damn," I said thinking that I should have gotten one of Reba's drawings when I had the chance. She never offered but I think, if I had asked, she would have given me one. She was nice like that.

I walked away but looked back a few times, expecting that I would see it this time, which happens to me sometimes, especially with house keys. I'll look right on the sofa hunting for them and they won't be there, and I'll look again a few minutes later and then there they are. It was easier to believe that I missed it the last time I looked than that an entire lighthouse just got misplaced.

I looked three or four more times and then just accepted it. Lighthouses, it turns out, don't disappear and reappear the way house keys do.

I stopped into a store kind of near the river and asked the storekeeper if he knew what happened to the lighthouse.

"The restaurant closed. They owned it. When they moved, they took it with them. It wasn't a real lighthouse, you know. Real lighthouses are bigger."

"Really?" I asked, but I wasn't even sure what I was saying really about. I knew that lighthouses were taller, but I thought that lighthouse was at least tall enough not to be able to pick it up and move it.

"There was a story about it in the local newspaper. Pictures of it being moved and everything," The store clerk told me.

"When the hell was that?" I protested, "I would have seen that."

"You read the Nyack news?" He asked.

"The what?" I asked, playing with my cigarette package, but not taking one out.

"The local newspaper, you know, the Nyack newspaper," He said like I should have known what he was talking about.

"There's a Nyack newspaper?"

"Yep."

"News to me."

The store clerk then said that the only people who knew about it were the business owners that got hit up to advertise in it.

"You buy an ad?" I asked.

"Yep."

"Has it generated much business?" I asked.

"Not one customer."

"Still advertising in it?" I asked.

"Well now there, the thing. I keep saying I won't but when the ad salesman comes around somehow he walks out with another check."

"He's either a very good salesman, you are an idiot," I responded.

"Some combination of the two," He laughed.

Up the street, closer to my apartment, I noticed two children pushing a shopping cart around the street.

They were going downside streets and coming up other ones and all like that, so I didn't see them constantly as I walked up the hill, but I saw them.

Near the top, I could tell they were like nine or ten.

A few yards closer and I could also see that they had a kind of beat up cardboard box bouncing around inside their shopping cart.

They were a boy and a girl. They didn't look as much alike as Suz and Reba did, but they looked a little the same. They looked enough the same that they could have been brother and sister, not that that really mattered.

From three blocks away I could also see that they were approaching people on the street and talking to them.

The people for the most part, shook their heads and got away from them. One or two lingered for a minute telling them something but walked away quickly too.

"What the hell are those dumb kids up to?" I asked a parking meter.

I wasn't really in the mood, but I figured I had to go see what they were doing before they got abducted like Suz and Reba.

I walked a little faster and was close enough to talk to them after they had talked to two more people, an elderly woman and a twenty something woman in a business suit.

The funny thing was that we were just in front of my apartment at that point. I mean, ten steps from my stoop, twelve tops.

"What are you two doing?" I asked.

"Say, mista, won't you take a little kitten, give her a good home?" The little boy asked.

"Pappa says he'll drown them in the tub, please take one," The little girl added.

"I don't think you father will really kill them," I told the little girl.

"Oh, he will, he will, these kitties will be goners for sure if you don't help," The little girl insisted.

I looked in the box and saw four, no, five tiny, black and white kittens squirming around in the box. They were climbing over each other searching for the absent mother cat.

I'm telling you; these little bastards weren't old enough to be away from their mothers. The ones I could see faces of hardly had eyes open. I mean, like, their eyes were open just a slit's worth. Some had one eye open more than another but still. It wasn't right to take them away from their mother.

"Ok," I said.

"Which one, mista?" The boy asked.

"Yes, please, which of these darling innocent babies

will you spare from the doom that will surely face the others?" The girl added.

I scowled at her.

"Does your father sell advertising for the Nyack newspaper?" I asked.

"There's a Nyack newspaper?" The boy asked.

"That's the rumor," I said taking my box of five kittens and walking up the steps of my stoop to my apartment.

"Look at you little motherfuckers," I said to them, pushing one around with a finger, "not enough meat on the lot of you put together to make a decent snack."

"Reowl" responded one of the kittens.

"Don't get your panties in a bunch, I was only kidding," I told it.

I might as well tell you now that I don't know the first thing about taking care of kittens.

Sharon had to show me everything, and, of course, Sharon knew. Sometimes it really pissed me off that Sharon just knew everything all the time. Like Sharon knew about feeding the kittens with an eye dropper, and that wasn't so hard to know about, but she also knew about coaxing them to pee with a wet washcloth between their legs, and that was a pretty fucking weird thing to just know about.

Baby kittens, she told me, didn't know how to pee yet. Their mommies had to lick them to get them to pee. If I had ever thought I would have rather been a cat, I wasn't thinking that anymore.

One thing Sharon didn't know about was what getting separated from their mommy so early in life was going to do to their kitten self-esteem. I didn't either but I was sure that giving them lots of attention would help.

Another thing Sharon didn't know anything about was naming kittens. She actually wanted to name them individually. I mean, names that didn't have anything to do with each other of all the stupid ideas.

Naming five kittens at once wasn't an easy task.

There weren't enough members of the A-Team and there were too many on the Starship Enterprise. Too many of the people on Gilligan's Island had stupid names and I couldn't remember all the names on M * A * S * H*.

I went through a bunch of cartoon ideas too, like The Jetsons and Flintstones before I gave up on television entirely.

For a few minutes I thought I had named them Hobo, Vagrant, Tramp, Vagabond, and Box Car Billy, but Sharon pointed out that Billy was a girl and rather than move their names around I gave up on the idea.

Don't get the idea that this isn't important because it is, it really is. When Sharon saw the kittens, just about the first thing she asked was what their names were, and that was going to be the case for everyone these kittens ever meet right up into cathood. Their names were going to be very important to them and it was completely up to me to come up with them.

Finally, I told Sharon I had named them.

"Caesar," I said.

"Which one?" Sharon asked.

"All of them."

"You can't really name them all Caesar," Sharon protested.

"I can, and I have," I answered.

"But how will you tell them apart?" She asked.

"Oh, that's easy, one has a white stripe under his chin, and this one has three white paws and one black one..," Yes, I was teasing Sharon.

"No, I mean, you know what I mean Peter, you have to give them each different names," Sharon said.

"I have. Sharon, let me introduce you to Tiberius, Augustus, Claudius, Nero, Julius, and, of course, the one with the little boots is Caligula."

"You haven't changed one bit," Sharon said disapprovingly.

"Should I have?" I asked.

"Oh, Peter."

"Yes, my like?" I responded. I thought she would ask and I'd tell her |I couldn't call her my love because I didn't love her, but she said nothing about it.

I hate when she said that and might have thrown her out right then, but she brought a jug of cranberry juice over and hadn't opened it yet. I was afraid, if I'd thrown her out right then, she might have taken the jug with her.

"I like me. My sofa likes me, my bathtub likes me, I'm surrounded by like, so why should I change?"

"You are anthropomorphizing," Sharon said.

"Six syllables, you want a quarter?" I responded.

"Do you know what it means?" Sharon asked, thinking that I didn't.

"To attribute human characteristics to inanimate objects," I replied.

"How did you know that?" Sharon asked surprised.

"I've been reading the dictionary a lot lately," I answered and that was the end of that conversation.

That was one of the best things about Sharon. If I said something smart, she didn't say anything back. She just let me be smart. Most people don't do that, but Sharon did.

Not Okay

She started cleaning up and I went and tried C - H - E - S - H - I - R - E to C - H - E - S - S on my computer.

"You have dirty laundry everywhere," She yelled out to me from the bedroom.

"There's a Suds and Duds just down the street and left at the McDonalds. I'm going to be doing this for a while, I won't even miss you," I called back to her, and lit cigarette.

She came out at glared at me until I stopped typing.

"What?" I said and she started nagging about being my servant and shit. That really bothered me because I was doing important work.

"Yeah, you're my servant. I like it, it works for me, if you have a problem with it then don't do it," I snapped.

"Is that all you want me for?" She asked.

"Well, you could bring me a glass and that cranberry juice before you go," I said.

"Be serious!" She responded.

"I am," I said back.

She went to the kitchen, washed a glass and brought it to me with the juice.

"What about someone to talk to?" She asked, pouring the glass full and setting it next to me.

"I talk to my sofa; I talk to the TV," I answered.

"Everybody needs someone alive to talk to," She insisted.

"I've got cats," I said.

"Cats can't talk back."

"That's the best thing about them."

The next word was Chestnut. I had already typed in C - H - E - S and while I was saying the last thing I said I typed T and N.

"Could you look at me?" Sharon said, looking like she was going to cry or something.

I stopped typing again.

"Sharon, I'm fucked up. I just am and I'm not going to change. If you can live with it, do, and if you can't, get out, but don't make me feel bad for being what I am. Uncle Will did it."

"He should die," Sharon said.

"Yeah, well, he did," I answered.

"Really? When?" Sharon asked.

"When I stabbed him with the knife you gave me, or pretty soon after," I told her.

"Oh. Oh... Peter. I didn't think you had really..," She said.

"Shit, Sharon, what did you think I was going to do with that knife? I killed Calvin too. Shot him a shitload of times. These disks were his," I said.

"He was a…"

"You bet he was. So, what do you think? Should I be worried about doing my laundry or killing monsters?"

"You are right, Peter, I'm sorry. I should be helping you," Sharon said.

"You want to blow me quick before taking off with the laundry?" I asked.

I didn't think she would, but she did, she really did. I went from C - H - E - S - T - Y to C - H - I - L - B - L - A - I - N with her on her knees under my desk sucking me off. Really, it was the coolest thing. I only stopped typing to cum in her mouth.

She was still on it as I typed C - H - I - L - D.

I stopped to pull her off.

I grabbed my cock and held it as it went limp.

Sharon got up and looked at the screen.

I pressed the enter key.

We both held our breath.

"Invalid Password"

We looked at each other without saying anything. Sharon wiped her face with the back of her hand and went back to the laundry.

I kept on typing as she got what she needed ready. As she was walking out the door she told me to be sure and put the cranberry juice back when I was finished with it. I said I wouldn't, and she was off out the door.

She wasn't gone as long as I would have been gone if I had been doing my laundry, but she is better at a lot of things than I am, so I shouldn't have expected laundry be any different.

Once she was in the door with all of the laundry she looked at the screen as I was typing C - H - O - P - S - T - I - C - K - S.

"You did a lot," She said.

"Yeah," I said, pressing enter.

"Invalid password," Flashed on the screen.

"I could teach you how to touch type," Sharon offered.

"What are you talking about, I type 60 words a minute," I defended.

"You couldn't type sixty words a minute if all the words were 'the' and spelling didn't count!" Sharon zinged.

I laughed.

I hadn't really counted how many words a minute I could type. Sixty just sounded like an impressive number to me, I don't know, maybe it was.

Sharon pouted the kitchen floor while I typed in more words.

She cleaned the porcelain in the bathroom while I typed in letters. I don't even want to tell you how long it had been since I had cleaned anything in the bathroom.

She even folded all of the laundry she had washed, which was something I never would have done. Laundry gets unfolded when you put it on. I can't see how folding it serves any purpose.

She had lectured me a few times about sexist gender roles so it confused me that she was so willing to slip into them. It might have been my fault because I just didn't do that stuff, but I didn't tell her she should.

Around ten she offered to make us some dinner, but I told her I didn't want to stop working to eat, so she heated herself up a can of soup and sat down on the sofa with it on my coffee table.

She wanted to turn on the TV while she ate but I told her it would distract me, so she didn't. Actually, having her sitting there, slurping that soup distracted me, but I didn't say anything. I can be nice that way. I can be distracted by some slurping soup and just live with it and not say anything because I'm nice.

If I had been thinking about how I was a male and she was a female and I just expected her to do everything for me and she just did it I would have realized I was a sexist fucker. But I didn't think it was male privilege, I thought it was me privilege. That is the way male privilege works I hear. You just get it and you don't have to think about it. You just get it and you think you deserve it for a hundred reasons other than being male.

She finished her soup right around the time I was typing C - H - O - R - E - A into the computer and was in the kitchen washing the pan and bowl by the time I pressed enter and read, "Invalid password" on the screen.

I don't know what she cleaned next, but she went on another half an hour or so before she came in to tell me she was going to sleep.

Not Okay

When she did come in I was typing C - H - O - R - U - S into the computer. I stopped to say goodnight or something like it, then turned back to the computer and pressed enter. She was halfway to the bedroom when I read the computer's reply.

"Invalid password" of course.

I was tired too, but there were only 15 more words to do to get to the end of page 239 and I really wanted to cross off that page before I went to bed.

I worked a little faster than usual, hoping to get through those fifteen words before Sharon was asleep and maybe go in and fuck her. I was really into fucking Sharon around then. It was a real achievement, I thought, that I could do it after what I'd been through with Uncle Will and all. Fucking was kind of saying that he didn't beat me, that I beat him. I don't think I could have been as normal as all of that if I hadn't killed Uncle Will and Calvin Maldonado too, for that matter. Killing those motherfuckers was really therapeutic for me. I'd recommend it to anyone who'd been a victim of that kind of monster, I really would.

At midnight I was still typing.
C - H - R - I - S - T - I - A - N
Enter.
"Invalid password"
C - H - R - I - S - T - L - I - K - E
Enter.
"Invalid password"
C - H - R - I - S - T - M - A - S
Enter.

The red light on drive B lit up to the sound of gears spinning inside the computer and information filled the screen.

I stared, confused, and read, "Menu: Client List, Distributor List; Supplier List, Select Option."

Read it again and felt sick in my stomach. After getting this close, I mean, only three words left, I was not going to get to cross off page 239. Not ever.

Christmas. Fuck. That must have held special meaning to him, like toilet paper does to me. It made me wonder what kind of Christmas stories he had. It made me wonder, if I was coming up with a password, would I make it 'Toilet Paper' or something else. Would someone who knew me be able to guess it? Maybe I'd make my password 'I'm OK.' Who would ever guess that?

18.

I didn't like sleeping next to anyone, but it was a little worse with Sharon because, in the morning, she was bound to reach for my cock. It happened every time and every time I would try to explain again that I had a hard-on because my bladder was full and that's all there was to that.

This time, I slid out of bed quickly as she went reaching, and ducked right into the bathroom.

I wasn't completely awake yet when I started pissing, but after I'd gone a little bit I thought about all the work Sharon had done scrubbing the toilet and how rude of me it was to piss on that hard work. If I had thought of it before I'd started, I would have been more thoughtful of Sharon and pissed in the sink.

"You're a real bastard," I told myself.

"What?" Sharon yelled into the bathroom.

"I broke the code last night," I yelled back.

We had to yell to hear each other over my pissing.

"The password, that's great. Was what you hoped would be there on the disks?" She asked.

"Looks like it," I yelled back.

Whatever Sharon said next I didn't hear because the toilet was flushing, which was even louder than my pissing. I could have asked her to say it again, but I really didn't care much what Sharon said so I didn't bother.

I did put on clean clothes for the first time in a long time, which wasn't hard to do because the only dirty clothes I owned were the ones I had been wearing when Sharon did the laundry the day before.

Sharon was in the bathroom pissing while I was in the bedroom getting dressed. I was always considerate of

Sharon when I pissed and left the door open. Sharon wasn't though. We couldn't talk while she was pissing because she always shut the door.

I opened the door to go on talking with her, which was something that always upset the hell out of her. She didn't mind me seeing her with her mouth wrapped around my cock, which I think, is pretty embarrassing. But not squatting on the toilet, no way.

This time, she was already done with the toilet and brushing her teeth, which made me forget what I had opened the door to say.

"Where'd you get the toothbrush?" I asked.

"I'm using yours," Sharon replied.

"I've got a toothbrush?" I asked.

"Yes, silly," Sharon said, and then I remembered that yeah, I did buy a toothbrush once, about a month after I had moved in. It was that one time I told you about that I had tried to clean the bathroom. I used steel wool to get most of the yucky gunk off of the inside of the toilet but there were spots that I couldn't reach so I bought the toothbrush to scrub in the crannies with. It worked pretty good but it was too much effort to ever bother doing again.

I didn't tell Sharon why I didn't want to kiss her that morning, but I hid the toothbrush in the bottom of the kitchen trash can, wrapped in a paper towel as soon as I could, so she wouldn't use it again. That was later. Right then it was morning and we were talking.

I could hear the kittens meowing in the bedroom as I lit up my first cigarette of the day. Those kittens were smart. They knew we were up, and they wanted something or other from us really bad.

"So, what was it?" Sharon asked.

"What was, oh, yeah, the password, Christmas."

"Shit, really? Christmas... why?" Sharon asked.

"Damn, if I hadn't killed him, I could ask."

Sharon ignored that and went to tend the kittens as I got back on the computer. C - H - R - I- S - T - M - A - S worked again for the password, which I expected. When I clicked the Client List option it asked for another disk and I had to dig through the stack trying them until I found the right one.

After that though, the information really rolled out on the screen.

Calvin Maldonado's client list was sorted by subject of interest or state. There were 262 entries, each was numbered and came complete with addresses, and some had a phone number too, plus a list of transactions between Calvin and them and their preferences. More were man on girl than anything else. Some were Man on boy, some were boy on boy, some were girl on girl. And other preferences also. Sometimes I can talk about that without getting freaked out, other times I can't even say the words.

But what this meant, in case you were having trouble following, was that these 262 people paid Calvin for child pornography, most of them, several times a year. I'm talking 262 people that knew what Calvin was doing and paid to help him continue to do it. Are you following me now?

Try it this way: 262 people that enable children to go through what Suz and Reba went through, what I went through, and wouldn't be able to do that anymore if I were to relieve them of their lives.

I may not have had the list of words in the dictionary to work on crossing off anymore, but I had this list and it was going to be rewarding, crossing the names off of it.

"I put the cranberry juice back," Sharon said.

I turned away from the computer screen and looked at her, "what?"

"The cranberry juice," Sharon said walking closer.

"Yes," I answered, no less confused.

"I put it back," Sharon said.

I stared at her.

"In the refrigerator," she said, and I nodded.

"Oh. That makes sense," I responded, "You didn't put the cranberry juice back in the cranberries."

"Are you going to kill them all?" Sharon asked.

"There must be billions of cranberries. I could never get to them all."

"The monsters."

I turned and she was behind me looking at the computer screen as I scrolled down the list.

"I'm going to try."

"What about the authorities?" Sharon asked.

"I am the authority now. I am, dun duuu, Captain Authority, champion of the innocent," I said, standing up from my chair and making a pose like a superhero.

"Be serious, Peter, you could get into big trouble," Sharon said.

"Nah. They want me to do it. Really. Why wouldn't they?" I assured her.

"Are you sure they all deserve to die?"

"I'll make sure. I'll check them out, mostly, I'd say yes, they do. These monsters, they suck the soul out of children and leave an empty shell to carry on," I insisted.

"You don't look like a shattered, empty shell to me," Sharon said.

"I'm not fucking normal, Sharon, look at me, I'm a fucking serial killer, that's what keeps me OK. You can't expect every victim to do that. I'm a lucky one."

"But Peter, that list is so long, you are only one man," Sharon said.

"I thought about that. It'd be too risky to hire people though. I'm just going to have to have faith that there are other monster killers out there, like me, doing their part to make the world safe."

I clicked print to get the entire list on hard copy. It was over 10 pages and I didn't have that much ink or paper, but I didn't think about that right then.

"You're still going to need help. The longer it takes you to get to them the more innocent children will suffer."

She had a point, but I didn't want her with me.

"No. Actually, you should go home, not have anything to do with me. Don't fucking cry. We can't think about our feelings, we've got to think about what's best for those children and I need to be able to call you if I get in a bind. You have to be an innocent outsider in order to get me out of a fix if I get in one, do you understand?"

Somewhere around the end of what I said I took her by her shoulders and looked right at her. Really, I was being as corn ball soap opera as I could about it. You know, making fun, like I had done standing up like a superhero before, but she bought right into it. I could have been even more convincing by kissing her, but she'd just brushed her teeth with, damn, I don't even want to think about it now.

There were enough tears in her eyes to make them wet, but not so much that they came out, which, in some ways, is sadder.

"Take those kittens with you," I added, turning away from her and back to the computer.

She rounded four up but the fifth was missing.

When she told me this I looked in the box and said, "Well, Mr. Tibbs can stay with me then."

257

"Tibbs?" Sharon asked.

"Tiberius" I said, and then I went over the kitten's names a bunch of times and made her identify them back to make sure she had them all right.

"Are you sure you can handle a kitten by yourself?" Sharon asked.

"I handle you, don't I?"

"I'm not a kitten, I'm a tiger," Sharon replied, making a clawing motion with one hand.

You know she left me with some money. Not enough to buy a car, but enough to get me started. My plan was to rob the monsters I killed pretty good, like I've said and use the money to finance my project. I could allocate money for a car from the first hit or two, since it was a work expense.

As soon as she was out the door and gone, Tiberius came scampering out from under my sofa. He knew what was what. He wanted to stay with me.

I tickled the white fur of his under belly and watched him roll over, kicking his feet at my wrist and biting my thumb.

When I pulled my hand away from him he rolled over, pushed down on his front legs, shook his bottom, and pounced on my fingers.

We played together for a while before I poured myself a bowl of cereal for breakfast. Tibbs was drinking the milk from my bowl, sitting on the coffee table between my television and my sofa before I had gotten my spoon and sat down.

"I thought you were too little for that," I said.

You know how it took me awhile to get used to having Sharon around all the time, well, it was the same thing in reverse getting used to her being gone.

Not Okay

That cereal bowl, after I was done with it, sat on the coffee table for weeks. Every week there would be several more dirty bowls and spoons until I was out of spoons. Then, when I needed one, I'd look for the least encrusted spoon to wash. But after a while I was out of bowls too and then I went to eating Pop Tarts and donuts in the morning.

I was expecting Sharon to pop in now and again, but she didn't for a few weeks. The one time she did come in I may have annoyed her so much she decided not to come back for a while.

She brought be groceries in the morning, then left, and came back that evening. I was in the living room and I said, "Before you go in the kitchen, I need to warn you."

"What?" She asked exasperated, as if she was expecting it to be something horrible.

"Just that there are grapes on the floor," I told her.

I waited for her to respond but she didn't, so I just let her know what had happened.

"I thought I could throw a grape into the air and catch it in my mouth. That's all. I missed and it ended up on the floor. I tried a few more times and more grapes ended up on the floor."

Sharon made a face at me which was like a response.

"I was pretty sure, with enough practice, I could get it," I said.

"Are there any grapes at all left in the refrigerator?" She asked.

"No," I said.

"All of the grapes I bought you ended up on the kitchen floor?" She asked.

"And then some," I said.

She wrinkled her face at me.

"I went to the store and bought more grapes. I really thought I could learn to do it."

Sharon didn't clean up the grapes for me.

When she didn't come back, after a few days, I swept them into a corner, so I'd stop stepping on them. After a while there was enough filth piled up that you couldn't even see the grapes. Still Sharon didn't come back.

The first monster I went after on Calvin's list would be my third kill and my first one out of New York State. His name, as it appeared on my list, was Bruno Bellheim. He lived in Bel Air, Maryland, a suburb of Baltimore.

I didn't go down the list in order. It wasn't fair or anything, but I went for the ones that liked man on boy first. It was personal.

I rented a car for this one, which turned out to be a good move, and drove to his town.

He had a real cushy home on a nice street. Steady traffic, but not a main artery, and decorated really nice.

I staked out his post office box until he showed up to get his mail, then I followed him back to his place. Oh, Bruno Bellheim was a made-up name. The guy's really name was Keith Dimancescu. Don't ask me where Bruno Bellheim came from, I couldn't tell you, it was just the fake name he bought his kiddie porn under.

I staked out his house and watched his patterns for two weeks, sometimes following him, sometimes sticking around the house. He had a pretty regular job, as a parts expert at a Ford dealership six miles from his house. I think he was the head of the department because he wore suits and ties and a lot of the people he worked with wore overalls and shit like that. Plus, they got dirty, looked at cars and pulled things off of shelves and he mostly talked to those guys and sat at his desk in an office.

Not Okay

On the second Tuesday I went in his house, after he left for work and looked around. You can bet, I found kiddie porn. Some of it was Polaroids and a Polaroid camera was with them, so it was pretty likely he shot the Polaroids himself. You could see the inside of his place in the background of some of the pictures. Plus, little boys.

He had nice stuff, too. A couple of big Japanese swords hanging on a wall, antiques, paintings, things that were so nice they were displayed under glass domes and shit like that. Plenty of movies on videotape and records too, but not much of the kind of stuff I liked to watch or listen too.

The music was like, playing saxophones and trumpets and that kind of thing, judging by the pictures on the covers.

The movies were mostly martial arts films. Some were Bruce Lee. I knew his name but wasn't into that sort of thing at all. I mean, maybe I'd listen to those records, just to check them out, but there was no way I was sitting through a stupid kung foo movies. That was just lame.

There were some boxes in the living room with things in it that had handwritten price stickers on them, a roll of price stickers and a stack of things that weren't priced, set up like they were about to be. It was as if he did a little flea market selling on the side, which was strange for a guy that seemed to be doing so well.

In the box, there were several mugs in the shape of people. The stickers said they were Toby mugs, but the name printed on them was Bennington. They were all priced between ten and thirty dollars.

I heard the noise of a car outside that spooked me, so I didn't look around anymore. A peek out a window let me know that it was a neighbor driving away, but I still got out. I had seen enough.

261

On Thursday, Keith came home from work, was inside for an hour or so, then went out, on foot, with a heavy-duty stapler in one hand and a small armload of handmade, eleven by fourteen signs in another.

He walked to all the corners of his street and busier streets and put up signs with arrows, the dates for that coming weekend and, 'yard sale' on them.

I smiled because I had an idea but I'm not going to tell you what idea I had right yet, I'll just let you know what I did and then you'll know, if you don't mind.

On Friday, I let him get home and settled in a few hours after his day's work and rang his bell just as it was getting dark, like seven thirty.

"Yes?" He opened the door.

Keith was a pretty big guy. He had a chest, you know. I hadn't seen them yet, but he had a weight set in a room and must have used it often.

"Hi, I read about the yard sale, I know it is tomorrow but I can't be here this weekend and I was wondering, I'm really only looking for one thing, if you have any, I'd sure like a chance to buy them now."

"Any what?" He asked.

"Oh, yes, sorry, Toby Mugs, particularly Royal Doulton, but Bennington is good too, really, any."

He smiled.

You bet I had done some homework. I found out by calling an antique store in the phone book that Royal Doulton was a popular name in Toby mugs. It sure made my story sound good.

"Come on in, yes, I have seven Bennington Toby mugs, two plates, five crocks, a pitcher. My mother collected them, and she's passed on," He said, leading me in and closing the door behind us.

Not Okay

"I'm only interested in the Tobys, but I sure am interested in them. What luck, your mother was a collector," I said, playing my role a little bit longer.

He pulled out a box and put it on his coffee table, then sat down on his sofa.

I wasted no time.

I pulled my knife out and lunged for him.

"What is this?" He yelled as I tried to thrust at him with my big hunting knife, the black one that Sharon had given me, you know, the one I had killed Uncle Will with.

The fucker managed to dodge it though, and before I knew it he socked me one in the face.

I wasn't expecting to see my own blood and there I was bleeding from my nose and my lip. I was bleeding from my nose and my lip and that was from one punch.

I took another swing with my knife and got him in the leg, which really pissed him off. It also made me lose the knife. He pulled away and took the knife with him, sticking out of the meaty, upper portion of his thigh.

I swung a fist at him, which I guess was pretty stupid because I don't know how to punch, and I think it hurt my hand more than his shoulder, which is what I connected with. The only reason I connected at all was that he was pulling my knife out of his leg.

I grabbed him around his neck in something like a choke hold, but not as effective. He dropped the knife and reached with both hands to try to pull my arms off, but I didn't let go.

Then he was punching at my face with a fist and I was hitting him in his face with a knee and squeezing his neck as hard as I could. And then we were rolling around on the floor. We even knocked into the box with the Toby mugs in it.

263

After that, I was under him and my knife was under me, which was really uncomfortable.

I worked my feet into his groin and pushed, the way Mr. Tibbs did when he was pinned on his back, which seemed to work a little, but this guy was fucking strong. He was really hurting me bad.

I thought of wisecracks, but I didn't have the breath to say them and he went on hurting me.

He was pulling my top half up off the floor and then slamming it back down hard, which hurt my head each time.

Then I bit his arm so hard he let go of one of my arms and then, instead of swinging it up toward him, to hit him, I swung it behind my back and grabbed the knife before he had me slammed down again.

So now I had the knife in my hand, but my hand was pinned behind my back. This time, he didn't let me backup to bash the back of my head into the floor. Instead, he smacked his head into mine, which really hurt.

I took the chance that he would stop when he thought I was beaten, even though I wouldn't have, so I let my eyes roll up and acted like I was spaced. It worked, he let go of me long enough that I could get my arm out from behind my back and oh, boy, did I give him a good fat hole in his neck.

You should have seen him bleed. You wouldn't think there was that much blood in a person, but it shot out all over me, the carpet, the box. He wasn't dead, he wasn't even done fighting, but he was sure weaker after that neck wound was in him.

I stood up and kicked him and he fell right over. Then I stomped on his face a bunch of times and then I picked up a lamp and broke it on him. I was having some fun, I have to say.

Not Okay

There was so much blood it didn't even look like blood. It looked like someone broke a jug of cherry snow cone syrup on us. Maybe a few of them.

I pulled my knife out of his neck and tried to put it into his skull but that turned out to be impossible. The guy's skull was just too thick.

Trying got me close enough to him though, that he reached out and grabbed my hair and pulled.

I got him in an eye then, that made him let go, but it didn't kill him.

I took the cord from the lamp I broke over his head and tried to strangle him with it but that didn't work either. In the end, in order to kill him, I dragged his bloody, convulsing body into his bathroom and drowned him in his toilet.

I left his head in the toilet and went back into the living room.

There was a lot of blood and mess to clean up.

I did what I could with a bucket and brush but ended up needing to refill the bucket a bunch of times and that got the blood in the kitchen too.

I thought about how I was able to do this but let Sharon do all the cleaning in my house. I really could have done some of it myself. I wasn't incapable.

I started sopping up what I could with his towels and then going back and forth to his bathroom to get more which tracked even more blood around.

On one of the trips, I pissed into the toilet, which meant on his head. It was cool in theory, but in practice, it splattered my piss back on me which I didn't care for, and maybe left DNA on my kill. I really didn't know if you can get DNA out of piss. I still don't.

It took me three hours to get things clean enough

that it didn't look like there had been a murder in there. It still looked like something had been cleaned up, but it could have been anything.

At midnight I looked over the entire place and found a second bathroom with a shower in it. Even though I liked baths better, this time, I went for the shower. I was so covered with blood that I did it with all my clothes on, and that worked out pretty well.

After that I took anything I thought was salable out of the bathroom Keith was in, locked the door from the inside and shut it with the corpse inside.

I spend the rest of the night putting things for sale outside, as well as furniture that I could make into displays.

He had plenty of stickers so I priced more stuff than a typical yard sale would have out. Some things, like that signed poster, I just didn't know. Those things I marked, "Make offer," I figured the customers would tell me what it was worth. No matter what the first person offered, I wasn't going to take it, and then, if someone offered more, even if it was only a little more, I would.

At six I started setting up the sale on the lawn. It was a big fucking sale, like I said, since it was just about everything of value that the fucker owned.

I had a small pile of stuff I wanted to keep for sure, and I put most of that in my rental car trunk.

At eight in the morning the first few buyers showed up and I wasn't even done putting things out.

That poster sold for a hundred dollars. I don't know if that was good or what, but since it didn't cost me anything, I liked it.

Did I tell you; the guy had a wall safe? Yeah, he did. I tried to open it with a screwdriver and hammer, but it didn't do anything, so I gave up.

Not Okay

All day Saturday, only one person asked me where Keith was.

"Oh, you know Keith," I said, "Too good to spend the day stuck here, not when he can have me do it and he can go off and enjoy himself."

"Yeah, that sounds like Keith doesn't it?" He said.

Later, he picked up a club from the set of golf clubs sitting out there marked thirty dollars.

"I can't believe he would sell these, and for thirty dollars! He only bought them a month ago for over a thousand and he was so happy about it."

"No more golfing for Keith. He said he was sick of it and didn't ever want to see them again. But doesn't the tag say three hundred dollars?" I responded.

"No, thirty," He said.

"Oh, boy, that's a mistake, it is supposed to be three hundred," I said, writing a new tag and taping it on.

"Who did you say you are?" The guy asked.

"I'm Jerry," I said.

"You are his..," He said.

"Yeah. Three years now," I said.

"Oh," he said, "you are his…"

"Yeah. He never mentioned me?"

"Oh, well, he never, uh, I didn't know he was…"

"How could you not know, come on," I said, giving him a wink.

"Oh, well, yes, now that I know, it makes sense."

"And you?" I said, teasing him.

"Oh, oh, no, not me, no way," He said.

"Too bad," I said, pretending to eye his behind.

That was plenty enough to get him done with me and the yard sale.

I ended up getting an offer on the golf clubs and selling them for a hundred dollars too.

I know I shouldn't have stayed through Sunday, but I had made a thousand dollars and change on Saturday and I just couldn't resist.

It would have created suspicion if the yard sale advertised for Saturday and Sunday and then it wasn't open on Sunday, I reasoned, but really I was having a good time.

When it got dark I brought everything expensive back inside and covered the rest with tarps from the garage.

I spent hours digging the wall safe out of the wall. Since I couldn't open it there, I thought I'd bring the whole thing home and work on it as my leisure. It was heavy as fuck, but I struggled it out put it in the trunk of my rental car too.

Keith Dimancescu was also a smoker, which worked out for me because when I ran out of cigarettes, he had close to a full carton.

I got a good night's sleep on his bed and masturbated in it too. He had that good, expensive lube that was really good for masturbating, and there was something about Keith being in the bathroom, all bloody and dead that gave me a hard-on too.

When I washed off afterwards, I saw that one of my eyes was black and blue and I had a puffy lip too. Weird that no one said anything about it at the yard sale, but that is how people are.

I hadn't realized it, but Keith had really beaten me up bad before I managed to kill him. I put some ice on the eye, but it still looked bad in the morning.

I closed up earlier on Sunday, like three in the afternoon because there was really not much business up to that point on Sunday. I'd only sold another $220.00 worth.

The best of what was left, as much as I could fit, I put in the back seat and front passenger seat of my rental car and left the rest.

A part of me wanted to rent a U-Haul and really clean him out, but I'd taken enough risks with this job. I had done good and I needed to call it finished.

I got home Monday night, fed Mr. Tibbs, and tinkered with the wall safe. I wasn't able to get into it but I did get some ideas about how to.

On Tuesday, I went to Ace Hardware and bought an electric saw and blade specifically for cutting through metal. I told them I wanted to make a sculpture using some metal beams.

It did the trick, too. I had the back of that thing cut right off in fifteen minutes.

There was some money in there, about $2.000, and some jewels, a gold and diamond watch, and some coins and stamps that turned out to be valuable.

The best thing that was in there though, was a 22-caliber pistol. I felt so lucky. Better than lucky even. Like an angel intervened, or maybe God, and saw that I was properly armed.

A pellet gun, as it turned out, wasn't even worth bringing with me. But this, this was the real thing.

I smiled.

All in all, Keith had been a great job, other than getting beaten up, and I had an idea about how to keep that from happening again.

19.

A week after I had cleaned out Keith Dimancescu and killed him in his Maryland home, I was still feeling the bruises he had given me. My eye was still red and purple, too. It was embarrassing. Everywhere I went, from the supermarket to the movie theater, people saw me and knew I was beaten up.

That wasn't all there was bothering me either. I could have lost that fight, which would have really sucked. He was bigger than me and worked out, so he was stronger and all.

If I was going to be prepared in my work, I needed to be buff too.

What I did was, I went and visited The Jack Lalanne Fitness Center in Nanuet. It was only a few minutes from me in Nyack, and they told me on the phone I could check it out for a day for free.

When I got there, I expected it to smell like testosterone.

I don't know what testosterone smells like, but I figured I would recognize it when I smelled it. It would be a sweaty old smell, gym locker rooms and monster truck rallies, neither of which I had ever smelled either.

The place smelled like aerosol can instead. I don't mean air freshener, although it smelled like that too, but the whole place had a smell like the spray of aerosol cans if you know what I mean. The air smells like that sometimes after there had been a lightning storm. Not so much like something extra was in the air so much as like something that is usually there is missing.

No one else there seemed to notice, or care.

Tad, I swear to God his name was Tad, signed me up for my free tour.

He was really built and wore a tank top so you could see all of his bulgy muscles.

"I want to get in shape, you know, be stronger. Can I do that without coming out looking like a freak? No offense, really, freaky muscles looks great on you, I just don't think it is a good look for me," I said.

"You have to work a long time to get like me," He said proudly.

"Oh, good," I replied.

Tad showed me around the place, but he didn't stay right with me.

It was all pretty gross. Guys were all over the place sweating and grunting, all of them bigger than me. They were on machines pulling and pushing and flexing. They were on benches lifting and dropping, they were on stationary bicycles pedaling and no matter what they were on, they were grunting and sweating.

I walked through the place looking around as if I were in another world. I didn't touch any of the equipment or exercise or anything and I was back at the counter, ready to leave in twenty minutes.

"What do you think?" Tad asked me.

"I think I know how Diane Fossey must have felt," I replied.

"Who?"

"No one you would know."

"I hope to see you again."

"Yeah, maybe I'll come back with a National Geographic film crew."

That was how that trip went.

271

On my way home I stopped at a sporting goods store and looked around the guns. When a salesperson came over I told him I was just a little curious. He was very informative.

It turns out, you don't need a permit to buy bullets. You don't even need to show any identification. That was cool for me, but pretty fucked up, if you think about it. I told him what kind of gun I had, and I bought a couple boxes of the kind of bullets he said to get. I even joined a firing range.

I showed up at the firing range the same way I did at Jack Lalanne's, not knowing what to expect or what I would think about it, but I took to it right away.

Someone showed me how to shoot and I turned out to be a fairly good shot. The guys there were friendly enough and didn't seem nearly as stupid as the muscle guys.

The only thing about them is that they were Republicans and proud of it. I didn't know there was a difference between Democrats and Republicans. From what I knew, anyone who wanted to run the government was a piece of shit and I told them so. They didn't entirely disagree with me, but they still liked their pieces of shit way better than the other party's pieces of shit.

My instincts were right from the start. Fighting is fine, if you are into that, but smart people don't bother with working out or anything, they just shoot the bad guys. That's what I did, and I didn't have any more trouble with getting punched or anything.

I practiced shooting as often as I could, and I know I got to be fairly good at it. Not great, but good enough to hit someone if I were close to them.

Still, the beating I took from Keith made me hesitate. I went to a bunch of people's homes and I watched them, but I couldn't bring myself to make the move to kill them. It was like the time I couldn't leave my apartment. I knew I needed to get over that and fast.

I did cross off some that I didn't kill. Some that had died on their own, one that someone else killed, one that had killed himself which was really sporting of him, and like ten that were in prison. Justice only worked for about one in thirty-five, but for that one, I decided to let that justice system work.

You don't want to even think about breaking into a Federal penitentiary and killing anyone. Not even a monster. I'm sure it is really hard. I don't know if I could have pulled it off even with Sharon's help. I sure couldn't on my own, so I just let it go.

It wasn't like those particular monsters were out fucking children while they were locked up. It was safe to cross them off, you know, mark them as taken care of.

A lot of the addresses were post office boxes, so the first step was often staking out the post office to see who picks up the mail from that box and follow them home.

That was the first thing that was really different about this one stake out of a post office in Queens. The person who picked up the mail was a woman and she wasn't alone. Another woman waited for her in a running car.

I was pretty well stocked by then. I had a good car, a couple more guns, surveillance equipment, and a plastic bottle with a wide, screw on cap to pee in that was ideal for the job.

I didn't spend everything on myself either. Mr. Tibbs had a collar with a heart shaped tag that had his name, address and phone number on it. Well, the name he ended up keeping, Mr. Tibbs. Tiberius Caesar didn't stick.

I ended up staking that post office out for three days before I followed the mail, because I just couldn't believe I had seen it right, not even the second time. I thought the woman must have opened the box next to the one I was looking at with binoculars from my car across the street, even the second time I saw.

The third time I knew I had seen right; it was them that was weird. Hell, it was weird that someone checked a post office box every day. Like I said, I'd done this a lot. Normally, I had to wait a few days. Normally, someone would check their mail a couple of times a week.

This wasn't a normal case.

Big things were wrong, like two women instead of a man, this was the first time for anything like that.

It continued to be different from other cases all down the line. When I followed them, they didn't go far. When they parked, it was in an underground lot in the middle of a busy city street. I thought I had lost them then. I parked and got out, planning to go into the lot and find their car but I found even better, the two of them walking out of the lot entrance talking to each other.

They stopped at a coffee shop and came out with what I would assume was coffee, then continued around a corner and into the front of the building they had just parked under through the back.

It was an office building.

"These two had to be big time dealers in the child pornography business," I said to a parking meter as I walked by it, "when I get their client list I'll have work for the rest of my life."

I saw the two of them get into an elevator as I got to the glass doors.

Not Okay

Did I tell you my car was a sweet, black Grand Am? I think I did. Oh, yeah. I love my car. Did I tell you it had cup holders? Yeah. It was a nice ride. The thing had 7000 miles on it when I got it, that was all. What it didn't have on it was a scratch. At least not until I got it.

I didn't go right up the elevator after those two then. I went back to my car instead.

I moved my car around so that I could watch the doors and see when my targets left. The next day I watched for longer.

I watched them individually arrive in the morning, I watched them go out in the afternoon, and I watched them come back an hour or so later. This time, I saw them coming and I went into the building ahead of them.

If you want to follow someone really close, and you don't want them to know you are following them, you should try this. Be right in front of them, then it'll seem like they are following you.

We all got to the elevator in a line, with me in front. I pushed the up button and we waited together. When the elevator came, I let the women get in first.

I had a loaded 22 caliber pistol in my pocket and twenty or so extra bullets in my front pants pockets just in case.

One of the women pressed the button for the seventh floor. I didn't press a button at all, and we all rode up together. I looked at them, but I didn't say anything.

Once off the elevator the women disappeared behind a door after being buzzed in by a receptionist who sat behind thick, bullet proof glass.

In every direction I saw a gold emblem and logo with the words, "Federal Bureau of Investigation."

On one wall was a picture of President Carter.

275

I hadn't pressed a floor button because I was planning to get out with my targets and follow them, but that plan had to change fast. I waited until the doors closed again, which they did, and then I breathed.

The elevator went back to the lobby all by itself, so I didn't have to press anything, which was good because the FBI are all into fingerprints and stuff like that. If I had left a print I could have been in trouble.

A few minutes later, sitting in the coffee shop where the two FBI women bought their coffee, I sipped a hot chocolate that was too hot and ate a corn muffin that I should have asked to be toasted but I didn't think of that until I'd already taken a bite out of it.

I smoked a couple of cigarettes in there, thinking about Calvin and the FBI.

If Calvin Maldonado had been selling his child pornography to the FBI, that meant they were on to him. I suppose that meant, too, that they would have made a case against him and put him away if I had just left it alone.

In the meantime, girls like Suz and Reba were getting victimized. It kind of made me want to kill all the FBI people anyway, for being so damned ineffective, but I made myself let it go.

Back at home, I fed Mr. Tibbs, who appreciated it after my being gone nearly a week. I also cleaned the litter pan and threw some trash in a can. All of this only took fifteen minutes, if that, but it made me feel like I was keeping the house even though there were piles of mess in every direction that would have taken days to clean all up.

I picked up Mr. Tibbs, who had gotten big and fat over the years, after he finished eating and gave him a playful shake.

"Good thing I didn't just shoot them," I said.

The FBI did give me the idea that I needed more sophisticated gadgets, you know, like the FBI and Batman uses. The next time I was in New York City I looked in a phone book under 'Spy' and would you believe it, there was a store called, The Spy Shop.

I went right over.

It turns out that you can't buy wireless transmitters, that is, bugs, because they are not legal. I tried anyway, saying, "Come on, you can sell them to me, I've got plenty of money" but the store clerk would have none of that.

I did get a parabolic amplifier that did a fairly good job of listening through doors and windows. Plus, it looked really science fiction.

It had a dish that was three feet across, with a microphone extending out of the middle of it. It had really sensitive aim but let me tell you, when you had it pointed right, you could hear everything. That thing set me back a few hundred dollars.

At home, I told Mr. Tibbs that I needed to practice with it, but he wasn't very cooperative. I pointed it at him from fifteen feet away but every time he would either not say anything or run up to me.

It was four in the morning and I was just starting to get frustrated when I heard the garbage truck outside.

"Perfect!" I yelled, pointing the device out the window at the garbage men. They made a thunderous noise that hurt my ears and I pulled the headphones off, hyperventilating.

I opened the window and yelled down to the garbage man.

"Hey, asshole, it's the middle of the night, watch how you're smashing those motherfucking cans around!"

"Screw you!" Came the reply as a second can was thrown on the sidewalk, this time, hard enough to dent it.

The can rolled to the grassy edge of my neighbor's lawn, I thought about yelling at him more, but before I started, I remembered that the garbage men were out there picking up garbage, which meant that I had, once again, missed the weekly pick up.

A minute before I yelled at them, I might have been able to call down and ask them to wait as I ran and brought mine down. That wasn't an option now. Now, all I could do was wait until they were out of sight and put my garbage in the neighbor's cans.

20.

The Hudson River has this weird way of flowing in September, where, if you watch you'll see, it picks up these brown and yellow leaves from a bank, carries them a ways down, then deposits them on another bank. Later maybe it'll pick some of those leaves up again and leave them somewhere else.

It made me feel like a songwriter again to see it, but I couldn't get the words I thought up to rhyme so I didn't write anything down.

If Suz and Reba had still been around I would have pointed these leaves out to them, maybe they could have been drawn, but no, they were long gone. They'd be adults now. At least Reba would be. This spot, where you could see where the lighthouse that used to be there was, it was more their spot then mine, but over the years I bet I'd gone down there to think about them more than I expect they ever were actually there.

There was such a pile of cigarette butts in the one spot. Most of them, maybe all of them mine. It was years of accumulation and some were so old they looked like a part of nature. No one ever cleaned them up.

I was feeling uneasy and I think I knew it was because of all the work I put into the Queens job, and all the anticipation that goes along with the work. I missed the payoff. You know, the end. I really missed doing the kill.

That's what I tried to come to terms with down the river. I really liked killing people. The truth is, it was fun. Killing someone and making them die felt great. I would say it was the ultimate orgasm but really, killing people is more fun than orgasms, and the good feeling lasts a lot longer.

I had a car, of course, but I still walked down to the river and back when I was done. This time, when I got back in my apartment, I was resolved to start a new project right away and I hadn't given up on my idea for a new song yet, so that was also a lift for my spirits.

I hadn't crossed out the address that turned out to be the FBI and I didn't think I wanted to. At the same time, I couldn't leave it with nothing, so when I looked at the next name I wrote, F - B - I in block letters over that one.

My next target was John Noland of Green Bay, Wisconsin.

I still had a good amount of money but I was worried that it would run out if I didn't watch my spending, so rather than taking a plane and renting a car, I decided to make a road trip of it, and drive my own.

Come to think of it, at least some of the other kills had to have been real, or I wouldn't have had any money at all at this point.

Before I left I was going to get a good eight hours of sleep, before I did that, I tried to write that new song.

I hadn't finished one in a long time, but I still thought I would finish this one this time.

What I wrote really sucked ass. It was worse than things I'd already thrown away and after screwing around with it for an hour and getting kind of mad, I crumpled the paper tight and threw it across the floor.

Mr. Tibbs watched the paper skid along the floor like a stone on a lake, putting himself in position as he had done since he was little. It really is something to see though. It is part of what makes Mr. Tibbs such a great cat.

First, he leans on his front legs with his bottom up in the air and twitching. You can tell when he's going to pounce because his front half gets even lower and then, zip!

Mr. Tibbs intercepts the paper wad well before it can hit the far wall.

He bats it between his front paws, not so much chasing it as guiding it like a hockey player with a puck down the hall and back up, under the coffee table, off the TV stand and back to me.

Paper ball in his mouth, Mr. Tibbs looks up at me and shakes his head.

"Stupid cat!" I say, taking it from him and tossing it in the direction of the kitchen where, somewhere, there is a trash can. Mr. Tibbs scampers after it and in a few minutes he has brought it back to me.

"Dogs play fetch, you are a cat! You are supposed to be above such canine foolishness."

He was right though. I unfolded the crumpled paper and gave the lyrics another go.

He wasn't so right that the song ever amounted to anything, but I did finish it before throwing it away, and that was important.

I shouldn't have jumped into the next job so quickly, but I was, like I said, eager for a kill. Other times I'd done more research and come more prepared. This time, I just drove to Wisconsin with my car full of equipment.

The home I followed him too was in a middle-class suburban development and came complete with an overweight wife and daughter. The guy went to work, he came back from work, and he checked his mail in his post office box two or three times a week.

For $2.00, every post office will tell you the home address of the renter of a post office box. People like John Noland, you know, monsters with families, they don't give their home address when renting a post office box. I paid the $2.00 to find out what address he did give.

It was a cabin in the woods. I got there at night and let me tell you, it was really secluded. I mean, the mailbox was at the bottom of a driveway that was a quarter of a mile long, and dirt and mud the whole way, with three different sets of gates you had to get out of your car and open and then get out again to close.

Not only did I drive up and park right there, but I broke in and started snooping around. It was kind of cold and there was a kerosene heater right in the middle of the room, so I lit it, then lit a cigarette.

I wasn't even trying to avoid my target knowing I had been there, which would give me a lot less time before I had to kill him. I didn't care, I wanted to get to the kill.

There was some porn there. Mostly straight stuff you could buy anywhere but kiddie porn pictures, magazines, and a few unmarked video tapes with them that were most likely more of the same. All the porn was locked in one of two footlockers, which I broke the lock off of. There were sex toys in there too. Basic stuff. Dildos and all, and the kind of expensive lubricant you could only find in an adult store.

It was just luck that as I was looking at this stuff, I saw a flicker of light outside.

I looked out and listened and I heard a car too.

I moved fast then! I ran to my car, turned it on, said a little thanks that I had a pretty new Pontiac Grand Am that was quiet, and moved the car to the back of the cabin. I didn't turn my lights on either. I was smart that way. I didn't want to totally scare him away.

John drove a Mercury Topaz, which is a kind of nice car. It was brown, but in the dark it could have been any color. As it got closer I could tell it was him and when it got closer still I could tell he wasn't alone.

Not Okay

This was exciting. I mean, once John Noland got in his cabin he'd know someone was there, that's how little time I had.

At the last gate, his passenger got out to open the gate and I could see that it was a young boy. Thirteen, maybe. He got back in the car leaving the gate open and they drove up the last few yards and parked right in front of the cabin.

I was really close to them too, and I could smell the kerosene heater. If I had been them, I'd have known as soon as I got out of the car that someone was there.

"Go shut the gate," John told the little boy.

John took some things into the cabin and the boy went toward the gate.

As soon as John was out of sight I went for the car. I could have stabbed the tires but, if you think about it, you can still drive on flat tires and I did not want my target to get away.

Instead, I went into the front seat, pulled wires down from under the steering wheel and used my knife to cut a shitload of them. You cut a bunch of wires like that, and I promise you, that car isn't going anywhere.

The boy must have seen me, but I went right for him anyway. In the time it took to sheath my hunting knife and pull out my gun I was to the boy.

I had my hand around his mouth and the gun at his head fast, before he could say anything.

"I'll let go of your mouth if you promise not to scream," I said.

The kid nodded.

"You gonna be quiet?" I asked.

The kid nodded again.

I let go, he took a breath.

283

"Are you a cop?" The little boy asked.

"Something like it," I answered.

"Are you going to arrest Uncle John?" He asked.

You don't even want to know how it felt to hear that boy call his monster Uncle John. It didn't matter if it was really his uncle or not. It made me a little crazy. I almost couldn't ask the kid any more questions I was so upset. But I needed to. And John had to know by now that I was around.

"I'm going to ask you some questions and you need to know that I already know the answers. If you answer one wrong, I'll know, and I'll kill you. Do you understand?"

The kid nodded again.

I totally wasted the first question.

"What's your name?"

"Kevin," He told me.

"Kevin!" John Noland yelled from inside the cabin.

I told you. Had I waited two seconds longer I would not have needed to ask.

"Don't answer," I said.

"How old are you?" I asked.

"Thirteen," I got back.

"How do you know John?"

"He's my scoutmaster," I got back.

"Has he hurt you?"

"No, he would never hurt me."

"One last question. Has he touched you in your private area?" I asked. I really couldn't believe I said it that politely, but I did.

Kevin didn't reply. Instead he looked at the ground.

"You are going to run down that driveway. When you get to the road you are going to keep running, do you understand?" I said.

He nodded again.

"God damn it Kevin, where are you?" John yelled.

The kid was off down the driveway. He didn't even open the gate again. He climbed right over it.

John Noland had to be shitting his pants.

And that was before I was in front of him on the porch of his cabin, pointing a gun in his face.

"Kids not coming back," I told him.

"Who are you? What do you want with me?"

"I am that little boy, thirteen years older."

"What the fuck are you talking about?" John demanded, and it was kind of like how Uncle Will talked to me too.

"You fuck little boys, *Uncle* John," I said, following his head with my gun as he trembled.

"Oh, God, please. I have a family. If my wife finds out I'm a dead man."

I laughed.

"Hadn't you noticed? You're a dead man. Do the math. My gun plus your face, it can't be hard to figure out,"

Then fear really came over him.

"You aren't the police?"

Damn, I thought, no one ever mistook me for a cop before and now twice in ten minutes.

"You always been this quick?" I asked.

"Wait, please, don't kill me, it isn't my fault. I try to stop, I really do. It's an addiction. It's a sickness. I can't control it, I need help. Don't kill me, God."

"You,..," I started, but I was so flustered.

"You're sorry for what you've done?" I asked.

"Oh yes, God yes, I'm so ashamed..," He wailed, dropping to his knees with real, honest to God tears on his face. There's no faking that. This guy was really remorseful.

I was having second thoughts. Even though I was all pumped up to kill someone, and even though I extra hated him for being some kid's fake uncle, he was getting to me. Lucky though, what he said next was this:

"Can God ever forgive me?"

"I don't know, why don't you ask him yourself?" I said, pulling the trigger on my gun and shooting Uncle John smack in the forehead.

It was funny. That's the thing. He set me up for a funny kill and then I just had to shoot him. I love being funny when I kill someone.

The shot was clean too. There wasn't much blood and he was dead right away. No more of this long drawn out dying shit. I wanted to think I had gotten pretty fucking good at this work, but maybe it was just luck. I never hit the target that well when I was practicing.

At first I had worried about the noise of a gunshot, which was really loud. But then it occurred to me that it was a hunting cabin. The sound of gunshots had to be kind of normal there.

I drove away from the cabin expecting to find Kevin walking down the driveway, or on the road. When I didn't I turned and drove the other direction for a few miles and still didn't find him.

I was worried about it.

That kid could be wandering around lost in the woods. He could even die out there and that wouldn't be good at all.

I saw a roadside payphone, pulled up to it and called the police.

I gave the police the address of the cabin and told them about the boy, and that John Noland, the pedophile, was there waiting for the cops. I called him by the word they like, rather than monster, but they still acted like I was talking in Martian.

"Could you please repeat that?" They asked.

"No. Rewind and listen to your tape if you need to hear it again. I'm hanging up in 30 seconds, do you have anything to ask me?"

"Your name is?" The voice on the other end of the phone asked.

"I am, um, Captain Authority, champion of the innocent," I said.

"How do you know all this?" He asked.

"I shot him. The pedophile that is, not the kid. 15 seconds,"

"You shot him, then he needs an ambulance?"

"Hell, no. He needs a hearse. seven seconds," I said.

"Don't hang up," I heard.

"I won't," I answered.

I left the phone off the hook and drove off.

10 miles down the road I stopped for gas. I didn't see a cop car until I was in Milwaukee and the sun was up.

I was tired then and looking for a motel sign on the highway. That's when I thought about money.

I didn't make a cent off of that job. I didn't even check the guy's pockets. It was sloppy of me, really sloppy. I might have made it home on the money I had left even with hotels, but I didn't take the chance. I pulled into a rest stop on Route 90 just past Chicago at like eight in the morning and slept in the car until afternoon.

I felt bad about how roughly I had treated the boy and thought about it most of the drive back. Around Pittsburgh I slept again, just for a few hours, and I didn't think about it then, but I was right back to thinking about it when I continued on my way, and all the way home too.

Not leaving garlic stones as a calling card was still bothering me too, but it wasn't the same. Not leaving garlic stones, that was bothering my ego, but terrifying the boy, Kevin, who was just a victim, and then leaving him to run away in miles of nowhere woods, that was more bothering my conscience.

After I had been home and had plenty of sleep in my own bed it was still bothering me. I was also out of money. I may have had problems all along but when I've got money, I can buy things or go to movies or get into another case to distract me until it goes away.

This time it just went on bothering me.

I would have gone to therapy if I hadn't been through that before and learned how far doctor patient confidentiality doesn't extend. To sort things out, I might need to talk about my work and some people might not see it as humanitarian as it really is.

Instead of a shrink then I found a support group that met in West Haverstraw twice a week for "Adult Survivors of Child Sexual Abuse," It was listed in the local section of the daily newspaper. I must have seen it before without really registering it because I knew right where to look and kind of what I was looking for.

I still was planning to listen more than talk, and when I did talk, to talk in general terms rather than talk about specific details of things I had done. I figured I could get away with that better with a support group than a psychiatrist, and I was right.

There wasn't even a facilitator. There had been, I learned, when it started but she didn't stick around, and the group continued to meet. If they followed anything at all, which they didn't really, it was a book called *Courage To Heal*. The book focused on women survivors, but a lot of the same things applied. The thing is, there were more men in the group than women.

"Just think how we feel," A woman said to me when I was talking about the fact that there were so many male victims of child sexual abuse and rape and there was hardly anything acknowledging us at all in research or print or anything. She was from a support group for women with heart disease and I didn't know what she was talking about.

The other men in the group were Dell, Don, Dean, Dan and David. This was a coincidence that I found absolutely hysterical but no one else did.

"Don't you see, all the guys have D names," I tried to explain.

"No, we don't, your name is Peter," o ne protested.

"Oh, that doesn't count, I'm Peter," I went on, but it was no use.

The first time Don started talking I wanted to ask him if his name was Roche. One of the things about the group was that it was first names only but damned if I didn't get to thinking it was Donny Roche, the kid who was with Uncle Will at the fireworks seven years earlier. I took him for 20, which would have been about right, and for a while I got surer and surer until he started talking about the person who victimized him, and it was all wrong.

We were all smoking up a storm, too, and at some point someone came in to tell us that this coming Thursday would be the last day we could do that. She said that starting the first of the next month, the entire building was going non-smoking.

That was a bitch because we were on the third floor. The women didn't mind even though both of them smoked, but the guys were pissed.

Yeah, I should have told you, there were 2 women in the group too, neither of them had a first name that began with D. I thought about saying so, but I thought maybe someone would think that it was offensive, so I didn't, just to be sure.

One was Betsy, the other I got the name of at least twice, but it was so unmemorable that I forgot it immediately after she said it each time.

Betsy was large. She was large enough that any 2 of us could have fit inside her. I mean, 350 pounds, maybe 400. To hear her tell it, she was fat because of what happened to her. I don't know if I buy it though.

I did end up saying something that offended her even when I was watching what I said so carefully so that I wouldn't. It was the second time I was there, and she was talking about eating and being fat for like, the third time.

"I guess I eat so much to make me unattractive to men," She said.

"Looks like it's really working!" I offered.

Sometimes people can be so sensitive that even a compliment upsets the shit out of them, like Betsy at the survivors meeting.

Someone pointed out that there used to be groups like this for people who had '70s been in concentration camps during the holocaust and they were called survivor groups too. They pretty much died out though, as the survivors of the holocaust got older and deader.

Back in the '70s though, there had been lots of them and quite a few of these groups handled their grief much more proactively. What I mean is, the hunted down old Nazis and saw that justice was served.

"They had them arrested?" I asked.

"Sometimes. Other times they just killed them."

"Well, you can't be too careful, don't want one to get away again or slip through the cracks in the system," One of the others added.

I smiled and for the next 20 minutes we were really talking about stalking and killing monsters. That was great. I didn't tell them that that was what I did even though I really wanted to, and I bet I'd have been the hero of the day if I had told them. Well, I really was the hero of the day, and every other day too, even if nobody knew about it.

The next meeting, that Betsy woman, you know, the fat one, was saying that until a month before she didn't know that she had been molested by her stepfather until she was, like, six years old and he died from liver failure.

"Excuse me, how can you not know?" I asked.

"I had suppressed it. I didn't remember it happened until my psychiatrist drew it out of me," She said.

"How can you not remember?" I asked, "It isn't, like, a little detail that can just slip your mind."

"It happens," Someone else is the group chimed in.

"If a trauma is too hard for someone to remember it can just get blocked out. They call it repressed memory. I had a hard time believing it at first myself. It took some convincing, but my therapist finally got me to accept that this is what happened to me. I can remember when I was molested now, although it's still a little hazy," David said.

"What happened?" I asked him, completely taking the meeting away from Betsy, who I didn't like anyway.

"I started going to therapy because sex didn't turn me on. I'd have an attractive girl in my bed and…"

"Lucky you," I interjected.

"Not lucky. I couldn't, you know, I didn't."

"No lead in the pencil, huh?" I asked.

"It was because of something that happened when I was eight. I learned that under hypnosis," David went on.

"I was an altar boy in my family church and the priest took advantage of me," David told me, because he had already told all of this to the rest of the group before I had joined.

"A priest? Fucking really? A fucking priest? How does a fucking priest do that? What about God and shit?" I asked.

"Some people go into the priesthood because they feel a calling from God, others because it is a good way to get the trust of children," The woman who's name I didn't remember said.

"Monsters," I said.

The rest of them looked at me like I was strange, so I didn't try to explain.

When David got himself together again he told about going to the church in Goshen and confronting his abuser with what had happened.

"Yes, how did that go?" Betsy asked.

"He denied the whole thing. The bastard tried to tell me it never happened, he just tried to negate my entire existence. It was awful," David said.

"This guy is still a priest?" I asked.

"Yes. He's still in the same parish, 20 years later," David answered.

"That's awful. All those children he's damaged since you, all of the ones at risk now," I said.

"There's nothing I can do to stop him," David said
I smiled.

David got upset, but not with me.

"I'd like to kill him! If I could, I'd kill him, I would fucking kill him with my bare hands!" He yelled.

"It's not so easy to kill a guy. You'd be surprised how much it takes to kill them and have them really be dead. You don't want to try it with your bare hands. It would be like building a treehouse using your fists to drive in the nails rather than a hammer," I said.

The group looked at me.

"So, I've heard," I added.

The conversation shifted again, to confronting victimizers and how that was supposed to help.

"It helped me," I said, thinking about Uncle Will's eyes when he knew he was dying. It just made me smile all over again thinking about it. Shit, this whole meeting was making me smile.

After the meeting, I caught up with David at the door and found out where exactly the church was, and the priest's name, Father William Buckner. I could have added him to the end of my list and maybe gotten to killing him in a year or two, if he didn't die of old age waiting for me to kill him, but I knew right away I wasn't going to do that. I couldn't allow a priest, someone who was entrusted to guide people, to be a monster instead. He needed to be taken care of right away.

21.

If there is anything creepier than a Catholic church, it is a Catholic church where the priest is a child fucking monster. I came in on a Sunday and sat around the middle and listened to evil Father Buckner give his sermon.

I wanted to hate every word he said, because he was saying it, but when I was paying attention, I had to admit it was pretty good stuff. If I hadn't known he was a fucking monster I might have even been moved.

My eyes drifted around and rested on the many strange decorations in the sanctuary. They were frightening things that conjured up images of gothic horror for me.

The nastiest of it I asked someone about after services, and they said it was the stations of the cross. What it was was images sculpted right into the walls of this guy getting the shit beat out of him and crucified and all like that. I knew it was supposed to be Jesus. I'm not dumb, I know about the whole crucifixion story, and it is a story, right, that's why they call it 'fiction,' but let me tell you, when you see it on the walls like that, it doesn't feel like fiction. That makes it seem like some guy really lived and had that happen to him and that really bites.

There was this material like silk, or maybe linen cloth, with two stripes on the bottom running the length of the floor and hanging over the lectern and marble altar.

On top of the altar, on one side was an open book on a cheesy stand, I guess it was a bible but really, it could have been a book of Norwegian wedding cake recipes and none of us would have known the difference.

On the other side of the altar was a cloth covered box of some sort, which, at one point during his performance, the priest removed the cloth dramatically, the way a magician might reveal that a rabbit, that had been under there earlier in the show, was now gone. I had gotten there a little late and missed the first few minutes so, for all I knew, that was the case.

What was under there now though, was a carafe of wine and a roll of round, white discs about the size of a half dollar coin.

The priest put a disc on the tongues of a bunch of people that came up and he touched their foreheads and stuff. It was all really creepy. I couldn't watch, so I was looking around again.

Did I say that there were words on that altar cloth? If I did, I was wrong. There was a bunch of letters, but it wasn't a word I know of.

"XPICTO"

That could have been the priest's home planet. It could have been the name of the company that made the cloth. Or maybe it meant that people shouldn't pick their noses in church or something like that. There's a lot about God and church and stuff that I just don't know anything about.

I was so caught up in trying to figure it out that I was caught by surprise by droplets of water hitting my arm.

I thought it was raining inside the church.

I looked up, expecting to see a leaky roof, or maybe dripping pipes running along the ceiling. It wasn't pipes though. That crazy ass priest was doing it.

Father Buckner was walking down the aisle with a foot-long soup ladle, swinging the damned thing at the audience and hitting them with water.

This wasn't a normal ladle either. Damn. Nothing was normal in this place. First of all, it was brass, or brass colored. And the end of it was more a big tea ball than a cup. Really fancy. I was right on an end, so I got a good splash of it compared to those who knew enough to sit closer to the center of a pew.

After he passed I leaned toward the next person in my pew, who was sitting far enough away to not get wet.

"Thanks for warning me, fuckhead," I said.

He scowled at me but didn't say anything.

Church, it turns out, is kind of like Six Flags. There's food and drink, weirdos in costumes, and if you don't know the safe places to sit, you are going to get water splashed on you during the show.

There was more annoying shit to come though.

After the water thing, the priest was swinging around a covered brass incense burner suspended on three metal chains and damned if inside it there wasn't burning the stinkiest weeds. A good whiff of that and I bet you you'd sneeze.

"The only reason people come to this show," I thought to myself, "is they don't charge an admission."

As soon as I thought it, wouldn't you know, they were begging for money too.

The collection basket was on a long pole and the boys in gowns were able to push them so that they lingered in front of each person without having to step over anyone. They really had this part down.

I looked at the kids who were helping in the services. They were all about ten years old and cute. Prime candidates for victimization by monsters, and all of them subject to that victimization by the one person no one would suspect.

Those poor kids.

I was on the case though.

Not Okay

When the collection basket landed in front of me I felt on the spot. I reached in my pocket and pulled out the first coin I found. It was a nickel.

I put it in the basket.

"There, satisfied," I said.

I didn't want to give the fucker anything, but I was under cover. If I hadn't given them anything I would have attracted attention to myself.

So that's how church services went.

There were too many people milling around to kill Father Buckner then, so I left and came back the next day. That was Monday.

There were still people in the church.

Two of them were playing some kind of game with a wrought iron rack full of candles. Each, on their turn, would light one of the candles using a stick that was provided. I watched for a while, but I couldn't make sense of what move meant what or how you would win the game.

I came back every day but nothing much happened until Saturday.

There were more people in the church on Saturday, and a line for the bathroom.

There were two doors, but everyone was using just the one.

The priest wasn't around so I spent some time sitting there hoping he would show up. I really wanted to take care of my business with him and have the rest of the day off.

Maybe five people went into the bathroom and came out a few minutes later.

A five minutes after the last person came out and there was no one left waiting, the priest came out of the other door. He had been in there half an hour easily.

297

"Constipated?" I asked.

I'm sure he heard me, but he didn't respond. Instead, he politely asked, "Do you wish to make a confession young man?"

Right then I thought aloud, "Well, if that's a confessional, where's the damned toilet?" But really, I was glad it was the confessional. It was a dumb place for a bathroom anyway.

I went into the confessional on the side that the other people had gone in and out of before and he went back in on his side.

I really had to go, I really did, so I figured it was bathroom enough. When a small wooden gate opened in a window between us I was standing, pissing against the wall.

"Hey, Father Buckner, I'll be with you in just a minute," I said, shaking it off.

While I was zipping up, Father Buckner said, "There is no need for names in here, my son."

I grumbled.

"But you are Father Buckner, aren't you?"

"Yes, my son, what is your sin?" He responded.

"Oh, well, um, I'm not Catholic so I don't really know how to do this," I told him.

"What is troubling you?" The priest asked.

"Well, it is like this, see, there is a bad man, who does really bad things, and I have the power to stop him," I said.

"What sort of bad things does he do?" He asked.

"He fucks little boys," I said.

"Are you certain of this?"

"Pretty sure."

"You must tell the authorities," The priest said.

"Oh, authorities don't do shit," I insisted.

"It is in their hands, my son, and God's."

"Father, why do you do it?" I asked.

"Do what, son?" He asked back, playing dumb right to the end.

"You know what you do, you use your position to take advantage of little children, isn't there some commandment of some kind, thou shalt not be a fucking pedophile bastard fuck head?"

"Me? I have not..," The priest started to deny it and that was really pissing me off.

What was pissing me off even more was how calm he was about the whole thing.

"You are a filthy scumbag monster; I am a messenger of God and this is my message!" I yelled, bringing my gun up to the mesh screen that separated us and firing.

As it turned out, this was a really bad way to try to shoot someone.

I fired all of the bullets in my gun and all of them missed. I didn't even nick the bastard's ear with one.

I reloaded and got out of the confessional. I was going to open his side and shoot him that way but, as it turned out, he got the idea of leaving too.

He made it about twelve feet.

I fired twice, hitting his leg with the first shot and missing with the second.

On the floor now, holding his bleeding leg with one hand, he turned around and faced me.

There must have been a dozen people watching us, one or two even, that had just heard the shots and come to see what was going on.

One of them screamed as the priest held a hand up, blocking his face, as if a hand could deflect a bullet.

I was a few feet away and not going to miss again.

"Do not do this, my son, it is a grave sin," He said.

"Coming from the sin expert," I said, pulling the trigger and getting him good, in the chest.

You know, when I think about it, if you are ever in a situation where someone like me is wanting to shoot you, the best thing you can do is shut up. I mean, I always take that shot after someone says something that kind of invites the bullet, if you know what I mean. Shooting him becomes, like, punctuation giving the last thing I say to the motherfucker that much more kick.

A couple more shots and I had him real dead.

I think the one that really got him was high, up in his hair. The way the blood came down his face was cool.

The monster priest fell, but I fired more bullets into him just to make sure he wasn't going to get up.

There were witnesses all over the place.

I looked around and saw fear on all of their faces. A couple of them looked like they would jump me if I gave them enough time to get their nerve.

They were all stupid sheep. The thing they should have been afraid of was the monster I had killed.

I thought I was going to get caught right there. I walked out of that church thinking the police were going to be outside those doors. They weren't though.

Then, I thought the cops would be catching up to me on the throughway back to Nyack. Somebody had to have seen me get into my car and drive away. I made it home safely though.

Once I was inside I locked the door and felt safe.

Safe or not, I was still shaking all afternoon.

After the first few kills I had come to take them in stride, you know. I just didn't shake like this anymore. But that one was so close. I really could have gotten caught right there, in the church, with the gun in my hand.

"Shit Mr. Tibbs!" I yelled, looking for my cat.

"I forgot about money again, I'm fucking broke and I didn't get my monster to pay for killing him."

I decided I wasn't going to be so sloppy again, no matter what, and that made me feel a little better.

I stayed close to home for the next couple of days, skipping the meeting that night, but making it to the next one, on Thursday.

I was looking forward to the meeting and seeing my friends there again. When I passed the sign that said welcome to West Haverstraw I really felt welcome.

That was where I got arrested.

David, after hearing about the priest's execution, thought the killer's description was a lot like me, which it was, since it was me. He told the police about me, of all the dumb ass things to do.

When I had talked to him, David agreed that Father Buckner needed to be killed. He changed his attitude about that after it really happened though.

What a fuck.

"I didn't mean I wanted someone to really kill him, it was just something you say when you are upset, only a lunatic would take it seriously," It turned out he told a cop.

Maybe if my car didn't match too, or if I had been wearing different clothes than the ones I was wearing when I filled Father Buckner, they might have asked me some questions and moved on.

Instead, they put me in cuffs right on the spot and took me to their police station.

"Damn you, David, you stupid son of a bitch!" I yelled as they put me in the police car, "Now I'm going to miss the meeting."

I was taken to Goshen that night and arraigned, not because the killing took place in Goshen, but because that was where the courthouse was for all of Orange County.

The judge set bail at some absurd amount and asked me if I had it.

"Sure, you can take a check, right? If it bounces you can dribble it on back to me," I said. I was only trying to make a joke, you know, lighten things up. I don't even have a bank account, I never have.

I was taken to the police station and kept in a holding cell until two officers from the sheriff's department came to pick me up and drive me the distance of one hundred yards, to the county jail.

Handcuffs alone were not good enough for them. They had to put me into a belt apparatus with cuffs attached in the middle. That should have been plenty, but just to make sure, they chained my legs together too.

"What, are you afraid I'm a threat to you?" I asked.

"Why? Are you?" One of them responded.

"That depends, do you fuck little kids?"

Neither replied to me but one told the other that I was insane. That might have been true, but it wasn't the point. Everybody has a few little shortcomings. At least I was doing something good for the world.

We arrived.

"This is it? We're here?" I asked as we pulled through the first set of chain link fences onto the grounds of the Orange County Jail.

"This is it," An officer said.

"Oh, hell, if I had known we were this close I would have walked, you didn't need to go through all the bother of coming to get me," I told them.

I think one of them rolled their eyes, but I could only see the backs of their heads, so I didn't know.

I was strip searched in there. This was an experience that I didn't care for when I was admitted to the mental hospital and I liked a whole lot less now.

After that, I was interviewed by a guy who said he was from the jail's forensic clinic.

"Forensic, you mean like Dr. Quincy? I love that show, does that mean I'm dead? Come on, doc, you can tell me, am I dead?"

"Do you feel dead, Peter."

"Well, I've had better days, but no, I feel like pitching skee ball at the Jersey Shore," I told him.

I was still amusing myself two hours later, cracking my wise remarks, some of which were really good.

It wasn't that I was having fun. It was really kind of a bummer of a time, but making jokes was my way of dealing with stress.

Still, as the night went on I found fewer and fewer things to find funny. I needed a cigarette. I wished I had my copy of I'm OK - You're OK to read again. I needed a little help to feel OK right then. I worried about what was going to happen to my responsibilities if I wasn't around to take care of them.

There were still a bunch of names on my list. If I was stuck in jail, who would kill all those monsters?

"Hey guard, who's going to feed my cat?" I yelled.

I listened for a response but didn't get one.

I yelled about my cat needing to be fed for over an hour until someone answered.

303

"Will you just shut up in there!" A voice called.

"Ha! I knew someone could hear me out there!" I yelled back, encouraged.

"My cat is going to starve to death without me there to feed him, you have to let me out of here. I'll go feed him and come right back; I promise."

"Dream on," The voice said back.

"My cat is wasting away, and you don't even care!" I yelled. I was doing a lot of yelling.

"Shut up!" The voice yelled again.

"I won't, I won't, I'm going on until I'm tired of doing it and let me tell you, I won't get tired soon. I have amazing reserves of energy; I can be yelling until this time tomorrow and later maybe. Just see, I'm going to yell and there isn't a fucking thing you can do about it."

"I'll give you 20 more seconds to shut up, then I'm going to knock all your teeth out with my Billy club, how does that sound to you?" The voice said back.

You want to know; I didn't say another word the rest of the night.

22.

"The next morning was the morning they brought me to this room, I met you, and you know everything from there on," I finished.

The room went silent.

"Is that it?" Sabrina asked.

"Isn't that enough?" I asked.

"It is plenty," She replied.

The room became silent again. Maybe because of the concrete, silence was quieter in there than other places.

"So, what do you think?" I asked.

"It doesn't look good," She said.

"I have a strong case, don't I?" I asked.

"They have you nailed, Peter. The gun in your house with your fingerprints on it, you and your car seen by a dozen people."

"They searched my house?" I asked.

"Of course, they did," She replied.

"What did they do with my cat?" I asked.

"I couldn't tell you," She said.

"That's just great. I hope he isn't in some evidence locker somewhere, that would really suck for him."

Sabrina looked at me.

"I think we should have a full psychological evaluation done."

"I don't want to plead insanity," I insisted.

"It is your only chance, Peter."

"No!" I said firmly.

"You must realize you're not well, Peter," She said.

"I wasn't, but I dealt with that myself. I know I'm OK, I know you are OK," I said.

"You are not, Peter, you are really not," She said.

"It's an unrelated thing, like being left-handed or having brown hair. Even if I am crazy, I don't kill monsters because I'm crazy, I kill monsters because they are a threat to children. It is the sanest thing I do."

"First of all, you are only charged with killing one person. There is no reason to tell them about any others if they don't put it together. If they do, then we will deal with that," Sabrina told me.

"They can't be that stupid, I've got a list, I told you, with the people I killed scratched off, if they can't figure it out from that, they can't wipe their own asses."

"You would be surprised," She said.

After a pause, she went on.

"For now, you are charged with killing one man, William Forester Buckner. You don't want to plead insanity, which is insanity itself I could try to bargain you down to twenty years. It is going to be hard, the man you killed was a priest, but I think the DA will do it. We don't want to get this in front of a Jury, they will bury you."

"Wait just a minute, I don't want to plead guilty either," I said.

"But you are guilty. You don't want to plead insanity, it wasn't self-defense, that doesn't leave much in the way of options does it?"

"I want to argue a point of the law," I said.

"What point?"

"How humanity is defined."

Sabrina lit a cigarette.

"In order for it to be murder, the thing I killed had to be human."

"Of course, the victim was human," Sabrina said.

"By what method are you defining humanity? Is

there a legal definition of the word, if so, can't it be challenged? If not, then it is subjective. Don't you see, I want to argue that Father Buckner, by being a predator of children, gave up his humanity and became a monster. I didn't kill a human being; I slew a monster."

"You can't expect to win in court with that defense," Sabrina said.

"No, but should that matter? It is the truth. Wouldn't it be unethical to present anything other than the truth, no matter how likely anyone is to believe it?" I asked.

"You may feel it is noble, but what will it accomplish other than sending you to jail for the rest of your life?" Sabrina asked back.

"It could attract some attention. It might make a few more people aware of the problem. It could put a little fear in the hearts of some of the monsters I never got to. If we are really lucky, it could even inspire a few new monster killers to pick up where I left off."

"You want to be a martyr?" She asked.

"It wasn't my first choice, I wanted to not get caught, but if being a martyr is the best I can do, I'll have to settle for it,"

"But Peter, I have nothing to support your claim even if I wanted to. If you were molested by Buckner when you were a child, maybe I'd have a tiny thread of something, but all I have is a big pile of nothing here."

"You have the guy, David, and those altar boys, now that he's dead a lot of people will come forward, and he must have left pictures behind, these bastards always have pictures."

"No, Peter, nothing," Sabrina said sadly.

"Why the hell not?" I demanded.

"Because there was nothing. The police checked it

out, I did as well. No one was molested by Father Buckner."

"How can you say that, what about David?" I yelled.

"David doesn't believe Father Buckner molested him either. Not now anyway," She told me.

"That's ridiculous," I said.

"No, it isn't. Repressed memories brought out under hypnosis aren't reliable. They can be false memories, unintentionally suggested by the psychologist. This psychologist thinks everyone was molested as a child, he has a dozen patients who aren't sure about their fathers, uncles, priests, teachers. I'm so sorry Peter, but you killed an innocent man. He was a good man, an innocent man.

I took Sabrina's cigarette out of the ashtray and started smoking it.

"Shit," I said.

"Yeah."

"Can you just tell them it was a mistake?" I asked.

"I can certainly try, but it would help if I could explain how your mental condition contributed to your making such a mistake."

"What's going to happen to me?" I asked.

"You could get help. I'm sure it would take some time but one day, if you cooperated with the doctors, you might be better."

"Are you saying I'm the monster?" I asked.

"You killed an innocent man."

"Stop saying that, shit, I know that, do you think I don't fucking know that?" I yelled.

"What would you like me to do?" Sabrina asked.

"Leave," I said.

"And your plea?"

"I need to think about it a while, I'll tell you tomorrow," I said.

Not Okay

"I'll be back tomorrow," Sabrina said, getting up.

"Are you sure he wasn't..," I started to ask.

"I'm sorry Peter, I'm really sorry," She answered.

This time, my lawyer left the conference room first. I sat alone in there for a few minutes waiting for the guard who would bring me back to my cell, where I belonged.

I was an animal, needing to be locked up where I couldn't hurt anyone.

Not a human. A monster.

"Uncle Will, you shit son of a bitch!" I yelled.

"You did this to me, you infected me with your evil and turned me into a monster just like Sharon said. God damn you! God damn you! God damn you!" I screamed until my throat was hoarse.

Then, in the lowest whisper I had, I cried for myself. I didn't cry for Father Buckner. Not then. I did sometimes later, but not then.

That sounds kind of over dramatic now, but I said, "God damn me," I wouldn't have said that if I'd thought about how over dramatic it would sound later. Oh well, you can't be cool all the time.

That's about everything. Thanks for listening, if you listened to these. When you picked me up from the hospital I was so happy to see you.

I was happy to see anything outside. I'm glad you took care of Mr. Tibbs while I was inside. I missed him.

Thanks for telling me I look good, even though I know I don't. Six years, shit, I'm old now. Not as old as you, but old. Sharon, honey, you've been a real friend to me. I don't blame you for not killing anyone for me while I was in the crazy hospital. I shouldn't have even asked you.

The most valuable thing I own is my story, I am giving you these tapes. The second and the fourth ones are the ones Sabrina recording in the jail when I first got arrested. I wasn't on meds then. Some of it must sound pretty crazy. I added some clarification for you on the first, third, and this final one. I'm giving them to you.

You deserve something, and it isn't like I'll ever be able to use it.

If you type it up maybe someone will want to publish it. Maybe you'll get some of the money you spent on me back. Just don't change anything. Don't make me sound like a better person than I was, don't make me sound like a terrible person either. Just leave it the way I said it.

I realize I made a big mistake killing the priest and I'm sorry. I'm changing right now though. I'm improving myself. For starters, I quit smoking. I know, it's only been a few hours, but I know I can do it.

I'm not going to give up killing monsters. You know I can't in good conscience do that. But I'll be much more careful not to get caught.

I don't have my list anymore, but I'll find another way to figure out who the monsters are.

I'm sorry if an innocent person ends up killed once in a while, but they have to understand, it is better than letting the monsters run around fucking kids.

If Father Buckner knew that sacrificing his life could spare hundreds of abused children I'm sure he would have volunteered. Apologize to Sabrina for me. I hope she doesn't get in too much trouble for my jumping parole. I can't be a serial killer and report to the parole board twice a week. I'm going to have to be really careful now. If I slip up, they won't let me out so easily.

Oh, it was easy too. Once I was on the medication I really sounded OK. Thank God I read that dumb book so many times. I knew just what to say and what not to.

Not Okay

Funny thing is, I think that one psychiatrist, the one that signed my release papers, I think he really liked the idea of a monster hunter out in the world killing pedophiles. I think maybe he released me hoping I would go back to work.

You know I can't tell you where I'm going or what name I'll be using. Chances are, this is really goodbye. You'll know I'm out there somewhere though, stalking those monsters, making the world safer for children.

I'm sorry I wasn't better to you. I really am. I'm sorry I didn't love you. I wanted to real bad. I know it would have made things better for both of us I did.

I'm turning this tape recorder off now. I hope I don't say anything after that. I hope I just walk away so you can have the whole story. This is the last thing I want to say. It's cool. It's a good way to end my story. A cool thing to be the last thing I say before I just turn off the tape recorder and walk away:

If you ever have children, keep an eye on them.